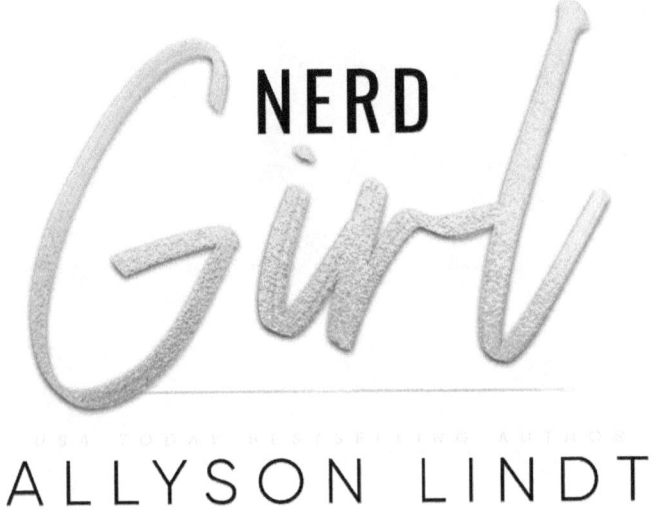

NERD *Girl*

USA TODAY BESTSELLING AUTHOR

ALLYSON LINDT

acelette press

For all those readers who take the time to read the dedication. This is for you. Imagine this says something raunchy about sex or foul language or something catchy like that.

1 /
gage

There was some saying about the early morning hours being for specters and otaku —or I made part of that up. But as I walked through the small town where I lived, at two in the morning, I was fairly sure even the ghosts and fanboys had gone to bed.

Even on a Friday night, a place like Haddarville was completely closed down before midnight.

I'd lost track of time, working in the burger place I'd inherited from my grandfather, and turned into a grill and microbrew when I took it over. Rather, I'd told myself I was working, I even had a fantastic plan for remodeling the back banquet room so I could reopen it, if I could get the idea on paper.

Mostly though, I'd gotten lost in thoughts of five years ago. When my wife told me she was leaving me.

Worst. Birthday. Present ever. *We wasted so much time. This way, maybe we can get some back.* She'd said that to me when she told me she'd been sleeping with another doctor she worked with.

She'd said it again when she called earlier this evening to let me know the final payout from selling our house had cleared and my half was on its way to me.

The first time I heard those words I'd asked her if the time was really wasted if we enjoyed it? In my mind, no good times were without merit. She disagreed, because our time together hadn't led to anything.

I couldn't get the differences in opinion out of my head.

My walk home took me past the graveyard, and rather than linger in the past any longer, I searched for those supposed two am ghosts.

Or maybe they didn't come out until three. I was an hour early, and that was my problem. My ex would've hated knowing that I did this. That I'd wasted precious time wandering and searching for something stupid like *specters in the graveyard.*

A pale figure caught my attention, but she was definitely corporeal. Evie was sitting on a stone bench a few rows in, legs crossed and gaze turned to the ground.

Her shoulder length hair was pulled into a short ponytail, showing off the shaved sides of her head and the layer of blond she had bleached under the natural black on top. She looked captivating and lost.

I had a rather good idea what she was thinking about, because it had been on her mind a lot. She owned the local hardware store, and they were struggling.

She'd been here for me since I moved back. A lot of the time in the subtlest but best ways. I'd spent my first few months in town with my head down and not wanting to talk to anyone.

Because a guy could only listen to *I heard you and Grace split. Always thought you'd be together forever* so many times before it felt more like a mental tick than a well-meaning comment.

But Evie would show up with supplies and coffee at the most random but convenient times, and she never pushed me to talk. She never brought Grace up.

Maybe I could offer at least a little bit of a similar distraction for Evie tonight. I followed a path around graves, and settled on the bench next to her.

She didn't look up.

"Did I get here in time for the show?" I asked softly.

She almost smiled. "What show is that?"

"Whatever one has you staring so intently at that spot of dirt." I'd grown up here with her—the town not the graveyard—and because our last names were Young and Zabriskie, we always found ourselves grouped together in class.

When we hit our teens, I was taller than everyone else and she was shorter, and we were both convinced we were way too ugly and nerdy to find true love.

Yup, that was our biggest concern at thirteen and fourteen. What a life.

She and I had made a pact that if we hit forty and were still single, we'd get married. That way we wouldn't be alone forever.

Back then, forty seemed like it would never happen. Now it was two days away.

I had gotten married though, and Evie had enlisted, both of us right out of high school.

"I don't think the show is happening tonight," Evie said. "The headliner stepped into the light and their understudy has a bad case of the..." She frowned.

"The what?"

"I was going for one of those puns, like on a candy wrapper, but I got there, and—"

"It ghosted you?" I offered helpfully. The pact we'd made was a ridiculous one anyway. It wasn't like people got married because there was nothing else to do.

Evie grinned. "There's my pun. Thank you and you win." Her glee was natural. Bright in the dark night.

No, people got married because they thought they were in love and planned to have kids, but not until Grace finished school. And then there had been late nights and early mornings and grad school and residency, and I'd been fine with that. I wanted to see Grace achieve her dream. "Go me. What do I win?"

"I hear the ghost theater needs a new headliner." Evie sounded thoughtful. "But I wouldn't do it if I were you."

"Why not?"

"I hear the audition is murder." Evie laughed.

I joined her. Bad joke, but I'd started it and it felt good to release the happy sound into the night.

When thirty hit, when we blew past it, Grace had realized she tied herself to me and wasn't sure she wanted to. That was what she'd told me five years ago. She said I didn't understand what she was going through.

"Someone else's murder or mine?" I asked.

"What do you think?"

"Papa always said I killed it when I was in the school musicals."

Evie straightened and leaned her weight against her wrists instead of slouching in on herself. "Was that when you played the tree or townsman number seven?" The light slipping into her tone brightened my mood.

"I was the best fucking tree there ever was. And I was also townsman eight, not seven. What are we actually doing out here?" Not that I was complaining. Evie's company was one of the best parts of my life.

That had been part of the problem with Grace. Not Evie, but the fact that once Grace's schedule shifted, once she finally had a moment to breathe after years of school and residencies and finding her place in the medical world, she and I realized we hadn't spent any time together since we got married. We didn't know each other as adults, and we didn't really like each other as lovers.

There was that and the whole she'd-been-fucking-a-colleague thing.

"I'm feeling my age," Evie said. "Thinking of better times."

"Which better times? Puberty? The bullying that came with it? Living on someone else's schedule?" *Way to be a downer, me.*

She didn't look bothered by the commentary, though. "We run businesses. That require customers in order to survive. We still live on someone else's schedule."

I couldn't argue that. "So you're basically pondering mortality."

"Basically."

Yeah. Me too. Since I returned to town, I'd poured myself into restoring my business. Gage was my grandfather's name too, which was why it was on the sign—Gage's Grub. Like it was meant to be mine all along.

I wanted to be here for Evie the way she had been for me over the past several months. I wasn't sure I could be, but I wanted to try. The last few months I'd been climbing more and more out of the bitter haze of the way my marriage ended, and seeing more and more what she'd done for me while I was a grumpy bastard.

I also remembered how many times she'd cringed over the last year whenever I said *it should've been you*. Because in a lot of ways I felt like that—I should've married Evie instead of Grace—but I was also hurt and pissed off and Evie deserved better than to be treated like an afterthought to my divorce.

"When's The Nerd Herd taking you out for the big four-oh?" If we were talking mortality, I might as well bring up our birthdays directly, and she and her girlfriends always celebrated their birthdays together.

Evie rolled her eyes. "We don't call ourselves that anymore."

Uh-huh. "Does Aubrey know that?"

Evie twisted her mouth, but it didn't hide her amusement. "We're voting on a new name next weekend, and I figured we'd tell her then." Teasing lined her voice. "And they're taking me out on Monday. Alys said it doesn't count if it's not my actual birthday."

"Your friends are dorks." I meant it with all the affection.

Evie's grin was back. "Takes one to know one."

"Let's go to Wendover." I didn't know where the

suggestion came from, but it sounded like a random, obtuse, and therefore wonderful idea.

Because fun wasn't time wasted, it was time enjoyed, and damn it the world needed more of that.

Evie looked as surprised at the suggestion as I was. "What? When?"

"Now. We'll drive up tonight and spend tomorrow living on comped drinks and buffet food, and celebrate our fortieth the way we should've celebrated our twenty-first." But hadn't, because she was doing MP duty at Fort Knox, and I was figuring out if I needed a third job to pay for Grace's junior year and still make our rent.

"You're an absolutely ludicrous man." She made it sound like the best thing ever.

"That doesn't sound like a *no*." I stood and offered her my hand.

She accepted, and I pulled her to her feet. She came up to just below my shoulders. Perfect height for top of the head kisses, and hugs plus chin rests.

Not that those things were us.

"It's a definite *yes*. Who's driving?" Evie asked.

Tough question. "Not sure Lemmy is going to make it to Wendover." I loved her truck, but she'd named it Lemmy because—according to her—it was ugly as sin, purred with the voice of an angel when it was in a good mood, and was only still running due to acts of God.

Logic that didn't make sense to most, but it worked for her, so it worked for me.

Evie puffed out her cheeks and they deflated as she let out a long exhale. "Sounds like you just volunteered."

It did, didn't it? "Pick you up at your place in thirty minutes?"

"Don't be late."

This was going to be fun. Excitement bubbled inside while we walked side by side toward our houses. The trip wasn't a big thing, the kind of drive people made on a whim all the time.

But the getting away, the impulsivity and the idea of spending the next day or so with Evie, no constant reminders of the past, and not giving a fuck... That sounded wonderful.

We went our separate ways at her place, and I had to force myself to not sprint back to mine. Twenty-five minutes after the decision was made, I'd thrown a change of clothes into a bag and pulled up in front of Evie's house, to find her already waiting on the porch.

She tossed her bag in back next to mine, and we hit the road.

The next hour and a half was a lot of empty freeway, random tangents, and car karaoke. We reached Wendover at an ungodly hour, but there were still people in the casinos, playing the slots.

We picked a hotel that had fewer cars in the

parking lot, and agreed there was no reason to waste money on two rooms. We did get two beds, though.

"Sonya would be both disappointed there's more than one bed, and pleased we're sharing," Evie joked as I took the key from the woman at the front desk. Sonya was one of her best friends, and loved any real-life thing that had the flavor of an overdone book trope.

I steered us in the right direction. "Then Sonya needs to remember we're the most boring, platonic friends ever."

"Totally, yes."

Totally, yes. Evie's agreement echoed in my head. Just friends. Nothing more.

2 /
evie

Green eyes stared back at me from my reflection in the hotel bathroom mirror, and wet strands of black and blond hung straight around my face, framing the accusation I cast at myself.

I should've turned down this trip. Gambling, even just slot machines, was the last thing I needed to be doing, given my money problems. But the small amount I'd spend here was a drop in the bucket of back taxes, overdue interest, and past due invoices.

Falling behind was never part of the plan, but I'd had to miss a couple of invoice payments here and there. I was honest with my suppliers and negotiated new terms each time.

Until they couldn't—wouldn't—give me any more breaks. Then I'd gone for a high interest loan. A big sort of debt consolidation thing. At the time, I thought it was my only choice, and I used the store as collateral. I was making enough that I could pay it back no problem.

But money wasn't coming in the way it had a few years ago, and once again, I found myself falling behind in payments. I'd reached a point where I owed too much to catch up, and the bank was tired of waiting. They'd given me a few short months to make things right, or I'd lose it all.

My past due bills would be waiting when I got home. I was here and should try to enjoy the day. I wrung out the water from my hair one more time before pulling into a ponytail, adjusted my light-weight peasant top, and emerged from the bathroom.

"All yours," I said to Gage.

He stepped around me. "Give me like ten minutes, and we'll go get breakfast."

"Yup." I made myself comfortable on my bed, grabbed the remote, and flipped through the TV. Nothing held my attention, and on the third time through, I settled on *CSI:Oompa Loompa Ville*, or whatever flavor of the show this was.

To be honest, I was grateful Gage suggested the trip. The distraction was a nice idea, and I liked his company. My friendship with him was different than with the women in the Nerd Herd, in a way that was hard to define.

Come to think of it, what was different about Gage?

Beside the fact he was a six-plus-foot wall of muscle who was just gorgeous to look at when I needed a distraction? Hmm...

Some days he was more of a beacon of hope when I wanted to pretend things weren't all doom and gloom. His marriage. Possibly my hardware store.

There was a peace in admitting that failure was an option, and the world wouldn't end because of it. The future would just carve a new path.

Did that mean I was giving up on the family shop? Rolling over and letting it die after more than a century because *everything would be all right?*

No. Absolutely not.

But today I wasn't in the mood for *it'll all work out, you'll see.* I was more in the mood for—

The bathroom latch clicked, and Gage emerged. Ten minutes already? He was wearing jeans and sneakers, his short, dark hair stuck up like it had been towel-dried but not combed, and he wasn't wearing a shirt.

He had a tattoo sleeve on his left arm, an Escher-like staircase that climbed up his arm, and around his bicep, and seemed to go everywhere and nowhere all at once—great metaphor for life. He was built, far more than a micro brew pub and grill owner had the right to be, given he was his own top taste-tester.

And I always enjoyed the view—that was some-thing else I didn't get from my other friends. They were all gorgeously fuckable, but not in the same way Gage was.

"You done?" He crouched to meet my gaze. "Can I finish getting dressed now?"

I pretended to consider the question. "I'm not sure. Could you stand there a little longer, let me figure it out?"

He snorted a laugh. "No. I'm hungry." He grabbed a T-shirt from his duffel bag and pulled it on.

That wasn't bad either, especially the way the fabric stuck to the still-damp parts of his skin.

"You wanna hit the buffet for breakfast?" I glanced at the clock. "Lunch?" That was what I was in the mood for—food.

"You know it," Gage said.

We collected what we needed for the day—purse, wallet, phones, keys—and headed downstairs. The voucher we got when we checked in gave us two for one on breakfast, and that almost made me feel like I was being practical, money-wise.

Almost.

In the hotel restaurant, we paid for our plates, then piled them high. I added pancakes, eggs, bacon, and sausage. More than should stay on the plate.

Another thing I liked about Gage's company, unlike any guy I'd ever tried to date, he never commented on how much I ate. Before I joined the Marines, I'd adopted a heavy lifting routine that stayed with me through my twenties and part of my thirties. I didn't stick to it religiously these days, and my metabolism was starting to slow, but I still needed a lot of calories.

The place was more crowded than I expected, and we snagged a table the moment it became available.

"Are we actually doing anything today?" I asked between bites of food. "*Is* there anything to do here besides gamble?"

"I hear the Air Force base is haunted."

"I thought we left the ghosts behind." I meant it to be a joke, but my words fell flat.

"You're a spooky gal… Besides, maybe the new ghosts will help us forget the old ones."

It was impossible to miss the sadness that leaked into Gage's voice. I could do spooky but, "We might need something stronger. We can tour the base, but you need a lap dance after." Half the signs leading into town had boasted about the local strip club. That sounded like a great distraction.

Gage stared at me in disbelief. "Your leap of logic is impeccably flawed."

"Not really. What better way is there to forget your problems than paying some woman you'll never see again to grind her ass against your junk? Hell, I'd *pay* to see that." Maybe it was kind of a weird thing for me to suggest. Was it?

Gage rolled his eyes. "You will pay. That's the point."

So much for being frugal. My mind was running with the idea though. It did this to me—my mind did—when I spent too long spiraling. It latched onto some random thought and refused to let go. Apparently today that was strippers. "You don't want a lap dance, I'll take one."

"You can't have my birthday lap dance. Get your own."

"Excuse me." A male voice interrupted the conversation. "There are no other empty seats. Do you mind if I share your table?"

I looked up to find a gorgeous specimen of a man standing next to us. The blazer over a t-shirt was a little iffy, but he was well-built, with dark blond hair and a hint of stubble on his jaw. I wouldn't mind a lap dance from him. Or doing one for him.

Gage toed an empty chair in his direction. "Sure. No worries."

The new arrival set a plate on the table that had a muffin and a small bowl of mixed fruit, plus a black coffee.

What was the point of going to the buffet if he wasn't going to enjoy it?

"Thanks. Sawyer, by the way." He extended his hand.

Gage shook it, and I did the same after, each of us offering up our names. Sawyer's grip was warm and firm. Like a man who was practiced in shaking hands.

Weird thought. At least my brain was moving on from naked people grinding against me.

Nope. That mental image was back again, and he was very much a part of it.

Sawyer glanced around the room as he picked at his muffin. "Is it always like this here?"

"Probably. We're not exactly regulars," I said.

Gage dug into his food again. "First time?"

"Yup. Popping my middle-of-nowhere Nevada cherry."

I liked it. "Technically, most places in Nevada are in the middle of nowhere. What brings you to this one?"

"I have meetings in Salt Lake City on Monday, and my brother told me this was a fun place to hang out." Sawyer frowned. "Pretty sure he was yanking my chain."

"It's not for everyone," Gage said. "But it has its high points. What kind of business?"

Sawyer opened his mouth, but a loud jangling filled the room, cutting him off. An excited sounding mechanical voice came over the loudspeakers and announced someone had just won the big slot machine jackpot.

A wave of cheers—some more enthusiastic than others—rolled through the room, before the conversation around us returned to a low roar of overlapping chatter.

"See. It's not all boring here," I teased. "That person's month was just made."

Sawyer smirked. "Fair point. Anyway, I'm in sales. Real estate. Investments."

I waited for a heartbeat to see if he would offer more. He didn't.

"That's pretty vague," I said.

He shrugged. "I prefer the term *diverse*."

Uh-huh.

"What about the two of you?" Sawyer asked before I could poke him for more info.

"I run a grill and microbrewery. Small town back in Utah," Gage said.

Probably no reason to keep it a secret since his name was literally on the place, and his face was in the ads.

"Nice." Sawyer sounded like he meant it. "What about you, Evie?"

I wasn't sure I liked the way he said my name. Rather, part of me imagined him whispering it in my ear, and the other half of me told me to stop swooning. "I tell you that and I have to kill you." I winked. Why did I say that? Why did I *do* that? I was so fucking awkward sometimes. "Kidding. I own a hardware store. Nothing nearly that interesting or deadly."

Sawyer's eyes grew wide. "Really?" Like that his tone shifted.

Why? What was so special about my revelation? "Are you surprised because you don't expect a girl to own a hardware store?" I hated to assume, but that was typically why people looked shocked when I told them what I did.

I'd hate to have to dislike this guy so soon in the conversation, if that was the case.

Sawyer grasped my fingertips, and I bit the inside of my cheek to swallow a gasp. *Knock it off, me.*

"Because people who work in hardware stores don't tend to have perfectly manicured nails. Not for long, at least," he said.

I pulled away, looking for that balance between casual disinterest and disdain. "I don't usually. A friend got me a manicure for my... day." I had a potent impulse to tell him anything he wanted to hear. To sit up and beg for attention and to be his good little girl.

And that just wasn't going to do.

3 /
sawyer

I should head to the roulette wheel and drop a couple grand on black, because this was one hell of a start to a lucky streak. Maybe I wouldn't retaliate against my brother for this bullshit after all.

It wasn't guaranteed this was the same woman I was looking for, but it seemed unlikely that there was more than one person named Evie who owned a hardware store in a small town in Utah.

Two choices sat in front of me. Introduce myself early, or spend a little time getting to know her and her friend, and feign ignorance when I met her again on Monday, and made my pitch.

I liked having surprise on my side, and knowing as much as I could before I went into a negotiation. Number two it was.

Was Gage a friend? A boyfriend? No rings on either of them, but that didn't always mean anything. He'd tensed when I took Evie's hand. Did she feel the same?

She was definitely interested in me. Was I going to use that to my advantage?

Fuck. Yes.

I wasn't going home without buying her land, because that was the best way to ensure Dad signed his commercial real estate company over to me.

"Is that why you're here?" I needed to keep this conversation friendly and flowing. "Celebrating your... day?" Birthday, I assumed. Anniversary? Maybe, but I was thinking no.

Gage shrugged. "Just seeing the sights. Living the life."

"Are you." Neither of those seemed like a real possibility here. "How does one do that here? *Live the life?*"

"Depends on your definition." Evie was making me uncomfortable with the way she was treating those link sausages. "Where are you from?"

Where wasn't I from? "Little bit of everywhere." When we were little, Dad moved us a lot depending on his current project. I managed to get over that wanderlust as an adult. All the way into my forties. When my husband left me a couple of years ago, when my father took the opportunity to remind me that was what I got for being *gay married*, I decided being tied to a place wasn't for me. "I suppose Atlanta most recently."

"Then no. You're not going to consider anything

here *living the life*," Evie said. "Especially not the strip club."

I had no problem embracing my preferences and depravities, but, "It's not even noon, and that's the first place you think of that's not a casino?"

"If you're not gambling, you don't have a lot of options." Gage wasn't bad to look at either. "It's that or the old Air Force base."

I didn't know a lot of couples who were fine with going to a strip club together, and even fewer who would admit it to a stranger. Did I need to change the direction of this conversation? Was she going to care if I hit on her? Was Gage more receptive?

Too early to tell, and I liked the puzzle in that. "You two have me intrigued."

"We're actually very boring, I promise," Evie said.

I shook my head. "Not true. You obviously knew what you were getting into by coming here, and yet you're here anyway. That's fascinating. I'd like to know what these exotic dancers have that's so compelling."

"It's best not to go in with expectations." Gage sipped his coffee.

Those were wise words in any situation. Never assume an outcome. The contract wasn't signed until the ink was dry and the check had cleared. "No expectations. Just curiosity. About both, actually. Old Air Force base?" Strip clubs were great for business trips. For getting potential contacts to let down inhibitions. A lot of people formed a strange sort of bond with another individual if the two watched strangers take off their clothes together.

A solid instinct for people told me that wasn't going to be the case for Evie. Or Gage. I didn't need to get close to him, unless it meant winning her over.

"It's haunted." Evie's expression and tone were serious. "The Air Force base, not the strip club." She furrowed her brow. "Maybe the strip club."

Gage shook his head. "Not in the same way. But the base—ghosts of those who came before. Lots of deep vibes there."

I looked between them. "Sounds… spooky?"

"Don't know. We typically stick to the museum," Evie said.

The longer I listened to her, the harder she was getting to read. I needed to stop making assumptions and observe for a while. She'd gone from shy to flippant and now she was stoic. "You ever get curious about if the rumors are true? About the ghosts?" In my experience, real life ghosts—our own pasts—were far more threatening than those who had passed on. Still… "What are the odds you'd give me a tour?"

"Yeah, okay," Evie said at the same time Gage said, "They have people on site for that."

They exchanged a look that spoke volumes without either of them saying a word. I could imagine the mental dialogue that went with the frowns, the abrupt nods in my direction and the widened eyes, but I'd just promised myself no more assumptions.

Gage clenched his jaw.

Evie raised her brows.

Gage rolled his eyes and sighed.

Evie turned back to me. "We were going anyway. You could come with us. See for yourself."

"That sounds great. Thanks." Though I wasn't looking for ghosts. As long as I came out of the afternoon with the best way to keep her on my side through Monday, this would be a far more valuable trip than Hudson meant it to be when he told me about this place.

As we finished eating, the conversation shifted toward stilted. Every question I asked, Gage was there with a brief reply, regardless of which of them I asked. By the time we all stood, Evie looked more frustrated than me.

We headed out to the parking lot. "You can follow us there," Gage said.

"Sounds good." I paused at my car.

Evie let out a soft gasp. "Is that yours?"

"It is. '73. Last year they made it." I was proud of my Datsun 240z. Bought it for next to nothing used when I was in high school. In my twenties and thirties it sat in the garage while I drove newer, faster, more expensive cars.

Evie hovered her hand over the body, never making contact. "You're restoring it."

"I am." And I wouldn't normally drive her cross country, but I was having some work done while I was here that I hadn't been able to find anywhere else. "Do you want a ride?"

Evie's grin was worth weeks of negotiation. "Fuck yes. I'll navigate."

"There's nothing to navigate," Gabe said with exasperation. "There's a main road and then a side road."

"And our new friend has never been down the side road." The way Evie walked around my car, her tone, it was all pure reverence. "This is going to be fun."

Yes it was. I held the passenger door open for her..

We navigated onto the main road, and Evie pointed me further into *town*. Was there really more to this place than a strip of casinos broken up by a grocery store and a couple of gas stations?

"That's Gage." She indicated the SUV that pulled in front of us. "We can probably just follow him."

Easy enough. He turned down a side road with a sign that said *Historical Museum*.

There were actually more buildings back here. Who would've guessed it?

We only drove for a couple of minutes before I saw the base ahead of us. This town was full of some interesting surprises. As we got closer, I had to admit the place looked pretty neat. Old abandoned buildings in the middle of the desert with a mini-Las Vegas only a mile or two away.

Gage turned left and I followed.

"Why isn't he stopping at the museum?" Evie seemed to be asking herself as much as me.

Which was good because I didn't have an answer. The building in question was a two-story box with a slanted roof and several windows. Simple. One of the cleaner buildings over here, down to the fresh coat of paint.

But we were continuing down the road, past a hanger with a big plane out front. Past buildings that looked like they might crumble in a strong enough wind. Past rows and rows of smaller box-shaped buildings that had probably been identical at one point.

Tall fences with razor wire up top surrounded those, and the entire vibe was a heavy *stay out*.

Which only made me want to see what was inside more.

Gage turned at the end of the fence, and headed down a dirt road that followed the chain link.

"Where is he going?" Another muttered question from Evie.

I had no idea, but my car wasn't going to appreciate that trip. I could make it on the packed dirt, but not if the rocks got much worse. We took the drive more slowly than he did, and fortunately, he stopped a few hundred yards in, before I had to suggest we get out and walk the rest of the way.

We were out of view of the main road, and if there weren't faint voices in the distance, it would feel like we'd left civilization behind. We weren't far from the freeway, but it was quiet out here. Eerie. Serene but haunting.

Evie walked up to Gage and smacked him lightly on the arm. "What are you doing? You're going to hurt the baby." She nodded at my car.

I swallowed a smirk.

Gage clenched his jaw. "Maybe *the baby* shouldn't be going off road then."

The longer I watched their dynamic, the more fascinated I was.

And Evie... I was glad I met her today instead of Monday, because she was fun, despite knowing her for such a short amount of time. I doubted I'd get to see this side of her in future settings. "Don't worry. I'll be careful pulling out."

Gage's scowl darkened. "I'm sure you will."

He was fun too, but not in the same way. More in that *I want her and she has no clue* kind of way.

"Forgive me if this is too personal, but are you two together?" I asked.

"As in, a couple? No." Evie's answer came quickly, before Gage could push out a sound.

"We could be," Gage said. "We did make that pact."

Did they now?

The look Evie gave him was similar to the one they'd shared in the buffet. The kind of thing that conveyed sentences in a glance. They were close, but she saw it differently than he did.

"Pact?" I was needling them on purpose.

Evie's *look* intensified.

Gage turned away from it. "When we were kids. We promised each other that if we weren't married by the time we were forty, we'd be together."

No shit.

"*When we were kids* being the key part of that phrase there." A huff worked its way into Evie's response. "Why are we back here? The fences are in place for a reason."

I was actually as curious about the place as I was the people. There was an energy here. It should be nothing. Dead. Flat. Lifeless. But something hummed underneath all of that. "We could walk around the outside edge. Get a closer look."

"We could go in if we wanted." Gage nodded at an opening in the fence a few feet away.

I should've noticed that. Someone had me distracted.

Evie worried her bottom lip, but there was curiosity rather than concern in her eyes. "Yeah, okay. I'm in."

"Me too." What the fuck was I doing? I was a forty-eight-year-old man, and I was about to creep around abandoned barracks in the middle of the day with two strangers.

But I couldn't ignore that the buildings and the company called to me.

Gage held open the fence. "Scout first. That's you." He looked at me.

Sure, why not. I crouched enough to slip through the opening in the chain link, then turned and watched them join me.

We started our way down one row between the structures.

"How did you know?" Gage asked as we walked. "That we weren't together?"

He didn't really want me to answer that. I was going to anyway. "You've spent at least a quarter of the time since I've met you staring at her tits and ass." At my words, pink crept across Evie's cheeks. "At least as much time looking like a dope when she says something, yet you do your best not to touch her."

Gage's expression was growing as dark as the shadows we crept in. "Not everyone is comfortable with public displays of affection."

"I don't mean that." I'd already started, I might as well finish. "I mean the little touches. The intimate finger brushes. The stolen kisses and tiny shoulder bumps. They're not only missing, but you're going out of your way to avoid them."

"You're more observant than I gave you credit for." Evie sounded thoughtful.

I shrugged. Best to set a low bar and exceed it every time. "I'm more a lot of things than you gave me credit for."

"We're here to see ghosts, let's look for ghosts." Gage's change of subject was less than subtle.

Okay. "How exactly are we doing that?"

"Urban exploration. We wander. We extend our feelers. We… listen?" Gage faltered.

Evie paused near a building and pressed her palm to the faded stain and splintered wood. "Sometimes the ghosts spill their secrets."

"What does that mean?" I asked.

She resumed walking. "Exactly what it sounds like." Her tone implied that was the end of that conversation.

We continued our stroll, down one row, and up the next. The conversation fell off as the barracks loomed around us, and even the voices were gone from the other people. The atmosphere here demanded reverence. Silence.

Clouds moved in above us, lengthening the shadows and making the air feel heavier. But not in a bad way. It wasn't a spooky kind of atmosphere, it was more like the three of us were isolated from the rest of the world, and wrapped in our own little bubble of discovery.

I shook the weird thought aside, and turned my focus to appreciating the view in front of me. Evie's fascination with each new spot, as well as the sway of her hips and her smooth, tempting exposed shoulders.

Was I looking forward to spending the next week or two in negotiations with her? Yes, I was.

"I want to look inside." At the abrupt announcement, Evie stopped next to one of the windows. It was nearly a foot above her head.

Gage dropped to one knee without hesitation, propping the other against the side of the house, and offering her a hand.

She knew they were friends, she may even know he found her attractive, but did she have any idea he'd move heaven and earth for her?

She took the step up, and wobbled before catching her balance on Gage and the building. She shifted her weight to get closer to the window. A few raindrops hit my nose. My neck.

Evie lost her balance again, and flailed for something new. I rested my hands on her hips before my brain could tell me it was a bad idea.

"Look quick." I kept my tone light, despite the sparks spilling between us. "It's starting to rain." Her heat seared through her thin top. Through my palms.

She rose on tiptoe and peered through the window, pointing her phone in as well and snapping a few pictures. "There are still things in there," she said softly. "Toys. A bed. Not a bunch of stuff, but —" The roar of wind cut her off.

More raindrops landed on us. And then the

deluge started, as if God himself had snapped his fingers.

Evie squeaked at the buckets of rain.

That was far more appealing than I'd expected.

She jumped, and I still held onto her, softening the short distance to the ground. Laughter shone in her eyes, and water poured around us. Her hair was plastered to her face. her shirt clung to her skin. Her pale bra was obvious, but her bright green eyes were the things that captivated me.

Her laugh caught in her throat when she met my gaze.

This was cliché. Idiotic.

Compelling. Intriguing. I wanted a kiss. Just a taste of the shine on her lips. She was so close. A twitch of my head, and I could claim her mouth.

Gage was on his feet, wrapping an arm around Evie's waist and pulling her away. "We should get back to the car before we get covered in mud." His heavy tone was a sharp contrast to her brightness, as he steered her toward the fence.

No. I grabbed Evie's arm and tugged her to face me again. "I had a lot of fun. Thank you for the invite."

This was where I should let her go. Watch them be on their way. Be grateful that Gage interrupted before I could make a potentially costly mistake.

Fuck what I should do.

I tugged Evie into me again, gripped the back of her neck, and crushed my mouth to hers.

This was better than I wanted it to be. Better than it had any right to be. Her mouth was soft, and her body molded to mine. The fire connecting us should be pulling steam from our clothes. I nipped her lips and devoured her moans and swallowed every one of her tiny gasps as the rain beat down around us.

Gage cleared his throat.

His loss.

Evie broke away from me with a soft smile, and hovered her fingers over her lips. "Thank you for being the random stranger in the buffet."

She was going to be so pissed when she found out the truth.

But I'd smooth it over, I always did. And that kiss was worth it. "Enjoy the rest of your weekend."

4 /
gage

A voice in my head roared *mine*, and I struggled to silence it. Evie wasn't mine.

Telling myself to chill the fuck out didn't stop me from glancing at her every few seconds as we drove back to the hotel. I couldn't help but notice the way her fingers hovered over her lips. The tiny smile that played on her face.

Because some asshole stranger kissed her in the rain. The same guy who was following us. Whose *pretty car* taunted me in the rear-view mirror, because he was going the same place we were.

A growl slipped from my throat, and I cringed at myself.

"What's wrong?" Evie asked.

"I'm fine." This wasn't me, and I needed to get a grip.

Evie's huff said she didn't believe me. Not that I blamed her. "Tell me, or I'll keep asking," she said.

I tried to hide another growl with a sigh. "Can we just make it to the parking lot?"

"Okay." The way she clipped the word, she wouldn't wait much longer before pushing the issue again.

I was overreacting, and I had less than five minutes to stop being a jealous ass. Knowing that and doing it were two vastly different things.

The one who got away.

Was I really going down that path? With my best friend? The woman who was my sanity and salvation over the last few years. Who had been there since we were kids.

I sure as fuck wasn't going to sit back and watch her with some big city asshole who had no concept of how incredible Evie was.

I pulled into the parking lot, and as I put the SUV in park, she was twisting in her seat to face me. "Gage, just talk to me."

Yeah. We should talk. I looked at her. Those eyes. That exasperation mixed with concern. The wet hair hanging around her face and the way her half-dry top still clung to her skin.

Fuck it. I cupped her cheeks between my palms, and my entire body roared in anticipation. When I found her mouth with mine, the thoughts vanished. The only things that existed were her and me. Her soft lips. The tiny sighs she was making. The taste of rain.

"Whoa." Evie pressed a palm to my chest enough to break the kiss.

I didn't want this to end. I needed more. "Do you want me to stop?"

Her pause was excruciating. Her, "No, I don't want you to stop," was my salvation.

I dipped my head to hers, kissing her again and again. Letting the pouring rain on the truck roof cut us off from the rest of the world. Nipping at her skin and swallowing her moans. This was more intoxicating than a good whisky. Better than...

There was no comparison.

"What is this?" Evie asked between kisses, but she didn't try to stop me again.

I wasn't in the right frame of mind to put a name to what we were doing. "Birthday present?" That was it. "Let me make this a fortieth birthday we'll never forget."

"With kisses?" Her laugh was light.

Not that I would mind, but I had something more all-consuming in mind. As in, I wanted all of her. I nipped her ear—the one Sawyer hadn't whispered in. "With mind-blowing sex."

"This is where I should protest, because sex ruins friendships." She tilted her head, giving me easier access to her neck, as I kissed along her jaw.

I scraped my teeth over her skin. "Is that what you're doing?"

Evie pulled away again, not from my touch, but

I couldn't kiss her anymore. "I don't want you to look at me differently when we're done," she said.

"City Boy already pointed out how I look at you *now*."

The corners of her mouth tugged up, I hoped at the nickname.

I trailed my fingers over her chest in a lazy *X*. "Cross my heart, this doesn't change the way I feel about our friendship." I dragged my thumb over her bottom lip, and her mouth parted in a silent gasp.

"You *are* hot." Her voice was breathy, but there was a hint of *I'm going to try to be rational about this* in her voice that was so very Evie. "And a really good kisser. As long as you're not bad in bed…"

"I'm not."

"Big words, big man." Her playfulness was back.

I was tempted to fuck her here. In the middle of the parking lot. "Room. Now."

In the short run across the parking lot, we were soaked all over again, and I couldn't think about anything but which piece of wet clothing I was going to peel off her first. This wasn't a big hotel, but when we stepped inside, the elevator looked like it was a million miles away.

Before we could cross the lobby, Evie yanked me to a stop. "What do you think happened there?"

Sawyer was a few feet away, having just emerged from the gift shop. He was as soaking wet as we were, and the suitcase he dragged behind him looked the same.

Was she serious? Who the fuck cared what happened?

"You all right?" Evie asked him.

God damn it.

Sawyer's smugness looked more like a mask than before, as he glanced between us. "Turns out my hatch leaks." He sounded seven degrees of irritated. "I was hoping they had enough souvenir clothes for me to wear so I could shove some things in the dryer."

"Any luck?" Evie asked.

"Nope. They had some great shirts." He tugged a bright orange hotel top half out of the bag he carried. "No pants or shorts though. I'll just air dry while I do some laundry."

Good luck with that. I so badly wanted to be the jerk I knew he would be if our roles were reversed. Especially given what he'd interrupted.

I couldn't do it. "I have an extra pair of sweats I can spot you." I hated myself as I listened to the words tumble past my lips.

Evie squeezed my hand.

That didn't quite help, but at least I knew she approved.

"I probably won't be able to return them," Sawyer said.

If he didn't stop talking, I'd have time to change my mind. "They're sweatpants. I'll find another pair somewhere."

"Thanks. I'll follow you up to your room."

Sawyer fell into step beside us as we resumed our journey.

While we waited for the elevator, he kept glancing at us, but didn't say anything. The ride up a whole floor was the same, and the silent glances were driving me nuts by the time I unlocked the room.

"What?" I asked.

"I interrupted something." He wasn't asking.

Evie stepped around us and grabbed her bag. "No. It was nothing." Her words cut through me. "I'm going to change in here." She stepped into the bathroom.

I handed Sawyer a pair of sweatpants, and turned to changing my own clothes. Could I wait until he was gone? Sure, but I wasn't above stripping off my shirt to prove a point.

Sawyer did the same.

Okay, so the guy was hot—I could admit I saw why Evie was drawn to him physically. That didn't mean he was worth her time.

He set his wet shirt on the bag his new T-shirt had been in. "Shared room. Holding hands. Swollen lips. I thought you two weren't together."

"We were about to be." I was more than happy to shove that fact down his throat.

"And yet you offered..." He held up the dry pants.

He couldn't even be gracious. I clenched my jaw.

"I wouldn't have," he said. "Especially if it was a

choice between being polite and having a woman like that."

"You say that like it should surprise me you think that way." I reached for a new shirt, but didn't pull it on.

Sawyer smirked. That infuriating look that seemed to be his resting expression. "You think you've got me figured out?"

"You think you've got *me* figured out?" I mimicked.

"Closer to doing so than you'd like me to be. Five more minutes on that base, and I'd have had her topless right there."

His arrogance sliced through me, letting fury spill free. I grabbed his bare arm and dug my fingers into wiry, corded muscle.

Sawyer didn't look concerned.

"You think so?" Evie's voice startled me. She'd emerged from the bathroom and was wearing an oversized T-shirt that almost hung past the edge of her cut-offs. "You were so far from getting in my panties..."

Sawyer jerked free from my grip and turned to face her. "I call bullshit. You were wet before the rain started, and long before the two of you made it out of his SUV. Which, I don't have to be any sort of observant genius to guess what you were up to. I walked right past the two of you steaming up windows like a dry cleaner's."

Good. Fucker.

"And you think she yielded to me because… Why? You warmed her up?" I asked.

Sawyer shrugged. "Your words."

"Does that usually work for you?" Evie countered. "The arrogance?"

"It was starting to with you," Sawyer said.

Evie shook her head. "No. It wasn't."

It had been, though. He intrigued Evie. The puzzle she couldn't solve at a glance. The problem with the Sawyer-puzzle was he resembled a box with gold inlaid designs. The kind that summoned demons when solved. *It's not hands that call us, but desire.*

"Fine." The smugness lingered in Sawyer's voice. "No one had any fun except me. I definitely shouldn't have interrupted what you two were up to. Don't let me stop you from picking up where you left off. Go ahead. I don't mind." He settled onto the edge of Evie's bed.

God this man was infuriating. Could I punch him here and now and get away with it? Evie would back me up if the police got involved. It was justifiable.

Evie's nostrils flared in irritation. "The problem with guys like you is that your ego is bigger than your dick, and the only thing more disappointing than the misplaced self-confidence is your performance in bed."

My snort slipped out, and I didn't make any effort to stop it.

But the unflappable Sawyer's feathers had been ruffled. Finally. His smirk vanished and he was on his feet again. "Really? You think your homegrown farm boy is better at fucking than me?"

I'd guarantee it. But my word didn't matter here.

"Yes," Evie said. "I'd bet my entire stack of casino chips that you're just bad in bed."

Another reason to adore her.

Sawyer crossed the room to her in a few short strides, and pinned her to the wall with his whole body as he pressed his hand to her throat. "I would ruin you for anyone else."

I was already moving, to yank him away. To physically throw him out of the room.

"Prove it." Evie's words stopped me in my tracks.

5 /
evie

I nside me were two Evies.

One was logical. Smart. Knew from her time in the Marines that it was a mistake to step between two men involved in a dick measuring contest.

The other knew that she was the measuring stick, and had locked the first in the closet to shut her up. The most gorgeous man in my hometown and the equally sexy stranger from out of town each wanted a chance to prove they could give me a better orgasm.

The way Sawyer's thumb pressed against the vein in my neck with just enough pressure to tease, the way Gage looked ready to rip him to shreds for daring to touch me…

Sawyer was right—it wasn't the rain that made me wet.

"What are the terms?" Sawyer asked. Because

of course he needed a bar to measure his victory by. He looked even better shirtless, and the tattoos dotted here and there added to forbidden air he radiated. I wasn't sure what to make of the Scorpions logo on his arm, but the entire package was sexy.

This was where Logical Evie would say *No bar. No deal. Stop acting like cavemen. Maybe hit up the strip club without me and get this out of your system.*

Good thing I wasn't listening to her. "Whichever one of you gets me off best, wins. I get to judge. Unless you're nervous about performing in front of another man."

"I'm not." Gage responded before Sawyer could.

Gage was the unknown in this whole thing. Those kisses. The hunger in his voice when we were in the truck. He wanted me?

He'd also promised me this wouldn't ruin our friendship. A teensy, tiny part of me wondered if he wanted more. Fortunately, that bit was also locked away right now. And this would make sure we kept sex in the realm of nothing-more-than-fun.

Sawyer pressed his mouth to the hollow behind my ear. Every time he did that, delicious shivers sped over me. "Stop me now if you're not sure."

I was positive. "Don't hold back. Gage won't." I was poking a bear. I knew it and was willing to do it again and again, to feed the thrill and want that was lighting my skin on fire.

Sawyer's lips were on mine again. This wasn't the flirty playfulness from the base, This kiss was possessive. Hard. Zinged through me from my head to my toes and everywhere in between, and made me feel like he'd staked his claim on me.

Which I wouldn't allow. Especially not with just a kiss. He had to earn anything he tried to take, and I was going to enjoy every minute of it. I used my entire frame to shove Sawyer away, and his eyes grew wide. His smirk never vanished, though.

He and his smugly sexy face could wait. I turned to Gage and crooked my finger. He was with me in an instant, crushing his mouth to mine. Picking up where we left off in the truck, but the playfulness was gone.

This was an intensity that stole my breath. Gage was craft beer to Sawyer's finely aged whiskey, and I didn't know which was better.

Both had their place.

Sawyer rested his hands on my hips to slide between me and the wall he'd pressed me into moments earlier. He pulled me into his bare chest, and his heat radiated through my shirt. His mouth moved along the back of my neck, licking. Nipping. At the same time Gage kissed me and sucked on my tongue.

Sawyer dug his fingers tighter into my hips, gripping me and refusing to let me go, while Gage lifted my shirt enough to hook a finger in my waistband and pull me tighter into him. We'd barely left first base and I was already losing myself in the myriad of sensations.

Gage dipped his finger lower, over my bare skin, slipping his touch down along my hip. "You're not wearing panties." His voice was a low growl.

Sawyer's grip tightened like a vice.

I smiled against Gage's mouth. "I only brought so many pairs, and I had to make sure I had one to wear home." That and walking out here in the middle of their less than subtle *conversation* in nothing but my cutoffs and T-shirt had made me feel deliciously naughty.

So did their duet of groans.

"There does seem to be a shortage of clothes going around." Sawyer let go of me with one hand. "And we wouldn't want your shorts to get dirty either." He undid the button on my pants with a flick of his wrist, and with a single yank, the zipper came down. He let the clothing fall to the ground.

The air teased my slick skin, but my shirt covered me.

Until Gage shoved my shirt up. "Barbarian." He glided his lips down my neck. "Going straight for the pussy like he's pillaging, rather than wooing."

The dry humor was Gage. The teasing was what I was used to with him. The words themselves... not necessarily. Altogether, his comment made for a unique flavor of temptation.

The thoughts vanished when he lowered his

head to my breasts and drew one nipple into his mouth. That was good. That was *really* good.

Sawyer remained focused on my neck, and the way he was biting I swore he was going to leave a mark. I liked that too. Really, I was enjoying all of it. Being caught between them. Feeling their mouths and hands roam everywhere, until the insides of my thighs were coated with desire, and I had to squeeze my legs together to suppress the throb of need.

Not that it was working.

Someone pulled my shirt over my head. Sawyer. Gage. Both of them. I was losing track of whose touch was whose, because why focus on one when it all felt so good?

Breaking away enough to work my shirt free meant a change in contact. Sawyer took the opportunity to spin me to face him, and cupped one of my breasts. He dragged his thumb over a still-damp nipple, sending a zing through my body. With his free hand, he glided down my arm to grab my wrist, and draw it to his erection.

New toy. I used the excuse to trace the outline through drying fabric. To feel how hard he was. How big, pressing into my palm, and twitching under my touch.

"In case you think I'm only doing this because you egged me on." His voice was low and rough. "You're not the only one enjoying yourself."

"I'd hope not." I was intrigued by this man. He was as fun as he was infuriating.

And he was slipping his fingers between my legs. Teasing his touch along my wet skin with a groan that promised delicious things still to come. "*Christ,* which of us did this to you?"

If I told him the truth, it would provoke him, so of course I was going to. "I don't know. I lost track."

"I'll have to try harder to keep your attention on me, then." Sawyer pulled his fingers back to his mouth, to suck them clean.

That was a good way to get me to watch him intently.

Until Gage glided his palm down my back and along my ass, between my legs, to slip his fingers into me from behind.

I whimpered at the slow, light penetration, and leaned into Gage's touch. The contrast between the two hadn't dimmed. Sawyer felt dangerous in a way I couldn't pin down, where Gage was safety. But they were both electric, and the way Gage pumped inside me was agonizingly delicious.

Sawyer stepped back, taking me with him and pulling me away from Gage. I couldn't help but pout at the loss of that penetrating touch.

Sawyer stopped at the end of the bed, and tilted my head up, forcing my gaze to his. "Reach into my back pocket, and take a condom from my wallet." His tone implied he wouldn't be ignored.

Okay. I'd play. I did what he ordered, tossed his wallet on the bed, and held the rubber up between two fingers.

He snagged it from me. "Now take off my pants."

"I don't let just anyone boss me around."

"I'd hope not."

I didn't have a counter to that, and I wanted to keep going, so I did what he said and pushed the rest of his clothes to the ground.

Sawyer sat on the edge of the bed and guided me to straddle his legs. I lowered myself into his lap, catching his erection between us, but not letting him slide inside. He knotted his fingers in my hair and yanked me closer to devour my moans.

I slipped against his shaft, grinding into him. Riding without penetration. If I shifted in the right way, could I get off?

From behind me, Gage glided his hands down my chest to between my legs, finally finding my clit. Circling. Coaxing. Drawing my orgasm to the surface. I came hard, losing myself in the pleasure. Not keeping track of how hard I was pushing or screaming or anything but how it all felt.

As the sensations faded, as Gage's touch fell away, Sawyer caught my bottom lip between his teeth and tugged before letting go.

"My turn." He scooted further onto the bed, coaxing me with him. He tore the condom open with his teeth and rolled it on.

I wanted to tease, but my body was hungry for more. Of everything. I hovered over Sawyer long enough to place his cock at the head of my entrance, and lowered myself onto him.

His strangled *fuuuck*… the way he dug his fingers into my thighs… the penetration… It was so good. He barely moved inside me as he pressed his thumb to my clit.

The fresh contact was too much, after… I couldn't… I whimpered through the discomfort. Was it more fun on the other side?

"Trust me," Sawyer said.

I raised my brows. "Never trust a person who —"

Sawyer shifted his touch, and hit a new nerve— an incredible spot that brushed the squirmies away and left ecstasy in its place.

Gage knelt behind me on the mattress, cradling my breasts, his cock pressing into my back. He kissed me. Ran his hands over my entire body. Touched anywhere he could reach.

Climax raced in again, focused on that almost-too-much-but-still-so-good feeling from Sawyer. I clenched around his cock, slipping, sliding, riding him like my life depended on it. I was barely aware of Sawyer's grunts changing. Shortening. Stalling, before he came, too.

Gage was making similar delicious noises, as he ground against my back. When he stopped, pulled away, the air cooled the wet spot he'd left on my skin.

This time when Gage kissed my shoulder, the

frantic hunger was gone. His touch was soft. Tender. "I made a mess." His words hummed through my skin.

Sawyer slid his hands up my hips to my shoulder blades, pulling me into his chest as he moved. "Guess you're staying here while he cleans you up."

I wouldn't complain about that. *Here,* pressed against Sawyer, was warm and cuddly and let me linger in bliss a moment or two longer.

When Gage returned, both men were gentle making sure most of the sticky was wiped off me. The bed wasn't so lucky. It had a huge wet spot where we'd been, and we opted to relocate.

I stood, and Gage's arm was around me in an instant, pulling me down next to him on the other mattress, Holding me tight. Not that I had a problem with that. The happy buzz in my veins wanted all of this, and for it to last for a million billion years.

Sawyer sat on the bed across from us, rather than joining us. "Well?" he asked.

Was he really...? Talk about a buzz kill. "Well what?"

"Who won?" Yup. That was what he was asking.

And I had the perfect answer. "Me. No question. Beyond that, let's call it a tie."

"Hmm…"

Sawyer's lack of comment had me curious, but I was keeping Smart Evie under lock and key a little longer, so I wouldn't have to think.

He grasped my fingers and kissed the back of my knuckles. "Happy... Day, Evie. Good luck to both of you on that pact." He let go of me to grab Gage's sweats from where they still sat at the edge of the bed. "Thanks for making this a memorable distraction." Sawyer dressed as he talked.

Um...

I didn't know what to think as he walked out of the room. That was abrupt. Definitely ruined the warm fuzzy glow in my core. Needy *fuck me* Evie was gone, and the part of me who could be reasonable and not much else was back.

I rolled out of Gage's arms and onto my back. "What did we just do?" I was asking myself as much as I was him.

"Had a lot of fun. Incredible. Fucking. Fun."

I almost laughed, though he hadn't said anything particularly funny. I just needed to find a light feeling again. "Incredible fucking. I get it."

"You *did* get it." There was an edge to his teasing, but it was faint. A whisper amid fun.

I rolled my head to the side to look at Gage. "I got a bit caught up..."

"In the challenge. I know. I was here."

The thing was, there weren't many people I'd trust with a conversation like this, and I was grateful Gage was on that short list. "Did we make a mistake?"

"Does it feel like a mistake?"

Why was I struggling to read him? His answer

was less than concrete, and certainly not what I hoped for.

"Only if you look at me differently now." It was the truth. The only answer I had.

He reached across the space between us. Less than a foot, but it felt like it spanned eternity. He grasped my hand. "I promised I wouldn't," he said.

"But now that it's happened…"

"To me, you're still the same Evie as you were last night in the graveyard."

Better. I could live with that. I was happy with that. "Then no, it doesn't feel like a mistake. You were incredible."

"So were you," Gage said. "But you always are."

Heat spread across my cheeks. I wanted to linger on Gage, not only on what he was saying, but on what he wasn't. What hid under the surface. What led us to this point so quickly today?

I wouldn't read between the lines though. Not today. Never with him. Doing so with someone else had gotten me in trouble once. It nearly destroyed me in more ways than one to assume a man meant something other than what they were saying.

I trusted Gage. If he said we were still friends, nothing more, I had to take that at face value.

6 /
sawyer

Sunday afternoons were the perfect time to catch up on paperwork. The world in general was a more subdued place, and that made a great atmosphere for sinking into the mundane.

Or it would if I could force my attention to my laptop instead of staring off into space thinking about yesterday. Again. Each time I let my mind idle, it raced off toward thoughts of Evie.

I'd had a lot of fun, but that didn't mean I needed to make it into a memory I moved into.

No, I already had those moments from my past that I lived in too often.

I had other properties besides hers that I was here to look at, and the details of those required my attention. I pulled up the list of mostly older businesses and family farms, spread across multiple towns and counties,

All of these were near bank foreclosure for

whatever reason. All in small towns that were on the edge of a boom of growth. My job was to figure out which were worth the buy, so we could resell the land right as the prices soared.

Evie's place was different though. Not unique, but rare. We already had a buyer, but it was someone who hadn't been able to or hadn't wanted to go to her directly. Given that said buyer was local, on top of everything else I'd learned about her yesterday, she may need to learn to choose her friends better.

Details like that weren't my problem though—I just had to get her to sell to us. Not just for the commission, but this was me proving to my father that I was the son he needed to sign the business over to.

It was a little late in life for me to play this card, and I'd missed out on years of chances thanks to...

A pain stabbed me in the chest, a spear penetrating my soul, and I turned back to work. I'd take daydreaming about Evie over this ache, any day.

My phone rang, and my brother's name flashed on the screen. Not the distraction I wanted, but probably the one I needed. Especially if he thought he'd gloat about sending me to the biggest little truck stop of a town he could think of.

"Yeah," I answered.

"Hey." Hudson's voice was warm. Friendly. Amused. "How was Wendover?"

There it was. "Absolutely loved it."

"Really." There was Hudson's shock. "You win at the tables or something?"

I had gambled... Though not in the way he meant. "You could say I won big."

"Uh-huh." In a single grunt, his interest had vanished. "You're not going to vague me into asking for details. If you don't want to share, I don't give a fuck."

I may tell him the story eventually. Like, as part of the story about how I landed this property. "Fine. What's up?"

"You know what's up."

I grunted and sank in my seat. Not this again. "Tell me why." He'd been trying to talk me out of making this deal since I made the plans.

"I told you why."

Because it's a bad idea.

Yeah, that wasn't going to cut it for me. "Give me the real reason."

"There's no better reason than that," Hudson said.

"This whole *I need to succeed so Daddy loves me more* motivation of yours is really childish," I said.

Hudson was silent for a moment.

"You're right, it is. And you're too old to be doing it," he finally said.

I snorted my amusement. "I don't need him to love me. I need my name in that *owner* spot on the paperwork when he retires."

"You don't want that. Tony wouldn't have wanted that for you."

That pain was back. The spear skewering me. Making it hard to breathe. I clenched my fist and jaw and waited out the feeling, but it didn't fade. Why did Hudson have to bring *him* into this? "Fuck you." It was a struggle to keep my voice even. Hard. "You don't get to say his name."

Because Hudson didn't take my side, he took Tony's when Tony go si—

"I need you to trust me on this," Hudson silenced the thought in a way I couldn't by myself.

"But I don't trust you. You see that's the issue, right?"

"Just—"

"Thanks for the Wendover recommendation," I talked over him. "Loved the score. Talk to you when this is over." I hung up before he could counter-quip me.

This hurt so much. If I hadn't dealt with it for months straight in the past, I'd think I was having a heart attack now. As I breathed through my nostrils and tried to count through forgetting the wonderful things, the way I lost them, that caused this pain, my gaze landed on my keys.

On the gold and platinum vial that hung with my keys. The object was custom made from his and my rings that held some of Tony's ashes inside.

"Why did you leave me?" I asked the empty

room. It wasn't the first time I'd needed to know that, and I didn't expect any more of an answer than I'd gotten in the past.

None of that eased the ache in my heart.

7 /
evie

I'd never been a morning person, but the military and then owning a store I would do anything for had me in before ten, doing the early opening ritual I'd learned from Grandpa as a kid.

I strolled up one aisle and down the next, checking each section and making sure it was all in order, that there wasn't anything out of place, or any low stock I needed to replenish. While I roamed, while my mind drifted over *so this is what forty feels like*, snippets of the past slipped in.

Originally, I wasn't Grandpa's choice to take over. A lot of the families around here had passed their land and businesses down through the men in their lines. But my mom and dad were career military—they met in the Navy—and they expected their sons would do the same.

Except the twins that they were told were both

male were actually one boy and one girl. They were never cruel about it, not even in a backhanded kind of way—Mom and Dad loved me regardless—but I wanted to do what Grandpa did. I wanted to build stuff and design things and figure out how the entire world worked.

I turned and headed down the aisle with the electronics components. This was the one I'd insisted we add years ago, after I realized I couldn't do career military. After I came back home with my tail between my legs, and discovered Grandpa had left me the shop when he passed.

In the years leading up to that, he and I found the things we had in common, and I taught him how to build small robots out of cheap RC cars.

I trailed my fingers over the shelf with the solder. Weird thing to be sentimental about, but I was.

My phone rang, yanking me from the clashing good and bad memories, and *Eddie* flashed on the screen.

"Yo." I answered my brother's call. Our real names weren't Evelyn and Edward, though we let most people believe it. I was Eowyn and he was Eomir—our parents were huge LotR geeks.

Probably better names than Boromir and Faramir like they originally wanted to give us.

"Hey, old lady. You get the walker I sent you yet?" Eddie was cheerful. The bastard had probably been up for five or six hours already.

Early mornings. Gross. "Is that what that was? I thought you sent me your scrap metal to make an obstacle course for Destructy."

"You pulled that poor thing out of retirement? He's the one who needs a walker."

Destructy was the biggest robot I'd built with Grandpa, and got his name not because he was meant to destroy things, but because I'd rammed him into a shelf full of hammers during his first test drive, and sent five aisles toppling like dominos.

That was the day Grandpa first mentioned me taking over—after we spent hours cleaning up and I figured out how to put the shelves up so it wouldn't happen again. That was also one of the happiest days of my life. I'd done everything for this place, and it was all going so well.

Until Travis.

No. What happened here was my fault, not anyone else's.

"He'd run circles around your ass," I teased.

"He wouldn't, because Destructy's not capable of turning in a circle, and that's what makes him terrifying," Eddie countered. "Seriously though, how's forty?"

"So far, same as thirty-nine, but with more nostalgia."

"Yeah, I get that." Eddie's shift toward melancholy was tangible even though I couldn't see him. "Look, I need to get back to work soon, but I wanted to see how things are going. Wish you happy birthday." He'd been promoted to Brigadier General a year ago—one of the youngest—and he was always busy. Not that he'd been anything but before that.

As for how things were going... *I'm about to lose the family store and I don't know how to fix it because I was thinking with my heart and vagina instead of my brain.* "Things are great here." The last thing I needed was his disappointment, or worse, his sympathy. "Happy birthday to you too, old man."

There was a pause. Was he distracted? Did he hear me?

"Next time I see you in person, you're going to tell me how things actually are." Eddie had always been able to read me too well. "Give Gage my wishes as well?"

"Of course. I'll tell him you called. Don't get hurt out there, and don't shoot anyone who doesn't deserve it."

Eddie chuckled. "You neither."

I hung up, trying not to let my mind wander down the path it was tugging me toward. Because Eddie had to bring up Gage. Of course he would. When we were really little, we were called the triplets, because we all had the same birthday.

But Gage and I were definitely not siblings. Even before this weekend, but especially now...

We were still just friends though. He'd said the sex didn't change that, and though there was a part of me that liked the idea of more, I didn't want to lose his friendship.

I didn't want him to become another Don. High school friend I hooked up with after I was discharged. A guy I thought was my best friend, until I found out he was keeping our relationship secret so he could fuck Alys, too.

I thought I'd learned after him. I was single for years after.

And I really didn't want Gage to be another Travis. The man I convinced myself for years that I was *with*, despite the fact that he said over and over all we had was sex.

No, I had to go and convince myself that Travis and I were more to each other, because we kept hooking up. He kept coming back and so did I. Hell, I even loaned him money when he asked. Let my cash reserves drop lower and lower until there was nothing left to account for slim months at the store.

When I pushed back on both—when I asked Travis about paying me back, about taking our relationship to the next level—he reminded me we weren't in a relationship. We were fuck buddies, and he pointed out I'd helped him financially because I could.

There were never strings attached to either agreement.

Travis's words, my idiotic misunderstanding.

So, I'd figure out how to fix the floundering store myself, and I'd take Gage at face value when he said the sex was just sex, because doing either thing differently would be a disaster.

I resumed my walk of the shop, making the occasional note here and there based on the sparse business we did Saturday while I was out. In the background was the occasional sound of someone coming or going. The voice of the employee working the register would drift back sometimes. A person in another aisle. The whirl of a cart's wheels on tile.

As I turned a corner, my brain stalled at what—who—I saw in front of me. "Sawyer?" My bitch of a body reacted instantly, heating at memories of Saturday. My brain veered off in a much cooler direction. It was definitely him. "How did you find me?" *Why* did he find me?

He wore the same smirk I thought was alluring before, that struck me as disconcerting now. "Not sure if you realize this, but your store address is listed online. On your website. Eowyn Young?"

I didn't like this at all. If I screamed, someone would be here in a blink. Sawyer wasn't advancing, but his posture was too casual. Too laid back.

"Let's try this again. *Why* did you find me? Couldn't stay away?" I kept my tone cool.

"Definitely couldn't do that, no."

What was he playing at?

He shrugged. "I'm not here for the reason you

probably think. Let's start from the top. I'm Sawyer Rawlings. I'm here to make you an offer on your property."

"My what?" That was less than brilliant. How did he keep scrambling my mind?

"Your store." He gestured around him. "I'm here to make you an offer. That's why I'm in town."

He wasn't surprised to see me at all. On the other hand, I was confused as fuck and just starting to catch up. A large piece of an otherwise incomplete picture slammed into my brain all at once. "You knew who I was."

"I did." There was no hesitation in his reply.

He came to town to try to buy my store. He knew he was looking for Evie when he met Gage and me on Saturday morning.

So… "In other words, when I introduced myself, your thought was *this is the woman I'm here to talk to. And instead of telling me so then you decided I should fuck her before I try to fuck her.*" It didn't matter that I hadn't heard his offer. I wasn't interested in selling, and definitely not to someone who entered the negotiation with—whose opening shot was—a deception.

Finally, I'd asked something that made him pause. "Yes. And then no."

Great. *Now* the asshole was going to be honest. My irritation climbed toward anger. "Why did you think that was a good idea?"

He stepped closer, and my body reacted again.

The scent of his cologne, his heat, it had my skin prickling at the reminder of his touch. How good the sex was. How much fun he was—

Nope. Wasn't going down that path, because this guy was a creepy asshole.

"I was going to pretend today that I didn't know the first time we met. But you had a great time this weekend, and you deserve the truth."

I raised my brows. Anger had become full-blown fury. "Super thoughtful of you." I like the edge slice through my words.

"I'm not here to fuck you," Sawyer said. "My offer is more than fair, and there's room for negotiation." He tilted his head closer, and his hot breath teased my skin. "Plus, we could have a round two. Back room is empty. We could relive this weekend before you sign anything."

Fuck this guy. I planted a hand on his chest and shoved him back.

He grabbed my wrist and held his ground. His grip was tight as he searched my face.

I was shorter. Smaller. But I was stronger, and I knew what I was doing. I twisted my wrist to grab his. I spun him away from him, pinned him to the closest shelf, and twisted his arm behind his back. "Get out of my store, and never come back." With a growl, I let go and put some distance between us.

He turned to face me again. "Beg and I'll think about it." He winked and blew me a kiss.

Was I more furious with him, or the itsy, bitsy part of me that liked this?

"*Get out.*" My scream came out more shrilly than I intended.

8 /
gage

I walked into Evie's store shortly after opening, her gift in hand.

Terrance, the guy she had working up front, nodded toward the back of the store. "She's in the stacks somewhere," he said.

"*Get out.*" Evie's scream echoed off shelves and walls.

"I've got this." I was already sprinting toward the shout. I passed someone as I ran toward Evie.

Sawyer? What the fuck?

Couldn't be, but I wasn't stopping. I reached her seconds later, standing in the middle of the plumbing aisle, fists clenched and face red.

"Are you all right?" I checked her for injuries as well as I could without making contact.

It took her a moment to focus on me. She worked her jaw. "Depends on how you define *all right.*" Her voice was barely controlled rage. She drew in a long breath and her nostrils flared. "It turns out the dick was good, but the dick life support system sucked."

What? "We're talking about Sawyer? That *was* him I saw. What did he do?" I turned to chase him down. Whatever it was, I'd knock some sense into him. Evie could explain later.

"Don't." Evie grabbed my arm. "I think he might enjoy it too much."

"What happened? Why is he *here*?" I set her present on a nearby shelf and reached out to rub her arm.

Slowly her fist unclenched. "He..." She sighed. "His *business*? Buying me out. He knew who I was. I'm assuming the instant I introduced myself on Saturday."

Now my anger had a focus. "I'll be back. I have a face to pound in."

"No." Evie relaxed further. "Seriously, that'll probably just provoke him. You do remember what happened, don't you?"

All too well. In fact it had been playing on repeat in my head for almost two days. A warring series of memories that soared high with how incredible it was to be with Evie, and crashed with the fact that I had to share that moment with—

"Yes." I could still find him later and deck him. Out of principle.

The rest of the energy seemed to drain from Evie as she sank to the ground and pulled her knees to her chest. "I can't lose this place, Gage. I can't."

So don't sell. I had a feeling from the despair bleeding into her words that it wasn't that simple. "Tell me what's going on."

"I owe so much." Her voice grew quiet. "Back taxes. Interest and late fees on a bad loan. I can't even dent the actual money owed, and I don't know how to climb out."

I'd known she was struggling, but had no idea how bad it was. "You should've said something."

She scrubbed her face.

It didn't matter now. That wasn't the issue. "We'll figure it out. I'll help. Aubrey and Alys. Deacon and Adam."

"You are *not* thinking of putting Aubrey and Deacon in the same room." She snorted.

"And you can't brush us off. If you need help, if your shop is in trouble, we'll help. It's what we all do." I wasn't letting her deflect.

"It doesn't matter." Evie sounded defeated, which I wasn't used to. "Even if I climb out, even if I miraculously find a bag of money under a rock, this place doesn't make enough without a cash reserve, and that's gone."

I sat next to her on the floor and wrapped an arm around her waist. She leaned into me and rested her head on my shoulder.

"There's an answer—there has to be—and we'll find it," I said.

"Thank you." The hopelessness lingered in her tone. "Eddie says *happy birthday* by the way."

I'd let her change the subject for now, but we were looping back to this soon. "Same to him. Have you had breakfast yet? Come over to the grill and I'll make you something."

"I can't. I have work to do." She didn't pull away.

"At least open your birthday present before you get back to it." I reached up to the wrapped, flat box, careful not to jar her, and handed her the gift.

She took it from me and set it on the floor next to her. "You already gave me an incredible present this weekend, plus I left your gift at home."

This weekend's present was tainted now. "It's a gift. You have to accept it."

"I don't think that's how that works, but I do like presents." Evie picked at the edges of the wrap, then grasped one and tore into the paper. She opened the box, and studied the framed paper inside, the creases in her forehead deepening. "Is this... the pact we made when we were kids?"

"Yes, but also no. Turn it over."

She extracted the image, which was pressed between two pieces of glass inside the wooden frame, and flipped it to see the other side. "Oh. Oh wow."

It was a rough sketch of a robot. The first she'd ever designed. She'd made notes on the other side, which was why it looked like I'd framed our *contract* with each other to get married if we were both still single at forty.

"I can't believe this still exists." She turned it back and forth, looking at one side and then the other. "Why do you have it?"

"Confession. I kept it originally because it had the promise on it. But I found it a few months ago when I was going through some boxes Grace dropped off, and it reminded me of…. I don't know. More inventive times? Of what we were when we were allowed to just be."

"I don't think I was ever that." Her voice was quiet." She leaned into me again, this time squeezing my arm. "I love it. Thank you."

We were silent for a few minutes. Speaking felt like it might shatter whatever this was, and I didn't know if that would be good or bad.

"It's a good design." She was looking at her drawing again. "Simplistic, but I could totally see if we added a spinning blade, some side armor." She twisted her head sideways. "Have to decide between exposed wheels or hidden. Both have drawbacks…"

The cloud that was hanging over her faded, and one corner of her mouth pulled up. She was processing. Planning.

I could hear the gears whirring in her brain. "You should do it. Design it. Build it."

"No." Like that her creeping joy vanished. "Talk about frivolous and expensive." She set the picture on a nearby shelf and stood. "I need to get back to work, and I should let you do the same."

"You need to not shove this idea aside so easily." I climbed to my feet as well. "You were almost smiling just now."

Evie twisted her mouth. "And then adult me woke up and realized that was in the past."

How was I supposed to counter that? Sit here and force her to build a combat robot? That didn't sound effective. "I'll let you go back to work then."

"Let me?" This time her amusement was dry.

"Yes. Let you. And make sure you have fun tonight with the Nerd Herd. But tomorrow, if we're not building robots, we're figuring out how to make sure you keep this place."

"Is that an order?"

"Yes."

Her almost-smile was back. She clicked her feet together, stood at attention, and saluted. "Yes, sir."

I grabbed her salute hand and squeezed her fingers. "As you were, Marine. I'll see you soon."

As I walked past the front register, I told Terrance, "Call me if that guy comes back." Because fuck Sawyer.

My thoughts were a jumble as I stepped outside. If Sawyer was staying in Haddarville, his car was going to stand out. He'd be easy to track down. If he had any brains at all—which I was questioning—he left town when Evie screamed at him.

Which brought me to how was I going to help

Evie? Coming up with a solution didn't seem as daunting as getting her to accept the assistance.

When I saw a familiar car—not Sawyer's— parked outside my grill a few doors down, my brain stalled.

That was Grace's Chrysler. What was my ex-wife doing here?

I didn't have many feelings around seeing her again beyond curiosity and a little bit of resentment. I'd learned that I didn't miss her, but I did dislike her. The faster I found out what she wanted, why it had to be in person instead of a phone call, the faster I could shoo her out the door.

As I approached the restaurant, I had a good view inside through the large bank of windows. She sat at the front counter with her back to me. Knox, my business partner, stood across from her, watching her with a scowl on his face, and Rohde, stood next to him in his deputy uniform, wearing a similar look.

Friends. What would I do without them? I pasted on a flat expression for Grace's benefit and pushed into the building.

She whirled, and gave me a huge, sweet smile.

I used to melt for that smile.

"Gage, *hi*. I was hoping I'd find you."

I'd given up being surprised years ago that she couldn't remember my birthday. "You came to the right place. What can I do for you?" I wasn't friendly or rude or much of anything.

Some of her cheer faltered, but she kept that fucking mask in place. The same one she'd worn while she fucked around on me. "I'm leaving."

"You already left."

Her scowl peeked through. "As in, I'm moving. Out of state."

That explained why she'd been so eager to put our house on the market, out of nowhere. Funny how she'd refused to give me details before now. "Hmm. When?"

"Now. The moving truck is on its way to Idaho Falls, and I'm driving myself up there. I wanted to stop in and say *goodbye* before I left."

If she was trying to bait me into asking where the new-old boyfriend was in all of this, it wasn't my problem. "Okay. Goodbye."

"I'm going to miss you."

Behind her, Knox rolled his eyes and Rohde made a gagging gesture.

I tucked away my amusement at their support, and I seriously doubted Grace would think of me again once she was on her way. This was the longest conversation we'd had since I signed the divorce papers. "Okay."

She huffed. "Do I get a hug, for old time's sake?"

"No. Best of luck, Grace." I stepped aside and held the door open for her.

She narrowed her gaze, and I stared back.

Seconds ticked away. She walked out of the shop, got in her car, and left.

"Want me to make sure there's someone waiting for her somewhere along I-15?" Rohde asked as I took the stool next to the one she'd been sitting in.

Waiting. I liked his phrasing. "Nah, but thanks. I just want her to find a life away from me, so I can do the same."

"Super mature of you." Knox didn't sound convinced.

Once upon a time I might've wanted vengeance, but it didn't seem worth it anymore.

"You never let me have any fun," Rohde grumbled. "A guy turns fucking forty and suddenly you think you're a saint."

"He's got a point," Knox said. "You're an old man now and that made you soft, Birthday Boy?"

Inspiration struck. "I'll give you something almost as good. There may be a new guy in town. Drives a Z24. Looks like he bathes in smug. Probably steals candy from babies."

"In other words, he pissed off Evie?" Knox snorted.

"What?" My feigned confusion didn't sound believable in any way. Yeah, he totally did. "What gave me away?"

"Lucky guess," Knox said.

Rohde's radio buzzed at the same time the phone on the shop wall rang. Rohde excused himself, talking into the mic on his shoulder as he walked onto the street, and Knox grabbed the receiver. "Gage's Grub."

I kept half an ear on the call as my mind wandered back to the weird shitstorm of a morning. Why did Grace show up now?

And more importantly, how was I going to help Evie?

9 /
evie

My day was a not-so-lovely blend of work, plus me slipping into distraction every few minutes. Thinking about Sawyer and how furious I was. Thinking about the money and wondering if I was going to have to consider his offer...

I had a couple of hours before I met up with my friends, which was the perfect amount of time to take care of the bills for the shop. I'd reached a point where I had to pay some of these in a specific window of time—after a credit card was paid or a deposit landed and before the bill in question reached *we're going to charge you a fee or shut something off* past due status.

It was a delicate balancing act, but one I'd perfected.

I wished I could understand why there was a consistent drop-off in revenue over the past several months. If sales were like they'd been a couple of years ago, things wouldn't be so tight. I might still be at risk of losing the store, but I'd see a light at the end of the tunnel.

No matter how many times I looked, though, I couldn't figure out what happened. What I did wrong to tank the family business.

Beyond trusting Travis, of course.

A knock startled me from my work, and I looked up to see Aubrey standing in my office doorway. She leaned against the frame when I looked up, in a pose that looked practiced specifically to show off her tall, slender frame. She owned the vintage clothing shop on Main Street, and this afternoon she wore a fifties-style swing dress. The lack of sleeves showed off the ink that trailed along her arms and back.

"You haven't gone home to change yet." Aubrey's tone was as much teasing as accusation.

Because I'd gotten distracted chasing a rabbit down a hole that didn't lead anywhere. "I would've gotten there soon."

"How much longer do you need?"

I loved her for understanding. "Fifteen minutes. Tops."

"I've got you covered." Aubrey pushed away from the door and her skirt flounced with each movement. "I'll be back then."

I dove back into the accounting as she left. But I was still working when she came back.

"I'm sorry. I have to wrap this up, though," I said.

She held up a bag, and crossed the room to stand behind me. "You work, I'll do your hair."

"I can't work while you're fiddling with my head. What are you doing to it?"

"I promise nothing you won't agree with. Work." Aubrey placed her hands on either side of my skull and pointed my gaze at my computer screen.

Fine. I tried to ignore the tugs on my scalp, and let Aubrey do what she was going to do while I paid a couple more bills and recorded the transactions. When I finished she was still going, but a moment later, she handed me a mirror. "All done."

She'd put my hair into short spiral curls and I had no idea how since I didn't feel any heat. I *did* look pretty cute. "I love it. Thank you."

"Clothes." Aubrey handed me a folded stack.

"I'm all gross from work."

"Then I'll wash them tomorrow. I have to anyway."

Fair logic. I did a subtle sniff test of me—I should be good to go in public, and it wasn't like I was getting laid tonight.

The thought flashed a pair of images in my head—Sawyer and Gage—and I hid a wince. I was never touching Sawyer again. Never talking to him if I could avoid it. And Gage was working tonight.

Not that I'd be sleeping with him anyway.

Dressed. I was getting dressed. Right. I unfolded what Aubrey brought me, and scowled at the crop top and stonewash jeans. "Oh."

"What is that? *Oh?*" Aubrey asked.

I shrugged. "I expected something vintage." Not that I minded. This was cute and practical.

"Early eighties, doll. It *is* vintage." Aubrey grinned.

I scowled, but locked the door to my office so I could change without being interrupted. I didn't care if Aubrey saw me—we'd all been friends long enough that changing in front of each other wasn't new.

"I told Alys to meet us at Joystick's instead of your house." Aubrey perched on the edge of my desk, and the petticoat under her skirt flounced.

Fun. "Trivia Night?"

"Trivia Night." Aubrey grinned.

"You do love me."

Joystick's was new enough that he was trying to cement the best nights for each theme or game. I don't think he expected Trivia Night to be such a big hit, as he'd started with it on a Saturday. His themed restaurant had filled with a line out around the corner, and he'd had to turn people away.

Since then he'd hosted the game on random days, trying to find the least busy one for the activity. Apparently we were a town full of dorks—which I loved. Also, people would drive for an hour or two, to visit the famous former child star's restaurant, so that meant it was typically crowded anyway.

When I was ready, Aubrey and I headed out. We only had a couple of blocks to walk. While we strolled down the street, Aubrey asked, "What's your next free night this week?"

"None this week. Not sure after that. Why?"

"Gage has enlisted me to find a time we can all brainstorm."

Fuck. It had to be about the money. He wasn't supposed to tell people about that. "Brainstorm what?" I tried to keep my question casual.

"I didn't ask."

That wasn't right. I gave Aubrey a sideways glance.

She grinned. "More accurately, he wouldn't say. I tried to ask him why he couldn't schedule it. What the two of you got up to on Saturday. He clammed up about all of it. Said I had to ask you."

In other words, his way of getting me to accept help was to sic my friends on me. My curious, hound-me-until-they-had-answers friends.

He was a bastard, but I couldn't be mad at him for it, as much as I wanted to be. "I don't know. I'll have to check my calendar."

"Bullshit. You know your calendar for the year by heart. And speaking of things you need to tell me, what *were* you two up to this weekend?"

I wanted to tell her everything, but on the other hand, I didn't. Especially since we were at Joystick's.

"It's... a long story." We stepped inside to the packed bar. The front half of the business was an amazing assortment of all things geek. Movie memorabilia, gaming stuff, anime figurines... I could spend forever just browsing here. The other half of the building was the restaurant, and I assumed it was just as full.

We found Alys at a table near the stage. Sometimes there were live bands. Tonight, the trivia master would emcee.

She was wearing a stuffed top hat with pink polka dots that matched her hair. I assumed she'd stolen it from one of her boyfriends, Maddox. She gave an exaggerated pout when she saw us. "You dressed up."

"I've got you covered." Aubrey pulled something from her purse and handed it over.

Alys examined the black, lace, fingerless gloves and grinned. "They're perfect." She pulled them on and spent a moment checking out the look.

"Who's our fourth?" I asked, as Aubrey and I dropped into seats at the table.

One of Joystick's trivia rules was every team had to be at least four people, to make sure as many could participate as possible.

Alys shrugged. "Don't know. Adam is here."

I wasn't surprised. "Adam knows a *lot* of shit."

Aubrey scowled.

That was her *no*. Not that I expected otherwise. Alys adored Adam because he did a popular podcast with one of her boyfriends. Aubrey didn't like him because he'd *stolen* the man she'd been in love with since they were kids.

Not that Deacon had ever seen her that way, but I understood the broken heart anyway. "No Adam," I said. My birthday. I could be the tie-breaking vote.

"Doesn't matter." Alys nodded across the room with a scowl. "Sebastian and Eli just recruited him."

Ouch. That was going to be a hard team to beat.

"Doesn't matter. We need *him*." Aubrey pointed toward the door.

Alys and I followed, and my gut twisted inside out. Sawyer looked just as good as he had on Saturday when he approached Gage and me. Long stride, faintest hint of silver in dark blond hair, and a confidence that said he knew what kind of attention he drew.

"I'm in. Don't tell my guys," Alys said at the same time I said, "Fuck the hell no."

"Why not?" Aubrey asked. "He's got that older, *wreck you one night, sell you a bridge the next morning* kind of vibe."

"Exactly his problem," I muttered.

"You know him." Aubrey sat up straighter and fluffed her hair as Sawyer approached. "You owe us an explanation," she spoke through clenched teeth at me, never dropping the sweet smile at Sawyer.

I rolled my eyes and crossed my arms.

"Evie. Didn't expect to see you here." Sawyer's voice was warm and deep. "Who are your friends?"

Aubrey opened her mouth, and I kicked her foot under the table. "Ms. Young will work," I said tightly. "And whatever you're buying, we're not selling."

"Shouldn't that be —"

I shot Alys a raised eyebrow look, and she snapped her mouth shut.

"That's too bad." Sawyer didn't look fazed. Fucker. "I understand a team needs four people to participate in trivia night. You look like you're one short."

"They could use another player." Aubrey pointed at Adam's table.

And I wanted to hug her.

"We're set," Alys added.

Sawyer shrugged. "Your loss." He turned away.

"Tell me we just seriously handicapped them," Aubrey said, as Sawyer strode toward their table.

I couldn't promise that. Sawyer was observant. He was cocky. That didn't mean smart, but I'd already underestimated him more than once, thinking he was being honest with me. "We'll kick their asses."

"*Ravyn*." Alys stood and waved with her shout.

A tall, slender redhead strode toward us.

I'd seen Ravyn Miller around town a few times, but didn't know much about her except she was from one of the wealthier families in the state, and she'd recently inherited a large farm at the edge of town, where she lived alone.

That and she'd been a huge help to Alys during the scavenger hunt that happened last month.

Alys introduced all of us, and we passed handshakes around the table.

"Are you playing tonight?" Aubrey asked Ravyn.

"If you've got an opening I am. Otherwise…"

"We do." I was happy to have her on the team, and not a moment too soon. The game was starting in a few minutes.

Aubrey grabbed my arm. "Before the questions start flying, you have to tell us how much hate to lay down on Sawyer and why."

"Who's Sawyer?" Ravyn looked confused.

Alys nodded in his direction. "Sexy new guy."

"Who we hate?" Ravyn looked at me.

I sighed. "If I give you the thirty second version will that sate you until the game is over?"

"Are you sure you want to talk about this with me here?" Ravyn didn't make any move to leave.

It didn't matter. "By the end of the week, the whole town will know, even if no one tells anyone." I had no doubt this would get out and the stories would be wild and varied.

"If anyone else finds out, I blame Gage." Aubrey paused and twisted her mouth. "Wait. Gage knows, right?"

I was sure it was Rohde who liked to gossip, but

I kept that thought to myself. "Gage definitely knows."

"Of course he does." Alys rolled her eyes.

"Y'all don't do a fast thirty seconds, do you?" Ravyn said.

I liked her. "Fine. Fifteen second version. Gage and I went to Wendover for our birthday. We met Mr. Tall, Dark, and Stupid Liar Face there. We had sex and now Sawyer is here to buy my store."

Ravyn let out a slow breath, her eyes wide. "Fuck me."

"Exactly." Literally.

"Wait. What? Backup." Alys and Aubrey spoke in overlapping confusion.

I suspected they'd heard me fine.

"Dorks and Demons, welcome to Trivia Night." Joystick's voice carried over the loudspeaker, cutting our conversation short.

"Game time." The interruption would give me time to figure out what to tell my friends.

Maybe.

Joystick handed the mic to the night's trivia master and stepped aside to let the event happen. The first few times he hosted this event, people accused him of cheating because Eli liked to play, Eli was fucking good at this, and Eli was Joystick's boyfriend.

No surprise, even without Joystick in charge of questions and scoring, Eli's team frequently won.

Not tonight, though. *Sorry, guys.* Anyone with

Sawyer on their team had to go down. That was all there was to it.

The way the questions started, most of the teams stayed in the running for a few rounds. Joystick had some nifty tech in here that let the questions pop up at each table, and there was a time limit for each question, depending on how many answers it required.

We glided our way through things like name four presidents, name that tune, name the smallest state in the US...

When we started getting six to ten images on the screen, with things like *name as many of these movies as possible*, teams were left in the dust. Even we fell a few points behind our rival for the night, because Adam knew every single image.

Next up was *name the bands*. Most of the people in the image started making music before most of us were born, but that didn't stop Alys from picking up where the rest of us were lacking in knowledge. She got them all.

Problem was, as far as I could tell from the boys' table, Sawyer did too. High fives and fist bumps abounded.

But I made sure we kicked their asses on the question about identifying the logos of defunct electronics stores.

In between, Alys and Aubrey tried to get me to spill the details about what happened with Sawyer. I brushed them off again and again with *later*.

Fortunately, Ravyn seemed to have a strong competitive streak, and she took my side when it came to focusing on the win.

Two hours later, our team and his were tied. We'd left everyone else in the dust.

"We're going to do something different for the tie-breaker round," the emcee said. "Each team gets to help decide what it will be. Ladies, do you want a physical challenge or a mental one?"

We all exchanged looks.

"They don't actually mean physical," Aubrey said to Ravyn. "It's usually something like pool or a video game."

Alys scrunched up her face. "We always win in physical challenges."

"Not against Adam," I reminded them.

"And you don't know what this Sawyer guy is capable of," Ravyn said.

I had a fairly good idea, and I didn't like it.

"Time's up, ladies. Do you have an answer?"

I looked around the table. Ravyn pulled a game token from the top of the stack she'd been playing with. "Heads we go mental."

I snickered at the wording, and watched the longest coin flip in history as the token flew about a foot in the air, then clattered back to the table.

Tails.

"Physical." As I announced our decision, my gut clenched.

The emcee turned to the other table. "Gentlemen, they picked the how, you pick the what. Pool, darts, or Street Fighter?"

Please don't be Street Fighter. Adam could spend half an hour on a single game token.

There was a bowing of heads at the boys' table as they had what I assumed was a similar discussion to ours, though the murmurs of *Street Fighter* were distinct.

"Darts," Sawyer said, before anyone else could speak.

I hid my smirk, but Aubrey high-fived Ravyn, and the other men at Sawyer's table groaned.

He looked at them, exuding that smugness I already hated. "I promise, I've got this, guys."

Sawyer strode to join me in front of the dart board, with more swagger in his step than should be legal. He picked the game, so I got to choose who went first.

I moved aside and let him throw.

He was *really* good, landing all three shots near the center, including a bullseye.

As he moved out of my way, he paused next to me, and dropped his mouth to my ear. "Do any of your friends have any idea how desperate you are for cock?" he whispered.

I clenched my jaw and rage spilled inside. I didn't even make it to the line before tossing all three darts, one at a time.

My entire table erupted in a massive cheer, as

did most of the dining room, when I landed better shots than Sawyer.

I gave him a perfect smile. "They know I qualified expert as a marksman in the Marines," I said in a normal voice. "Which means they know me better than you ever will."

Sawyer turned away without a comment, while the emcee announced that we were the winners.

"Hey, drinks are on me." Sawyer rejoined his table, just as Alys walked away from Adam.

Adam shook his head. "Nah, we're good."

And like that, the boys' club broke up.

With the competition over for the night, people moved back to other things. Joystick insisted on singing me *Happy Birthday* when he brought out the cake The Nerd Herd ordered for me, and I couldn't maintain my scowl through any of it.

This was fun.

As we all laughed and joked, I completely ignored Sawyer walking out of the building alone. Nope, didn't notice him, not even for a second.

Aubrey pressed close to me, arm against mine, as we enjoyed cake and laughs. "You still have to give me your schedule," she said softly. "And you still have to tell me why."

I frowned.

"I'm trying to help." She pointed out.

"I know." I wasn't upset with her, but the reminder that I was at the point where I needed that kind of help made my cake sit heavy in my stomach.

10 /
sawyer

Who was hammering on my door at—I turned my head toward the clock on my nightstand—six in the fucking morning?

The noise stopped for a moment, then resumed again full force. "Sir. Haddarville police. Could you open the door?"

What the—?

I pulled on a shirt, rubbed the sleep away a little more, and moved to the motel room door. If the police wanted me, they could deal with me in my boxers.

A look through the peephole revealed that yes, there was a uniformed man standing outside my room. I opened the door. "Morning, officer. Is there a problem?"

He flashed his badge. "Sorry to wake you, sir. I'm Deputy Rohde Meier. We have a little girl in Two-oh-Three B who lost her octopus last night.

Have you seen it?"

What? I stared at him blankly. "Beg pardon?"

"An octopus. Stuffed. Maybe about ten inches at its largest. Purple. Well-worn around the ears."

"Do octopuses have ears?" Octopi? Octopods? "I'm sorry, did you wake me up to ask me about a child's missing toy?"

"She throws fits without it. Her parents are in a panic. You understand."

"Send them my sympathy." I actually meant it, but there was no reason to let him see that. "I haven't seen it though." I swung the door shut.

Deputy Meier stopped it from closing completely. "Thanks for your help anyway, Mr…"

"Rawlings. Sawyer Rawlings."

"Got it. And you're in town for how long?"

Only as long as it took and not a second longer. "A week or two. I'll be gone when my business here is done."

"I see. Well, you enjoy your stay and be careful out there. People in small towns tend to talk. Oh." He looked at my crotch. "Next time, keep the weapon holstered while talking to the police."

I wouldn't give him the satisfaction of looking. "Thanks. I'll keep that in mind," I said flatly as I let the door swing shut again. A glance down confirmed that yes, my dick was hanging out.

Fuck.

I already knew I shouldn't have egged Evie on last night, but when she hit that angry-enough-to-kick-your-ass point, her cheeks did a cute, puffy red thing and her mouth puckered in a perfectly kissable hard line.

If Deputy Meier was her way of pointing out whose town this was, she didn't need to bother. I was happy to close this deal and move on.

That might mean apologizing to her, but we weren't there yet.

Okay, maybe I could apologize for last night's comment. If she had the power to send local cops after me, she may not be as dick-starved as I teased her about. Not that I thought she was anyway. Gage would worship every inch of her if she let him.

I forced myself awake through my shower, and made myself coffee in-room. This wasn't The Four Seasons—the double queen beds were basic, and the *kitchenette* was a sink and a microwave. It was cleaner than a lot of four-star hotels I'd stayed in though, and the walls were thick enough I hadn't heard my neighbors last night.

That was all I needed from anyplace I slept when I was on the road.

First stop this morning was the hardware store. Again. I walked in to see the same young man working as yesterday. He nodded toward the back of the shelves. "Evie's stocking shelves, if you're looking for her."

"Thanks." I liked this guy. Nicest person in town so far.

Up until five years ago, my father's business

didn't matter. I'd been in real estate, but my husband and I were a team.

The memory—Tony's face in my mind—ached. It always did, but not the way it used to. Now the reminder felt more like an empty void than the kind of gaping agony that made me practically catatonic after he pass— left me.

Hudson helped me climb out of that pit and offered me a chance to come back to the family business. Back then I didn't care. I existed because there was no other choice.

How pathetic had I been?

I found Evie with the shovels, and the post hole digger in her hands was nearly as tall as she was. That didn't stop her from wielding it like it was nothing when she turned to face me.

"What?" she asked.

Here went nothing. "I wanted to apologize for last night. I was out of line during darts." How I managed to not gag on the words was a mystery to me.

"For last night. *That's* what you're sorry about." Her voice was as flat as her expression.

"Absolutely. I never should've said what I did. And you had your vengeance with Deputy Meier this morning. I appreciate a good tit for tat."

She frowned. At least that was a reaction. "No clue what you're talking about."

"Sure. Regardless, I'm here on business. Nothing else. I'd like a few moments of your time, and if you're busy now, tell me when to come back. I have an offer—"

Evie spun the post digger in her hands like it was a lightweight baton, and it swiped inches from my leg. The tip struck the concrete floor near my feet with a loud *clang*. "Let me make this clear," she said. "Pay attention this time. There will never be a good time. I didn't ask Rohde to pull you over this morning, but if you come back, I can make sure you and he become best of friends. Maybe you can turn him bi with the sexy charms you seem to think you have, and then you can fuck him too."

A uniformed man had never done much for me. "So you do think I'm sexy."

Evie narrowed her eyes and scraped the tip of her digger closer to my shoes. "Get out, Mr. Rawlings."

I wouldn't drive her to shout this time. Instead I gave her a bow and walked out. I'd give her time to cool down and come back tomorrow morning.

It felt silly to drive across the street to get wings for lunch, so I left my car while I walked to Joystick's. The food wasn't nearly as good as the night before, mostly because they gave me the wrong flavor the first time, and not nearly enough sauce when I complained. When I came back to my Z24, there was a warning ticket on the windshield, for *safety*. It said *get your tires checked*.

Was this going to be an ongoing issue? I couldn't wait.

The next morning I decided to drive one town over for coffee and breakfast. As I pulled back into Haddarville, the flashing blue and red lights appeared in my rear-view mirror.

The cop who pulled me over wasn't Rohde, and he ticketed me for having a taillight out.

The girl working the counter at Evie's was new to me, and she refused to give me any information. She also told me if I took one more step into the store, she'd scream and call the police.

Apparently, they had my number anyway, because *another* cop pulled me over on the way back to my motel for going twenty-seven in a twenty-five.

Fuck this. I was walking everywhere in this town, the rest of the week.

Thursday morning, I wasn't surprised that my coffee order was wrong—every restaurant order I'd placed for the last two days had been. I held the barista's gaze as I downed half of the too-hot, too-sweet drink in a single swallow.

I was cock-blocked at Evie's again.

I needed a different approach. Maybe going back to my room and slamming my head against the wall would work better. Then again, I'd probably get a ticket when the neighbors complained about the noise.

Sinking into self-pity wasn't the answer. Giving up was *never* the answer.

When I'd gone back to work at the family agency, it didn't take long to remember how competitive things were there. It was the reason my husband had asked me to leave originally.

I'd fallen back into the routine because it was better than staying locked inside my own head. The longer I worked there, the more I remembered why business came first. About six months ago, something happened between Dad and Hudson. Neither of them gave me details, but it was enough that Hudson stepped back in his role, and Dad talked a lot more about me taking over the business when he retired.

I felt a little stupid being closer to fifty than forty-five and just barely pushing for control of the family company, but better late than never. At least this was a chance to rebuild my life. Remember how to not give a fuck. Cement my place in the world.

Because one thing I'd learned from my husband's passing was that giving up wasn't an option. He had, and it cost me everything that mattered.

If I couldn't get Evie to talk to me, I'd go through one of her friends. The tattooed blonde who ran the clothing store was my first stop.

I had a foot in the front door when she kicked me out.

Adam had seemed nice, and on Monday night he mentioned he worked at the antique store. When I got there, Adam wasn't in. Deacon, the owner, made it clear I wasn't welcome.

Sebastian ran a new age tea shop. He sounded like a chill guy.

Nope. He gave me the cold shoulder too.

Fuck it. I'd start at one end of Main Street and walk up and down, going into every shop, until someone was friendly and willing to ask Evie to talk to me. But in the spirit of slamming my head against the wall, I was in front of her place again, I might as well give it one more shot.

I walked inside.

"Evie's not here." There was another person behind the counter. "And you need to leave."

Her voice drifted out from the aisles. I couldn't tell where Evie was, but it was near enough to hear her talking.

"*Evie*," I shouted. "I'm sorry. About all of it." Apologizing sucked. Surrendering sucked more.

"Fuck you," she yelled in response. "Get out of my store."

God damn it.

I walked out, and headed down the street. As I neared Gage's, he and Rohde were loading a cooler into the back of a pickup truck, next to a few other coolers and a grill.

"Mr. Rawlings." Deputy Meier greeted me with an overly friendly grin. "How is the man with a record-breaking number of tickets in a forty-eight-hour period?"

Gage fist bumped him.

They would *not* get me to react. I hated this place, and now I knew who sent the cops after me.

I played fake all the time to make sales and this was just another instance of needing to do so. "That's me."

"I'm gonna run this down to the park," Rohde said to Gage. "Want me to take out the trash on my way?"

Oh, real subtle and mature, asshole.

"Nah, I got this." Gage snorted a laugh.

Rohde gave me a wave and a wink, before climbing into the truck and pulling away from the curb.

"So good to run into you again." Gage was too warm and friendly. "Rumor is, you want to talk to Evie."

"That's the *rumor* huh?"

Gage nodded. "Tell you what. Municipal barbecue is today. Cops will be there. Fire. It's going to be a blast, and I'm catering. Come help me out, work for me for the day, and I'll think about putting in a good word with Evie."

If anyone could get her to listen, it was probably him, and I instantly hated him for it. I also doubted any bit of his offer was sincere. "I call bullshit."

"Do you have any other options?" Gage asked.

I hated that he was right, but I could charm the pants, skirt, or work boots off anyone, and if this was my way to get people on my side, or at least sympathetic to my cause, so be it. "All right, I'm in."

11 /
gage

Wen we arrived at the park, I was surprised to see we'd beaten Rohde there.

I pointed to several of the items in my truck. "These can all go by the picnic table," I said to Sawyer. "We'll set up in a few."

"On it."

That easily? I shouldn't question his willingness to take orders but, "Like that? No argument?"

"None."

"Why not?"

Sawyer clenched his jaw. "Because at the end of the day, if you decide to be an anal-retentive asshole and nitpick my work, you won't have anything to pick at. I may not like this, but I said I'd do the job, I'll do the fucking job."

"Great then."

Rohde pulled up, and I was about to give him grief about taking so long, when I saw his nephew climb out of the truck as well. Kurt had a box with him, the same one he frequently toted to the park, and he lugged it onto the grass a few feet from the pavilion.

Rohde joined me.

"Looks like you picked up a hitchhiker," I teased.

Rohde glanced past me to Sawyer. "So did you."

"I told him if he helped today, I might put in a good word with Evie."

"Will you?"

"No."

Rohde smirked. "Did he believe you?"

I shook my head. "Nope. He's out of options, though. Hey, Richie Rich," I hollered the last bit in Sawyer's direction. "Help me haul these coolers into the pavilion?"

He rolled his eyes, but didn't argue. As we hefted the first large chest to the ground, Sawyer said, "is that the deputy's kid?"

"Nephew." If he had any decency at all, warning him off should be enough. "Kurt lost his dad about a little more than a year ago, and they built that plane together. It goes everywhere Kurt possibly thinks he can fly it, and Rohde will publicly execute you if you hurt him."

"Noted. Not that I was planning on it."

"Good." I was grateful the conversation fell off as we finished setting up.

I dove into grilling as everyone else started

showing up with their families. One of my favorite things about cooking at these things was watching everyone play, have fun, and just set aside the stresses of life for a few hours.

Bonnie, who worked dispatch, approached Sawyer, and I couldn't help but turn an ear in their direction.

"Haven't seen you around here before." Bonnie's voice was demure and sugary and nothing like the stern tone I frequently heard barking for attention over Rohde's radio. "Are you fire or police?"

"Grunt." Sawyer sounded good natured. "Just here to serve the drinks and watch."

Bonnie giggled. "I hope you like what you see."

"Me too."

"*Bonnie*," someone called from the grass, where they were throwing a frisbee back and forth. "No fraternizing with the enemy."

Bonnie looked between the field and Sawyer. "He looks harmless enough," she yelled back.

"I promise you he's not." I couldn't help but interject.

The smile that tugged at Sawyer's mouth was almost snake-like. "I'd listen to Gage. He strikes me as a man who knows a lot about assholes."

Fucker.

"Hey, Richie Rich. We're running low on pop. Grab more from the truck."

Sawyer looked between the coolers he'd just

refilled a few minutes ago and me, his eyebrows raised. He gave a brief shake of his head, and I swore I heard him mutter *whatever*. "Yeah. Okay."

Bonnie walked away to join the crowd, and for the next little bit, Sawyer lingered at the edge of the pavilion, watching it all and occasionally playing *fetch* for me.

In between playing gopher, Sawyer lingered near the edge of the pavilion, watching.

I expected him to insert himself into a conversation, and try to make friends.

Then again, I did a decent job of turning half the town against him.

When the food was ready, everyone lined up to eat, and he waited. "Do you need me to grab anything else, Gage?" Sawyer hollered over everyone's heads.

He was acting awfully nice.

"I'm good," I called back.

He filled his plate last, including making sure I got something, and then he found himself a table with an obviously empty spot. "Mind if I sit here?" he asked the firefighters.

Clint was one of the nicest people here, and scooted aside to make room. His, "Not a problem," was clipped, but not severely.

"Thanks." Sawyer took a seat.

The entire table ate in an awkward silence, and I couldn't look away. He had to be up to something. But what?

"You a gymnast, Clint?" Sawyer's tone was friendly and warm.

I didn't think anyone but Bonnie had introduced themselves, so he must've been paying attention to names.

Clint raised his eyebrows. This used to be a touchy subject for him, when we were younger. Like a lot of us, he'd learned to embrace who he was. "Former cheerleader. Current dancer."

Was Sawyer about to stick his foot in his mouth? I didn't know if I wanted that or not.

"That explains the leaps." Sawyer stuffed a piece of burger in his mouth and swallowed before continuing. "During frisbee. You move like someone who's used to catching air."

Observant fucker.

"Do you watch all men that closely?" Clint's tone was guarded flirting.

Sawyer shrugged. "I watch most people that closely. You can learn a lot by paying attention to the right things."

"Yeah, you can." Clint had a similar philosophy. Did Sawyer know that? There was no way he could.

Someone shouted my name, and I turned away to talk to them. When I was finished throwing more brats on the grill, I gave my attention to Sawyer's table again. The entire group was laughing and talking.

That could be dangerous.

After lunch, a bunch of us wanted to play flag-football—police versus fire. But fire needed another person.

"Hey, Richie Rich," Levi, the fire department chief, called.

Was I pleased the nickname was spreading? I was.

"We're down a man. Come play skins with us," Levi said.

Sawyer seemed to consider the request for a moment before nodding. "All right, I'm in."

He joined his team, and tossed his shirt next to everyone else's. I hated to admit, he looked as good shirtless as he had in Wendover. It was obvious why Evie had been drooling over him, and I was considering doing the same. His ink was paint on a canvas of muscle.

He also had the palest city boy skin ever. Not even sleeve tan lines. Did the man not spend any time outside?

We were maybe twenty minutes into the game when Kurt yelled from across the field, "Uncle Rohde. My plane broke."

"Time out." Rohde jogged away from the group to meet Kurt halfway. "What happened?"

Kurt held up the controller in one hand and the plane in the other. "I don't know. It just stopped working. Make it work." His voice was hard and angry.

"I don't know how it works." Rohde stayed

calm. "We can take it to Evie later and see if she'll look at it."

"Fix it now." Kurt shouted.

"Can I look?" Sawyer stepped forward.

Rohde clenched his jaw. "Not unless you're an expert in remote control airplanes."

"No. But the tanks have a lot of similar mechanics."

Kurt's eyes grew wide. "You know about RC tanks?"

Was that a shadow that flashed across Sawyer's face?

"I do." Sawyer nodded at the controller. "Do you want me to see if I can help?"

Kurt shoved the device at him. "Yes."

Rohde looked like he was torn between yanking Sawyer back, and relief that someone might have a solution.

"We playing?" Someone called from the field.

"Go," I said to Rohde. "I'll sit out, so the teams are even, and I'll watch him since I brought him." Besides, football wasn't really my thing. I was more of a hockey guy.

Sawyer, Kurt, and I moved back to the pavilion, and an empty table, with Sawyer carrying the plane like it was precious cargo, and Kurt hovering inches away.

Sawyer set the vehicle down, and reached for a series of metal objects attached to one of the wings.

"Pretty sure these aren't standard issue for an F4-U."

"They're the zombie bombs," Kurt said.

"Nazi zombies?" Sawyer looked completely serious.

Kurt shook his head. "Zombie Nazis."

"What's the difference?" I couldn't believe I was asking this.

Sawyer gave me a look of disbelief. "Nazi zombies became Nazis after they died. Zombie Nazis were Nazis who became zombies."

Kurt grinned. "Exactly."

"Don't the bombs kill all of them?" What was I missing?

Kurt huffed as if that was the dumbest question he'd ever heard.

Sawyer sighed and rolled his eyes. "Be useful. Hold this right here." He pointed me toward one of the metal things.

The way Kurt watched me with expectation, I didn't have a choice but to comply.

"Here's the thing about zombie Nazi bombs." As Sawyer talked, he pulled out his keys, and removed a small pocketknife from the ring. He flipped the blade open. "Sometimes they interfere with radio signals."

"You can't remove them." Kurt's shout drew glances from the field.

"I'm not taking them off. I'm moving them."

Sawyer's tone never dipped toward frustration or condescending. "Gage is friends with Evie, right?"

Kurt nodded.

"And Evie knows how to fix the plane?"

"Yes," Kurt said.

Sawyer moved the pocketknife toward the piece I held. "So Gage will make sure I do things right."

There was no way his logic made any sense, but I wasn't going to argue.

"Okay?" Sawyer asked.

Kurt scrunched up his face, and after a moment, relaxed his expression. "Okay. As long as I can still bomb the zombies when you're done."

"Of course." Sawyer relocated the *bombs* one by one, with me holding them exactly as he instructed each time.

During the entire process, Kurt watched closely. "How do you know how to do all of this? Are you smart like Evie?"

No.

"Definitely not." Sawyer saved himself with the answer. "But someone really close to me, someone I loved and lost"—was that a hitch in his voice? A chink in his armor?—"used to make zombie crushing tanks. And he taught me a lot about them."

"My dad made this with me." Kurt's voice grew soft. "But he died."

"I'm sorry. I know it's hard when they never come back." That was definitely a catch. A fumble in Sawyer's tone. "But if we keep this running, in a way he's always with you."

We finished rearranging the plane's armaments, and carried it to an empty spot in the park. When it took off, Kurt grinned broadly. "It works."

"You probably need to secure those bombs better than we did," Sawyer said. "I'll make you a list of what you need to tell Evie."

Kurt's attention was mostly on his plane now. "What if she asks how I know all that stuff? Grownups never believe kids."

"I do. But if she asks, tell her your Uncle Rohde's friend said so."

That would've been the perfect chance to send the kid to get Evie on Sawyer's side. Have Kurt mention his name. Hell, I was almost impressed with the way Sawyer handled the whole situation. He was still a bozo, but he had a soft spot or two.

Sawyer spent most of the rest of the picnic helping Kurt fly the plane, and as everyone left for the day, he helped me clean up. I got a good look at him under the pavilion, and the fact that he'd never put his shirt back on shone in a glaringly uncomfortable red on his skin.

"That sunburn is gonna suck," I said.

Sawyer looked down at his arms, and at his torso as best he could, and puffed out a sigh. "Probably." He reached for his shirt, which someone had left on one of the benches.

"Don't put that back on." I could be a little nice, after what he did for Kurt. "Trust me."

Sawyer snorted.

"Dumb request, I know, but do it anyway, Richie Rich."

We climbed into my truck. I drove to the motel, parked in front of his room, and grabbed the aloe that I kept behind the back seat for things like grill burns.

He looked at the bottle with raised eyebrows.

"You have something to say?" I asked.

He bit his bottom lip. "I don't. Rather, I'd really love to make a joke about you finding an excuse to oil me up, but I'm not so arrogant I think this burn isn't going to hurt like fuck, and be even worse without help."

Good boy. I swallowed the words. If he could be civil, I could do the same. "This will be easier inside. Yes, I'm inviting myself back to your room."

"I knew I'd win you over." Sawyer's light taunt ended in a wince when he went to climb from the truck, and his back peeled away from the seat at a slower rate than the rest of him.

He let us inside, which was as neat and clean as if this was his first night in the room, rather than having lived here a week. There was nothing personal in view, aside from a glimpse of a suitcase peeking out from behind the far bed.

"Have a seat," I gestured to the closer bed.

Sawyer sat on the corner, back ramrod straight.

I squeezed a generous helping of gel into the palm of my hand. When I touched Sawyer's back, he sucked in a sharp breath swallowed by a low groan. Both sounds drove straight to my cock.

Nope. Not thinking like that. I was focused on getting this done, and heading back to my grill.

I'd figured out a few years ago that I was attracted to men, and Evie was the only person who knew. It wasn't something I'd ever had a chance to explore, marrying when I did, and dealing with the break-up after.

And this was *not* the time to start fantasizing about what I could get up to, with Sawyer of all people.

"A Scorpions tattoo?" I teased lightly as I worked over the worn ink on his bicep. "You a fan?"

Sawyer let out an amused bark. "No. But a girl I really wanted to fuck in high school was. Live and learn, right?"

"You could always get it covered up." This was good. Small talk. Something to stop me from thinking about how incredible it felt to slide my hands over the bulge of his bicep, and down the contours of his chest.

"Nah. Our scars remind us that the past is real."

"Wow. That's deep."

"That's Papa Roach."

Funny. *Ha.*

After I finished rubbing him down, I dragged in

a smaller cooler full of half melted ice. "You might want this tonight."

"Thank you." He sounded sincere.

"And I'll talk to Evie. See if she'll hear you out."

Sawyer instantly looked suspicious. "Why?"

Good question. What was I doing? He'd been so good with Kurt today. But he was still the asshole who lied about who he was to take advantage of Evie, and tried to do it a second time, too. "I want you to be done with her. I want you to leave town."

"I'm not leaving until I get a *yes*."

"Because you're an asshole." This was better. No repressed desire. No wondering if maybe he was an okay guy after all. "I'll ask her to hear you out, and once she does, and says *no* anyway, you leave."

If he stayed, if he won more people over, someone was going to end up liking him, and that was dangerous.

12 /
evie

The older I got, the harder it was to shake off a late night of work the next morning. It was going to take a lot of coffee for me to wake up today, and my brain fog was made worse by the fact I hadn't solved the problem that kept me at the hardware store late.

My books didn't balance. This was more than me having zero reserve funds and being behind on every single bill. What I was taking in, based on receipts, didn't match what I had going into the bank. I couldn't find the pattern, though. I'd spent hours going through sale by sale, trying to line up where the money was missing.

Fortunately, I could move around my kitchen when I was in the worst of conditions, so making coffee was an option. I had just set the pot to brew when the doorbell rang.

The story of Sawyer talking to Rohde the other

morning had made the rounds, and anyone who had heard it was either in the *but is he well hung* camp or the *serves him right* camp.

I was the latter, and I also wasn't making a similar mistake.

The doorbell rang. Who was here so early? A quick check confirmed my tits were secured behind my tank top, and my shorts weren't stuck in any cracks they shouldn't be in.

I saw a familiar outline through the frosted glass before I opened the door, so I wasn't surprised to find Gage on my porch. "Hey." I gave him a broad grin, as some of the fog seeped away.

"Morning."

"What's in the bag?" I nodded at the reusable grocery bag in his hand.

"Breakfast."

Ooh. Sexy. "Why?"

"Because I'm going to stuff you full, and then you'll be more pliable——" Gage paused.

I laughed. "Did you just realize what you said?"

"I did."

"I like the idea of being stuffed. With what?" I was already stepping aside to let him in.

"Pancakes. Strawberries. Whipped cream."

My hero. "More pliable for what?" I should probably know that before I agreed. But unless he was going to say *hear Sawyer out*—which Gage would never do—I was likely to agree to almost anything.

"Brainstorming session with Aubrey, Alys, and me."

Oh. Fuck. I managed to avoid Aubrey's pushing on my birthday and let myself keep putting the conversation off since. I did need to confront things though, and if my friends could help me, maybe it was time to suck it up and not shoulder this entire thing on my own. "Okay. But only because you're making pancakes."

"I knew it. Bribery works every time." He fell into step with me, and we headed back to the kitchen. He unpacked the bag on the counter—not that there was a lot in there. A glass mason jar full of an off-white powder that I happened to know was his homemade mix, a pint of strawberries, and a pint of cream.

"What can I do?" I asked.

He pushed the berries toward me. "Wash and slice."

"On it." I grabbed a colander, knife, and cutting board, and set about my tasks while he dove into his. "How was the picnic?"

There was silence.

I glanced over my shoulder. "Gage?"

"Sorry, what?"

"The picnic. Yesterday. How did it go?"

"Eh, fine. Boring, you know. Kurt is having problems with his plane, so expect to see him soon."

Fair enough. I liked working with the kid. He was bright, eager to learn, and slowly chipping away at my defenses. He wanted my help building a robot and I'd told him no, but each time he visited, he had new reasons it was a good idea.

If his plane wasn't working though, I had a hard time believing he wasn't melting down. "Should I call Elaina, see if he needs help today?" Elaina was Kurt's mother.

"He's squared away for now." Gage paused as he flipped a pancake. "Sawyer helped him."

I heard that wrong. How long would it be before Sawyer's name stopped making my gut curdle and my pulse race? I should've known he'd sweet talk a few people, but to land himself at the municipal picnic...

I wasn't going to ask who invited him, because I had to look all these people in the eye after he left, and I'd hate to resent someone for my mistake. "Oh."

"You okay?" Gage glanced over his shoulder at me.

No, but I would be. "Change the subject. Tell me... something else. Anything."

"Umm... Antiques Roadshow is coming to Salt Lake, and Deacon got tickets."

That was fun. A few years ago, Deacon discovered a large cache of furniture in the basement he didn't know he had. Most of it belonged in an old-fashioned sex dungeon. "Is he bringing one of the naughty pieces?"

"He hasn't decided yet." While Gage waited for

each hotcake to cook, he worked on whisking cream in a bowl.

"Fingers crossed we see him on TV in six months, while some antique appraiser tries to keep a straight face while they explain to the camera *and this seat was used for men to pleasure women, while their husbands were away.*"

Gage chuckled. "I can almost picture it now, but the reality would be much more fun."

"If you think about it though—"

"The chair? Have you been thinking about it a lot?"

I stuck my tongue out at the back of Gage's head. "Enough to feel that that could be really hard on a guy's neck."

"Does it matter if he has a magic tongue?" Gage asked.

Were we really talking about this? Of course we were. We'd always joked like this. It landed differently after our birthday weekend, though. Because now I was picturing Gage burying his face between my legs. After the way he kissed, I was quite sure he had a magic tongue—

"Earth to Evie." He snapped his fingers in front of my face, startling me. "Pancakes, and whipped cream are done."

Breakfast. Right. "Strawberries too." I grabbed us coffee, and Gage took the seat next to me at the four-person table.

We filled our plates. "A girl could get used to

this," I said as I shoveled a forkful of everything into my face.

"If you're not used to it already, I need to step up my game."

Did that mean something? Of course not. A week ago, I was watching him come out of the shower shirtless, in a shared hotel room, and we were joking about it. Just because we kissed… and groped each other until he got me off, and he came on my back while I rode— Just because of all that didn't mean I needed to start acting weird.

I shook the thought aside. Mostly. A piece of my mind refused to let go of the memory of what it felt like to have Gage's hands running over my body. When I looked up, the smear of strawberries and whipped cream on his chin jarred me the rest of the way back to reality.

"What's so funny?" Gage asked.

"You have something… Right…" I pointed to his face then mine. It would be easy enough for me to get it. Or to lean in and lick it away.

No. We didn't have that.

"Better?" Gage swiped the mess away.

I nodded.

"It's not funny," he said.

Was I still…? Yup, I was still smiling. "It's kind of funny."

He dipped his finger into the whipped cream, and smeared it on my nose. "You have something on your face."

Now I was laughing. "Meanie." I scrubbed my nose with a napkin.

"Takes one to know one."

"Oh yeah?" I grabbed a slice of strawberry, dipped it in cream, and stuck it to his cheek. It fell the instant I pulled my hand away.

And now we were both laughing like loons. It wasn't that funny, but the mood was right and the release in tension was exactly what I needed. "You have something…" I pointed at his cheek.

"Do I?" Gage dipped his finger deeper in the whipped cream bowl, this time drawing out a noticeable dollop. He reached for me, and I squealed and tried to duck.

Ooh, I had a better idea. When he moved to attach again, I dove in and sucked his finger into my mouth. I half-missed, and I felt the cream smear across my lips.

His groan made me freeze, and his heated gaze sent desire pulsing between my legs. I couldn't look away.

Fuck it. I wrapped my tongue around his finger, watching him the entire time. Falling into the way his lips parted slightly, and the incredible sounds rumbling from his chest.

When he finally pulled away, the air was heavy. Did he want what could come next as much as I did?

"You have something on your lips." The laughter was gone from his gravelly voice.

I consciously stopped myself from licking. "Where?"

Gage pressed his hand to my throat, dipped his head closer, and drew his tongue over my lips. "Right there." His words hummed through me. His grip tightened, and he crushed his mouth to mine.

Was it worse that I wanted to make this a habit with Gage, or that there was still a sliver of me that wanted another round with Sawyer? Something potent. Angry. A balance to the sugary sweetness of Gage.

I shouldn't even be thinking that. Ever. That thought needed to vanish from my mind now and never come back.

Fortunately, each time Gage brushed his mouth over a new part of my body, what's-his-name drifted further toward the back of my mind.

13 /
gage

Evie tasted so good. Sounded amazing. Felt incredible pressed into me. I wanted to drown in this feeling of kissing her. I'd never had this kind of intensity with anyone.

I dragged my mouth up her neck, planting kisses everywhere. The way she dug her fingers into my biceps made me think she was grasping to stay grounded as much as I wanted to let go. *Fuck*, I needed this woman more each time I was around her.

How did I survive for so long without being able to breathe in Evie?

I leaned in closer, and the scrape of casters on tile reached my ears. I felt the chair shift underneath me, and my brain caught up to what was happening right as my seat slipped from under my ass.

My knee hit the ground, and Evie giggled.

That look. That joy. I had to have more.

I was on my feet in an instant, finding her mouth with mine again as I gripped her hips and pulled her upright as well.

She hooked her arms around my neck, and as I lifted her, she wrapped her legs around my waist. Her heat pressing into my chest and stomach was intoxicating.

I carried her the few feet to the counter, and set her ass on the butcher block. Her tank top shifted in the process, teasing at what lay underneath, and I tugged the stretchy fabric down, exposing her breasts.

She rested her palms on the wood and leaned back, leaving her gorgeous assets on display without unhooking her legs from me.

This was so much better than strawberries, though... The table was close enough for me to grab the bowl of whipped cream. I scooped a generous dollop out with one finger, and smeared it across one of her breasts.

Her delighted laugh was enough for me to get high on. I dipped my head to lick the sweet cream off. Sucking and nipping at her skin, lingering even when the sugary flavor was gone.

While I lavished one of her nipples with my tongue, I kneaded her other breast with my hand.

"I think the other one is feeling left out." Evie's voice was playful and light.

"Can't have that." I grabbed more whipped cream and moved to the other nipple. I kept up the attention until Evie was moaning and squirming against me.

She held me tighter with her legs, working her hips. "Are we going to keep playing Nine and Half Weeks?" Her question was breathy and playful. "Because I have ice in the freezer."

"Only if we get to rewrite the ending." I wanted to draw this out and spend all day worshiping her. I wanted to give her so many orgasms she couldn't walk or remember Sawyer's name.

Evie pulled my face up to hers and crushed our mouths together. "Never mind. That'll take too long. Fuck me, Gage. Please." The begging in her voice combined with the way she ground against me.

I was either going to fuck a hole in the cabinet or come in my pants. Or both.

I tugged on her shorts and panties, and she lifted herself up for me to pull the clothing off.

As she undid my jeans, a new thought sank in. *Protection.* I couldn't stop my groan of disappointment. Letting go of her for even a second would be agony.

"What's wrong?" Evie asked.

"No condoms."

"Skip it."

God that sounded like a good idea. "Are you sure?"

"I have an IUD. I'm clean. You're clean unless *she* brought something home…"

No. I'd been tested and the unnamed *she* was the

last person I wanted in my head right now. "I'm clean."

Evie freed my cock, and her hand on my shaft was almost too much. "Skip it," she repeated.

I was done arguing. I slid inside her slick, tight opening. "*Fuuuck.*"

Her groan mingled with mine and raised the temperature in the room to scorching.

I wanted to go hard and fast and not stop, and she was working against me, urging me to do exactly that. "Stop." It hurt to say that word. "I don't want to come too soon."

"Don't make me wait too long." She draped her arms around my neck again.

Never again. I worked a hand between us to press my thumb to her clit. I didn't dare move inside her while I sucked on her neck and stroked her pulsing button.

Her breath caught, and her mewls grew faster. More punctuated. When she clenched around me, I used the last of my restraint to not finish then and there. As she reached that peak where her groans became cries of pleasure, I moved my hands to her hips, to hammer inside her, fucking her hard and fast.

The way her pussy continued to squeeze around me said this was drawing her orgasm out. Without a leash on what I was doing, I lost track of anything but the rhythm. The feeling. How we were tied together, and the rest of the world fell away.

Nothing mattered but how it felt to be part of Evie.

My balls tightened and desire mounted inside me. I swore the world ground to a halt, including my breathing and my heart, for a single beat.

I came hard, spilling inside her. Pounding even after I was spent, and only stopping when my cock protested at the overstimulation.

I leaned into Evie, digging my fingers into her legs for support while she rested her head against my chest.

"I'm going to be over here making you breakfast every morning if it makes you this kind of insatiable." This warm fuzzy feeling was incredible. I could ride this high forever.

Evie traced her fingers teasingly up my exposed ass, sending a shudder through me. "It's not the food making me insatiable," she said. "But we're still good, right?"

She'd asked that before, too. I was torn between a simple reassurance and telling her if I had my way, I'd never let her go.

Holy shit. Putting words to the feeling hit hard. I wanted her. I never wanted to lose her.

Coming on that strong probably wouldn't go over well. I had more wooing to do first.

I kissed the tip of her nose. "We're still good. Always."

We finally broke apart. While Evie went to get ready, I cleaned up myself and the kitchen, and called Aubrey to tell her we'd be at Evie's store soon. When we got there, Aubrey and Alys were already waiting.

The store was closed, like most of the businesses were on Sundays. Evie let us all in, locked the door behind us, and we headed to the large back room she used any time she needed a large space to work in.

The four of us gathered around a table that was frequently filled with snacks, but this morning held a notepad, and I had the pen.

"One of you needs to tell us what this is about," Aubrey said.

I looked at Evie. This wasn't my story to tell, but I had pushed her into the situation.

She twisted her mouth and stared back at me. Her nostrils flared. "Yeah, okay." Her sigh was long. "The hardware store is broke. Like, super broke. I made some bad decisions, I made those worse with a bad loan, and I thought I had it under control. I don't."

"How bad are we talking?" Alys sounded sympathetic.

Evie scrubbed her face. "I'm only a month or two from foreclosure, if I don't come up with a fairly large sum of money quickly." She grabbed my pen and scribbled a dollar amount on the notepad.

The number of zeroes caught me off-guard, but I kept my shock from showing.

Aubrey let out a low whistle. "How did you let it get this bad?"

"Hey." I barked out the reprimand. "This isn't on her. Travis. Predatory lending."

The pen clattered to the table when Evie dropped it. "No, this is on me." The energy that had been there an hour ago was gone. "Aubrey's right. I shouldn't have let it get this far."

"So let's fix it," Alys said. "Bake sale. Lemonade stand. Both at the same time. Whatever you need, we're here for it."

"We could get married." I shouldn't have said that. It wasn't a solution in any way, and the looks I got in return confirmed it, but now that I'd said the words—

I needed to dial it back. I wasn't ready for marriage again, even with Evie.

Aubrey screwed up her face. "Maybe he's onto something. Cash only registry. You could pay the bills with your wedding gifts."

Alys looked at the number on the page again. "Unless you both have more friends than we realize, and they're in the habit of giving *generous* gifts, that's not going to cut it."

"Plus, that drags you down with me, Gage. Thanks though." Evie looked bummed. "I've been going through a lot of old things. Grandpa's storage, some of the stock that's tucked away behind everything new. Deacon thinks he might be able to help me clear some of it out, and maybe get a decent price. It won't clear my bill, but it should buy me another month."

My mind skipped through the thought, from Deacon to Adam. "What about some sort of livestream fundraiser?"

"I don't have a channel to livestream on." Evie looked at me like I'd gone off the edge.

But Alys smiled. "Maddox and Adam… They'd totally dedicate time to you."

The two of them had started doing podcasts a few months ago that were basically squirrel-fueled streams of consciousness, and their viewer numbers had skyrocketed.

Evie's frown deepened. "I can't ask—"

"You have to." A hard edge slid into Aubrey's voice. "You need help, and we're your friends. We're here to help, and they'll want to do the same. We all stick together, right? Everyone on the street?"

"I'll talk to Maddox," Alys said. "Assume he's already said yes. You'll be on the show. You can talk about robots and they'll love it. This can work."

"Okay." Evie didn't sound convinced, but there was a hint of gratitude in her surrender.

We tossed a few more suggestions around, and set a time to regroup in a couple of days with Maddox, to make plans. Aubrey and Alys left.

Evie sank lower in her seat with a loud exhale. "I should be upset with you for ambushing me, but thank you. That needed to happen."

"You won't lose the hardware store. I won't let you."

She almost smiled. "Are you free the rest of the day? Want to watch zombie movies or something?"

"Absolutely." I had to tell her about Sawyer, though. I'd been putting it off on purpose, but I needed to get it out. "There is one more thing."

"No more things. I can't handle any more things." She rolled her head to the side to look at me. "Kidding. What's up?"

"Talk to Sawyer, so he leaves. Just hear him out."

Evie raised her brows and sat up straight. The humor vanished from her expression. "No."

"I told him you would."

"You..." She clenched her jaw. "When? No, wait. Yesterday. Are you the reason he was at the picnic?"

I could almost see the pieces slotting together in her head. "Yes," I said.

"I told him *no*. That should be enough for him and for you. I'm not going to hear him out, and you have no right to tell him otherwise."

Fuck. "If you do—"

"He'll leave town?" Evie said. "Do you think that? Because he hasn't gone yet, and I've already told him I'm not interested multiple times. Why, Gage?"

Good question. I was struggling to remember why I made the offer.

130

Right. Because he was good with Kurt. He may actually have a little bit of decent guy hidden somewhere in there.

Nope. Because I wanted him gone, and he'd told me he wasn't leaving until Evie sold to him.

"I don't know."

Evie shook her head. "I'm not going to listen to his offer, because I'm not going to sell to him. That's that."

14 /
sawyer

I should be driving home by now. Enjoying a leisurely ride across the country, contract on file and deal in the bag.

Instead I was sitting on a bench outside the motel laundry room, counting stars and pretending the direct view of the cemetery didn't bother me.

My phone rang. *Hudson.* "Yeah," I answered.

"You on your way home yet?"

What did he do, read my mind? Sense my frustration in some brotherly act of caring, from across the country?

No. He was calling to gloat.

"I like it here. Lots of potential. I'm sticking around for the scenery." Somehow I managed to keep any trace of sarcasm from my voice.

"Uh-huh. Can't close the deal, huh? That's not like you."

A fly buzzed around my head, and I swatted

ineffectively at the air. "How the fuck do you know what is and isn't like me?" We'd said more to each other in the last few weeks than in the last ten years. Why was I suddenly of any concern to him?

Besides the obvious answer of I was working to take his *birthright*.

"I know you hate an unjust deal, and something isn't right about this one," Hudson said.

"Like what? You keep calling me. You keep trying to talk me out of this. Tell me why."

Nothing.

"Great answer." This time I let sarcasm ooze in.

"Walk away, Sawyer. You don't need to prove anything to anyone."

Seriously. Like a broken fucking record. "I'm not giving up. I'm not Tony." I didn't mean to mention him. Not here. Not ever to Hudson. "I won't just surrender and leave."

"He didn't surrender anything." Hudson's voice was hard.

I could do that too. "He surrendered *everything*."

"No." Hudson bit off the word. "He got sick. He chose to live the rest of his life on his own terms, rather than being hooked up to machines and drugged out of his mind. He made the same choice Mom did, and then he died. He didn't give up. He didn't fucking leave you. My wife left me. I know the difference. Mourn him. Admit you miss him. Grieve so you can start to heal."

The ache that stabbed me through the heart

almost made me whimper, and I shut that part of myself down in a blink. If I chose to hear him, I'd curl up in my room and—

What did he say? "Your wife left you?" That was so much easier for me to focus on than the hole Hudson's words dug out of me.

"That's not what we're talking about."

It was now, because the clawing at my throat and my mind and my soul was too much, and I couldn't fall into it. "You said the words. Since when are you separated?"

He let out a heavy sigh. "Apparently, she's been fucking dad. She and I were fighting, she compared me to him, and I threw her out. But she hadn't been a part of *us* for a long time."

"Holy fuck." This was way better than my own misery. So why did part of me feel bad for my brother? "Why didn't you...?"

"Say anything? How eager would you be to tell people your wife was fucking your dad? You can't even admit your husband died."

Fuck this. Hudson didn't get my sympathy. "That's why you're not in the running to take over."

"It is."

"Good. That means I win."

"Don't sacrifice everything for this."

My laugh of disbelief slipped out before I could stop it, and the turmoil raging in my head threatened to become a spew of unintelligible words. "I know Tony is dead. I realize that." Admitting it out loud when I refused to let myself so much as think the words sliced through me. Could emotional wounds bleed? "I've already lost everything. At least this way, I get something back."

Because fuck the brother and father who pushed me out. Fuck them all.

"Sawyer—"

"Best of luck with your divorce, dude." I hung up before I had to listen to Hudson say anything else.

The dryer buzzed from the room behind me, but I was stuck in the mire of my thoughts. I was spiraling into a place I refused to be, and I couldn't stop myself. All I could think about was watching Tony become someone else as he wasted away those last few months. As he surrendered to the same type of cancer that killed my mother.

I didn't want to be—

"Mr. Sawyer?" Kurt was standing in front of me.

Great. The one person in this fucking place I didn't mind seeing was a kid who reminded me too much of myself at his age. "Why are you here?"

He pointed toward the front office of the motel. "My mom is the night clerk. What are you doing?"

"Laundry." I should get back to it…as soon as I pulled my head on straight again.

"So you're waiting? If you're not busy, can you answer questions for me about tanks and remote controls?"

I definitely could not, because that was Tony's

thing, and I needed those thoughts out of my head. "I'll try. What's up?"

"Did zombies kill your dad?"

Oh. Wow. Not what I expected. "No."

"Was it Nazis?"

This took an unexpected turn. "I'm not that old, and my dad isn't dead." Though I suspected Hudson wished he was. "You realize zombies aren't real, don't you?" Pretending was one thing, but reality had to be established sometimes.

Which was why there was a gaping hole in my heart I couldn't patch.

"I know." Kurt sighed. "But sometimes it's easier to make-believe."

"I understand that. Did zombies kill your dad?"

"No. If he had to die though, I wish it had been zombies. We're allowed to hunt those."

Whoa. Dark sentiment from a kid. I got it, though I shouldn't encourage it. "There have been a lot of times I wished I could get rid of the same thing that took my mom from me." I needed to move away from this conversation. I wasn't going to discuss death and life and everything in between with a ten-year-old.

As much as I'd wished back then that any adult would be that kind of honest with me.

"Are tanks more effective than planes?" Kurt asked.

I could do this. A neutral topic. Sure, I only

knew anything about it because of Tony, but I could stay removed. "It depends on what your goal is. Tanks aren't particularly good in urban environments, but planes tend to require more fuel and be less precise."

"Urban environments?"

"Like cities. Lots of close together buildings. Imagine trying to drive a big, huge thing down a narrow street with tall buildings."

Kurt wrinkled his nose. "Sounds scary."

Sure, *scary* worked. "I bet it is."

"Is that why robots fight in a big empty box?"

I assumed he had more background on his question than I did. "I don't watch a lot of robot fights."

"You should. They beat each other up, but people don't get hurt, and sometimes there are explosions. *Pew*." He made a broad gesture with his hands.

"That does sound pretty epic."

"So. Epic. I'm going to Evie's tomorrow," Kurt said. "She's going to help me make modifications to my F4U. You should come too. You know almost as much about robots as she does."

I doubted that. Apparently there was one line I wasn't willing to cross—I wouldn't argue with her in front of this kid who still had hope. "That's not a good idea. Evie doesn't like me very much."

"Evie likes everyone who knows about robot stuff. I bet if you tell her that, she'll like you, too."

"Kurt." A woman's voice carried through the parking lot. She strode toward us from the front office at a fast clip. "Why are you bothering this man?"

"He's not a bother. We're talking shop." I knew her—Elaina. She'd been sugar and sweetness when I checked in, then turned cold like everyone else within the next day.

"He's nice, Mom. Why doesn't anyone like him?"

I hid my smirk at the way Elaina twisted her mouth. She took Kurt's hand. "We're sorry to take up your time," she said to me. "Have a good night, Mr. Rawlings."

Kurt waved and I returned the gesture as he walked away with his mother.

I should be grateful to be alone again, but the silence left my grief an opening to rush back in. It was probably a good thing there was no place in this town that would sell me liquor at ten on a Sunday night, because I was tempted to buy the cheapest gallon of vodka I could find, and drown in it.

Instead, I grabbed my clothes from the dryer and headed back to my room. My earbuds sat on the nightstand.

Ignore them. See what's on HBO. Fall asleep to a stupid movie.

I grabbed the noise canceling buds, shoved them in my ears as they connected to my phone, and cranked the music. It would be loud enough to keep me from thinking, except that I picked a playlist I hadn't touched since Tony—

Since I couldn't hold the feeling back, I lay on the bed and let grief consume me as the series of metal ballads we'd played at our wedding wrapped me up in emotional agony.

15 /
evie

Alys texted me Monday morning to tell me Maddox and Adam were in to help. One of them would write up some text to warm up their audience, and I could approve it, and then they'd have me on Sunday.

I hated the idea of putting so many people out for my mistake, but I was grateful for the help. I thanked her and sent them thanks as well.

Rohde dropped Kurt off a little after ten. This second summer without her husband was proving hard on Elaina for more than just emotional reasons. She worked nights because it paid better, but with Kurt out of school, she didn't have anyone to watch him.

A few of us volunteered, and today I would help him make upgrades to his plane. Which so far had been as much talking robot theory as working on the RC vehicle. Not that I minded—I loved the chance to share my knowledge.

"What happened to your zombie Nazi bombs?" I asked when he and I were set up in the back room.

Kurt jabbed at the wings where the devices in question had been. "Sawyer said they were messing with the remote control, and they had to go."

Sawyer said... His name hit harder than I cared for. I was already over the conversation with Gage yesterday—I understood why he'd done what he did —but that didn't mean I was over hating Sawyer.

Disliking, maybe. It was hard to think one hundred percent poorly of him if he'd helped Kurt.

I couldn't believe I'd made a rookie mistake like forgetting that the bombs might interfere with the RF. "What if we used plastic instead of aluminum?" I asked.

"Will plastic still destroy the zombies?"

"Zombies eat brains, right?" Sawyer's voice came from behind me.

What the fuck was he doing here? Right, I left Terrence in charge this morning, and he didn't seem capable of stopping Sawyer from wandering through the store.

Kurt was nodding enthusiastically. "They eat brains and they bite people and they invade France."

"But they can't bite through plastic," Sawyer said.

"And they can't do anything if the bomb blows them up, regardless of what it's made from." I kept my voice pleasant but fixed Sawyer with a glare. "Can I help you?" I swore to God if he said *just hear me out*...

"I'm hoping I can help both of you." Sawyer's smile didn't quite reach his eyes. "This young man suggested that if I tell you I know a little bit about RC vehicles"—

"And robots," Kurt cut him off.

—"and robots, that you'd let me help with his project today."

No. Absolutely not. I was *not* spending the day doing this with Sawyer. I didn't want him tainting the experience for me.

"Can he please, Evie?" Kurt turned wide eyes on me. "He's really smart, and he also knows more about zombies than anyone else ever. I bet he's hunted them."

"I have." Sawyer hadn't moved past the doorway.

And I couldn't turn down Kurt. Not with such a reasonable request. "As long as Mr. Rawlings behaves, he can stay."

"I promise to be a good boy, Ms. Young." The smile Sawyer gave me was all smug, and did wicked things to my insides regardless.

"Kurt—go grab two-quarter inch-by-three PVC elbow joints from aisle seven," I said.

"Yes, ma'am." Kurt saluted and ran from the room.

I stepped closer to Sawyer, and ignored the idiotic way my body reacted to the scent of his cologne. I crooked a finger, and he bent his head closer to mine. "Truce for him. And then you go away." My voice was barely a whisper.

Sawyer stepped back. "I agree to the truce."

I'd take it for now, and kick him out when Kurt was gone.

There was one more thing I needed to do first, though. I called Elaina, to make sure she was okay with it... and possibly to let her be the one to tell Kurt *no* when she decided she didn't want Sawyer near her son.

To my surprise, Elaina said, "I heard Sawyer was really good with him at the picnic, and Kurt hasn't stopped talking about how much he knows about robots and zombies. As long as you're there with them, I'm fine with it."

"Okay. Thanks." I was too stunned to say much else.

Kurt returned quickly with the parts in question and handed them to me. "What are those for?"

"Not sure yet. But we'll figure it out as we go." One of the things I was trying to teach him was improvisation. Parts could be made specifically for a project, but they could also frequently be found in the most unexpected places.

"What's that?" Kurt pointed at the wall.

It was the framed sketch Gage gave me for my birthday, and seeing it hanging above my desk still made me smile. "It's the first robot I ever designed."

"Does it blow stuff up?"

Fair question. "Robots didn't do that back then."

Sawyer cleared his throat with a less-than-subtle cough. "Robots have always done that."

"Like Gundam," Kurt said.

Sawyer pointed at him. "Exactly."

I didn't care that Sawyer was familiar with cartoon mecha or RF or RC, or anything that I enjoyed. There was no reason at all for me to even notice that he knew those things. "How about this—back then *my* robots didn't blow stuff up." On purpose. "But I do know how I would make that one into a fighter." I shouldn't have said that.

"Can we build it?" The excitement on Kurt's face brightened the room.

I shook my head. "No. That would cost too much." I gave Sawyer a look that dared him to challenge me on this one.

He clamped his mouth shut.

"Okay." Kurt tended to understand the concept of *too expensive*. "Can we make landing gear for my plane now?"

A request I was prepared for. We'd been planning this for a few weeks, and I'd machined parts for him in my spare time. We weren't just replacing the wheels, we were running the mechanics to the cockpit that would let Kurt raise and lower the gear from the pilot's seat.

"Of course we can," I said. "And Sawyer can help us make sure we don't get any RF interference." If he was going to stick around, he could either prove he was worthy of the invitation, or he could fail, and I'd come to the rescue. Either way was fine with me.

Sawyer gave a sloppy salute. "Yes ma'am."

"Not like that." Kurt's voice was instantly stern. "Like this." He showed Sawyer the proper way to salute.

"You two practice that. Make sure he gets it right," I said to Kurt, then stepped away to grab the parts I'd made.

When I returned, Sawyer and Kurt were giving each other proper, firm salutes. They wouldn't impress a drill sergeant, but they were close enough for civvies.

"At ease, soldier." I set the parts on the table.

Kurt tried to fall into the at ease posture I'd taught him, but ended up giggling.

Sawyer picked up one of the wheels and turned it over several times as he examined it. "The precision on these is incredible. Where did you get them?"

I jerked my head at the CNC machine behind me. "I designed them. I made them."

"Wow." He sounded genuinely impressed.

"Hello— Whoa…" Aubrey called, and trailed off as she stepped into the room.

She glanced at Sawyer and then me.

I didn't want to get into *anything* in front of Kurt or Sawyer, and I hoped the look I gave her conveyed that.

She twisted her mouth. *Why?*

I tilted my head. *I'll explain later.*

"We still on for tonight?" Aubrey asked aloud.

"Always." Tonight was DJ night at Joystick's. Maddox ran the playlists because he had the most eclectic taste in music. He would pick a genre— country tonight—and play nothing but that all night. Aubrey and I loved it and went whenever we could.

The invitation was always open to our other friends too—Gage and anyone else who wanted to join us—but typically Alys was with Onyx, for Maddox, and Aubrey and I danced alone.

"What are you doing tonight?" Kurt asked. "Fighting robots?"

One track mind, this kid. I knew how to make him stop asking questions. "We're going dancing."

Kurt wrinkled his nose. "Gross."

Give it about three or four years, kid. "I'll be there," I assured Aubrey.

She gave one last look at Sawyer, and left.

I'd explain it all to her tonight. Not that there was much to say.

For the next few hours, I talked Sawyer and

Kurt through removing old parts or installing new ones, and they would reply, but other banter and conversation was all-but nonexistent.

Sawyer fitted a tiny cable to the stick on one end and the landing gear on the other. "Seriously, this precision," he muttered. "People pay a lot for this kind of work."

Heat flooded my face at the praise. Damn my body for reacting. "I don't do this professionally."

"Would you? Could you?" He held my gaze.

I blinked first. "I suppose, but there's not a demand for it."

Sawyer grunted and went back to helping Kurt attach a wheel to a leg.

I hated to admit it, but Sawyer was good with Kurt. Patient. Kind. Encouraging the kid's imagination instead of squashing it.

We wrapped up a few hours later, and sent Kurt on his way when Elaina stopped by for him.

Sawyer stuck around, diving into cleanup without pause.

Without a buffer here, I could tell him to leave. "Should I ask why you know so much about RC planes?" Not the way to shut down a conversation.

A shadow crossed over Sawyer's face before his expression went blank. "You really shouldn't."

Or maybe it was exactly the way to put an end to the day. I wasn't interested in getting personal with him. "How about cockpits?" Why did I go there?

Because my brain was a dirty filthy traitor.

"Do you really want me to answer that, or do you want to take it back?" Was that teasing in Sawyer's retort?

"I said what I said. If you're going to give me a take-back..."

"You'll what?" He paused in putting tools back in their places. "Take back the day we met?"

I stalled. The answer was *absolutely I would*. But I wouldn't. "I'm not the one who fucked up that day."

"Hmm..."

Infuriating. "That's all you have to say for yourself?"

"Why robots?" Sawyer asked. Was he serious?

"You're not even trying to hide that you're changing the subject."

"I don't need to hide it."

"I like to build things." Why was I still talking to him? Because I was enjoying the conversation, as much as it hurt to admit. "That's what I'm inspired to build. I also had a mild to medium fascination with mechs growing up."

"Gundam?" Sawyer looked amused. Not smug. Not like he was gloating. Just the faintest hint of a smile.

And fuck-it-all if that wasn't sexy.

"Voltron," I said.

"Why?" He sounded genuinely curious.

"Honestly?"

"Sure, let's do honesty."

"Can you handle that?" I wasn't ready to completely yield to his charm—so sue me.

Sawyer raised his eyebrows.

One point, me. "I didn't figure anything else was capable of protecting us from Godzilla." It was a fear I'd only had for a short while, but it left a lasting impression.

"That was a big concern of yours?" Sawyer's amusement was back. "Some people feared quicksand, but Evie was worried about Godzilla?"

"Exactly. I saw this documentary a few years ago about Jaeger pilots." I let the teasing slide into my voice with the *Pacific Rim* reference. In a way I hoped Sawyer didn't get it, because then I could say I wasn't having fun with him.

Sawyer chuckled. "I saw that one. I don't think Godzilla is a Kaiju though. Rather, not *that* kind."

Damn it, I was definitely having fun.

"I bet you'd drift perfectly with Gage," Sawyer said.

The comment struck me in a way I didn't understand. I wanted to love the idea and at the same time, it made my stomach churn. I doubted Sawyer was going for either reaction. "You haven't mentioned buying my place once today." I changed the subject on purpose.

"You called a temporary truce and I agreed."

"Are you done trying to get me to sell?" I knew better. If I pushed the issue, I could dislike him again.

"I've put it on hold for the night," he said. "And otherwise, not by a long shot." He checked his watch. "I should let you get ready to go dancing. Thank you for today, Eowyn."

I didn't care for how sexy my full name sounded on his lips or the conflict that raged inside me as he walked out of my store.

16 /
gage

I tended to turn down any offers from Evie to go dancing with her and Aubrey. I didn't mind the music, especially since Maddox had taken over DJing; he had decent taste in most genres. It was the dancing that I wasn't fond of.

Especially on a country music night.

I was going through Evie withdrawal, though. The best way to see her, to be close to her tonight, was to be at Joystick's.

When I walked in, she was talking to Aubrey and laughing. Evie's smile when she saw me, the way she broke away and crossed the room quickly to grab my hand, made the entire decision worthwhile.

"You're here. Holy shit."

I loved seeing her in such a carefree, good mood. "Surprise."

"Watching you try to line dance ought to be the highlight of the night." Aubrey's sarcasm was light.

"I exist for your amusement, ladies." I gave a deep bow.

Aubrey snorted. "Some of us more than others."

Pink dotted Evie's cheeks. "No clue what she's talking about. I'm sure you'll dance fine."

"Don't give me too much credit." I knew my limits. "But if you promise to teach me, I'll do my best to learn."

"Do you two want to be alone? I can ask everyone else here to leave," Aubrey teased.

I wrapped an arm around Evie's waist. "That would be rude. We can go."

"No." Evie laughed and yanked me to her before I could pull her away. "You're here, you're going to see it through, damn it." She was in a good mood tonight. Incredible, even. I hadn't seen this much recently, and it was a good look on her.

"Are we good with him yet?" Like that Aubrey's tone shifted to something less amused and more distracted.

I followed her gaze to where it was fixed on the door. Sawyer had just walked in, looking stupid-good in flannel, jeans, and cowboy boots. He even had the hat.

My mood slipped. "Why…?" Was he here? I couldn't push the whole question out.

"He overheard Aubrey and me talking about tonight." Evie was staring at him, too. "It's not like he's not allowed to be here."

"So we're *not* good with him," Aubrey said.

"No." Not ever.

Evie didn't answer, and jealousy clawed its way through me. "Overheard you where?" I asked.

"Howdy, cow people... That sounded better in my head." Alys joined us, draping her arms over Evie's and Aubrey's shoulders.

Ravyn was with her. "Are we drooling over Gage's new boyfriend?"

Like that, Evie's amusement was gone, replaced with a scowl. "What?"

"New guy comes to town, clashes with one of the local hotties..." Ravyn trailed off as she looked between all of us. "I *so* read that wrong. Ignore me."

Evie shifted her body, nudging the group toward the dance floor and away from Sawyer. "He can go wherever he wants, unless Joystick makes him leave. Free country and all that. We're here to enjoy the music."

"And dance," Alys said.

Evie nodded. "Exactly."

That sounded great, except that as the music started, it quickly became clear Sawyer knew what he was doing, and I had two left feet.

It might've been easier for me to hide it, if we weren't all doing the same dance, with me being one of the few people who couldn't seem to find the beat. Evie and Alys tried to coax me through it. Aubrey and Ravyn were too busy snickering.

Why couldn't I have picked the night with the mosh pit? The steps would be a lot simpler, and it would give me an excuse to elbow Sawyer one or five times.

About three or four songs in, I desperately needed a drink. A lot of what they served here was from the microbrewery Knox and I had, but I was in the mood for something stronger. I leaned my head close to Evie's ear. "Gonna hit up the bar. You want anything?"

She shook her head. "Alcohol won't make you dance better, it'll just make you think you are."

"Thanks for the tip." I cut a straight line toward the bar.

I downed a shot of tequila. Losing control of my senses probably wasn't as smart as it was tempting. I ordered a beer, and turned to watch Evie and the others. This was definitely a better way to participate—she made for an amazing view.

Sawyer stepped up next to me. "You were looking good out there. Why'd you stop?"

"Fuck you." Whatever affinity or tolerance I'd had for him the other day was gone.

"Ouch." Sawyer didn't sound even slightly offended. "Are you sore because you suck at this or because I spent the day with Evie without your intervention?"

He what?

No. That was bullshit, and he was trying to get a rise out of me. "You didn't spend the day with Evie." *He overheard Aubrey and me talking about tonight...*

Sawyer shrugged. "Believe what you want.

Doesn't change my life. You can join us next time though. Maybe watch us play zombies."

"How do you—" I wasn't going to ask. I didn't care about the answer.

Sawyer's smirk said he was going to give me one anyway. "She lies there and screams while I eat her."

Fury spilled inside me, but I wasn't going to lose it in front of everyone. The way my fist clenched around Sawyer's shirt, it hadn't gotten the message.

Instead of beating him to a pulp in public, I dragged him to a back hallway, away from everything but the room where they stored the booze. "Stay the fuck away from Evie." I spoke through clenched teeth.

"What happened to *I'll talk to her on your behalf?*" Sawyer forced my grip open and dropped my hand with distaste.

"I changed my mind."

"Uh-huh. Does she know how much you decide on her behalf?"

I didn't care for this conversation, especially the way Sawyer's words were similar to Evie's yesterday. "The point is, Evie's mine." I liked the way those words tasted. "She should've been a long time ago, and you need to leave her alone."

The way Sawyer smirked was infuriating. "Good for you. I'm here on business. She knows that."

"Do *you?*" The answer that I wasn't sure I wanted to hear was to the question *did she?*

"Are you really jealous because you want her? Or because you want me?"

Was he fucking kidding me? I let out a barking laugh at the question. He was trying to get under my skin, and I was letting him, but I saw more clearly now. "You're not the hot shit you think you are."

"I am." Sawyer didn't flinch. "And that's why you're jealous." He stepped closer. "But if she's not interested, you don't have to get all worked up." His voice slid toward ridiculous and seductive. "You could have me to yourself."

He gripped the back of my neck and crushed his mouth to mine.

What the actual fuck?

And damn it, why did this feel good? Why did I like the way his stubble scraped my lips and his fingers dug into my flesh and how hard his body was against mine?

"You have got to be kidding me." That was Evie.

I broke away in an instant, to see her standing at the end of the hallway, watching us with disbelief.

"It's not what it looks like," I said.

She sighed. "Could you be any more cliché?" Evie turned and walked away.

I didn't give a shit what Sawyer was doing—she was the only person that mattered. I sprinted to catch up with her. "He kissed me," I said as we reached the front door.

"You were *not* struggling." She didn't pause, cutting a path down the sidewalk in the direction of her house.

I fell into step beside her, and grabbed her arm.

She jerked away.

"Stop, Evie. Listen to me."

"No." She spoke through clenched teeth.

He kissed *me*. I'd said that once, it didn't work. "Evie."

"No."

We walked in silence to her place. We walked up to her door, and she never so much as glanced at me, while she shoved her key in the lock.

"I'll wait out here until you listen to me," I said.

Evie finally looked at me, but it was a withering gaze filled with hurt, which drilled a hole through my heart. "'Night, Gage." She walked inside and closed the door between us.

It was impossible for me to miss the sound of the deadbolt sliding into place.

How did tonight fall apart so quickly? I wanted to explain, but I was having a hard time wrapping my brain around what happened. I pressed my back to her door, and slid to the ground, landing with a *thunk* on my ass.

I didn't know how long I sat there, but my legs were asleep long before Rohde strolled up the walk toward me.

"Go home, Gage."

"I'm waiting to talk to Evie." I had to make this right.

He nodded. "I know. She called me."

I couldn't... I let out a heavy sigh. "I just want to explain."

"Let her cool off. This isn't helping anyone."

I raked my fingers through my hair. Why did he have to be right? It had taken me decades to realize I wanted more than friendship from Evie, and somehow I was throwing away all my chances, one after another. "Fine." I wasn't giving up on her, but he was right, this wouldn't get me anywhere.

17 /
evie

I needed two-point-seven liters of coffee to get started this morning. Why didn't anyone sell coffee by the liter?

I'd been up long after Rohde made Gage leave last night, wondering if I should follow. Should I text him? Did I overreact?

When I saw Gage and Sawyer together... *Kissing...* That image played over and over again in my mind. As I fell asleep. In my dreams. Now, while I tried to find enough consciousness to get to work.

I was definitely angry. Hurt. Jealous.

Turned on?

I had too much work to do today to deal with my brain acting like this. Gage and I were friends. *Just* friends. We both kept confirming as much. I wanted it that way.

In the name of getting anything done, I pushed the thoughts aside, and headed into my store.

I reached my office in the back of the hardware store, and my brain still wasn't leaving things alone. If I talked this out with Gage, maybe it would help. I hated the idea of being on the outs with him.

A text message should work.

> Me: About last night...

His answer came though almost immediately, which made me smile more than maybe it should.

> Gage: I'm sorry.

> Me: It's not my place to say who you kiss.

Typing the words didn't feel right, but it was true. I had no say in that.

> Gage: It could be.

What? What was that supposed to mean?

> Me: You enjoyed it.

Why did I say that? Did I need company in the fact that I still thought about the way Sawyer kissed? Did I want to keep being mad?

I really didn't.

> Gage: That feels like a trick question.

I wouldn't—couldn't do that to him. Make him walk into some sort of mind game trap.

> Me: No. Because we're friends. We don't do that to each other, right?

> Gage: No, we don't. So yes, I see what you found appealing about it, despite who he is.

> Me: So you did like it.

It kind of sucked that teasing didn't convert well to text, but I put a winky face at the end. So many emotions tickled my senses, wondering just how much Gage liked that kiss. Jealousy was back. So was desire. Happiness? That was a weird one.

Confusion.

"Evie, I need your authorization." Angela, one of my employees, called over the intercom in my office.

I set my cell aside and strode to the front of the store.

It turned out to be a return by Terrance. A manager's override was required to authorize this kind of employee transaction, and I was my own on-call manager today. I typed in my code, and let Angela get back to finishing the transaction with Terrance.

As I stepped away from the computer, a string of transactions under Terrance's name caught my attention. What the...?

All of my people got a discount, and some of them occasionally used it, but the list of sales under his name seemed oddly high.

How many hammers did one man need?

It was probably for a series of little things, but I couldn't leave the thought alone. I returned to my desk, and pulled up the employee customer accounts. Across everyone, there were a bunch of little sales—the occasional bottle of soda or drain cleaner. A plunger here, a snake there.

And there were a handful of bigger transactions as well. Someone needed a reciprocating saw or batch of Sheetrock.

Terrance's account looked different though. The biggest thing that stood out was the amount he'd cashed out in store credit. I did some quick math as I looked down hundreds of rows of numbers.

I was looking at tens of thousands in store credit. That he'd used to buy power tools, fixtures, lights, and so much more. Irritation and disbelief whispered through me.

This couldn't be right.

But if it was, it would explain why I couldn't balance my books, and why my store seemed to be hemorrhaging cash, even now. Something that tasted like anger tinged my tongue.

I called up to the front counter, and Angela picked up.

"Is Terrance still here?" I asked.

"No. Do you want me to see if I can catch him?"

"No, that's okay. But will you bring me the table router he just returned?"

"Sure." A moment later, Angela set the tool in my office. "Did you need anything else?" She asked.

Some fucking answers. "No, thank you."

I couldn't believe this. Terrance had worked for me for years. I hired him on Travis's recommendation, and even when I booted Travis out of my life, Terrance hadn't seemed upset. He'd always been a great employee.

What did one man do with seven industrial-sized air compressors, and why hadn't anyone noticed?

Because he mixed up the transactions. Bought from different employees...

Disbelief warred with my growing fury. He couldn't have. He didn't steal all of this from me, did he?

I frowned at the screen. Angela hadn't been working three months ago. She'd taken the entire month off, to go on vacation with her family.

So how did she sell Terrance a lawnmower?

I didn't want to believe this was true. The evidence was staring me in the face, though.

So far it was all circumstantial, though it would

be a pretty big coincidence if what was happening was anything different than what it looked like. I needed to be sure though. I needed hard, physical proof.

And in the meantime, I needed to keep my rage in check, rather than tracking him down on the street, and shouting about why he was fired in front of every single person in town within yelling distance.

Because when I called the police, I didn't want there to be any mistakes one way or the other.

I spent the rest of the workday ordering more cameras. Installing them in new places, and trying to do so without my employees knowing what I was up to. Thinking that way made me ill. What if more of them were in on this? The transactions were associated with Terrance's name, but what if he had help?

And how fucking arrogant was he, to not do a better job of hiding—

It didn't matter. After the store closed, I finished installing the last of the cameras near the register and the front of the store. I tucked them away, hiding them from view and pointing them at traditionally blind spots.

By the time I walked out of the store, I was exhausted both physically and emotionally. One of my people was ripping me off, and somehow I still felt guilty about the fact that I was about to ruin his life. What was wrong with me?

No. What was wrong with him?

How dare he?

I needed to get home. Or to the liquor store. Or to gorge myself on pizza. Or something.

My phone blinked with an unread notification when I picked it up, and I clicked on Gage's unread text message.

It just said *yes*.

My question was right above that, so easy to see.

> Me: So you did like it.

> Gage: Yes.

I couldn't deal with that tonight, on top of everything else. I just couldn't.

18 /
sawyer

Was I an asshole for what I did to Gage?
Without question.

I knew it. I felt bad about it, but I was trying so hard to shut the part of me up that cared. A therapist might call it self-sabotage... Pissing off Evie... Pissing off Gage... All of it pushed me further from accomplishing, well, anything.

It was a good thing I wasn't listening to that part of my brain.

Because on top of feeling guilty, I'd also be dwelling on the fact that I liked that kiss. I enjoyed kissing Gage as much as I did Evie, and I wanted to try both again. Maybe next time without pissing them off first.

Nope. I wasn't thinking about that, because that kind of infatuation was for teenagers, and idiots in romance novels.

I was also ignoring any feelings that the conversation with Hudson had stirred up. The reminder of Tony, and the nagging that said that Hudson had never actually been against us, it was just easier to tell myself he was.

Fortunately, I kept myself busy the entire day with work. Seeking out new opportunities, making dozens of calls, and setting up a string of appointments for after I bought Evie out and left this place.

I grabbed the stack of advertising materials I'd put together for mailing out, locked my motel room, and headed to the main office to drop them off. Last week, it had been impossible to get a solid answer about where I could mail or ship things from. I'd ended up driving to a nearby, larger city.

Elaina let me know earlier today that I was welcome to leave anything with her, and she'd make sure my mail and such went out with the motel's daily pickup.

When I walked into the front office, Elaina was working the front desk, and Kurt sat at a short table on the other side of the lobby, playing with Legos.

I handed Elaina my stack of envelopes. "Are you still here?" I kept my tone warm and friendly.

Her laugh was short. "Our night person called in. I get to pull a double."

"Ouch." I winced on her behalf. "Want me to take over for you for the night?" Who was I?

"Thanks, but I don't think that would fly with management."

"*Mr. Sawyer.*" Kurt's excited shout interrupted. "Come see what I'm building."

I looked to Elaina for an *okay*, and she shrugged. "He has to camp out on the couch tonight, because it was short notice. I don't have anyone to watch him. If you don't mind keeping him company for a while…"

What else was I going to do? Head back to my room and pretend a bit more that I was heart- and soulless? "I don't mind at all."

I joined Kurt at the coffee table, and listened while he explained how he designed his Lego fighting robot. It was easy to fall into the conversation, though a lot of it reminded me of the parts of life I'd been trying to avoid.

This time though, thinking about Tony and his RC tanks, made me smile. The memories were bittersweet, but more on the sugary side. It also reminded me of how much fun it was building with Evie yesterday.

"You've got a dumb goofy look on your face," Kurt said.

I shook the thoughts aside. "And you're probably up past your bedtime."

"I'm not."

"Sawyer's right." Elaina's voice came from behind me. "Let him get back to his room, and you go to bed."

I wished them both *good night* and stepped outside. I was ready to head back to my room, when a shadowy movement across the street caught my attention.

It was Evie, sitting on a bench in the graveyard. Good for her. I should leave her be.

My feet carried me in her direction, despite the decision.

She looked up as I approached and rolled her eyes. She stood.

"Wait. I'm not here to antagonize you."

"Why are you here, Sawyer?"

I had a feeling she meant more than tonight.

You know why. To buy your store. Nope. I wouldn't read into her question, but that didn't mean I had an answer for her. "I don't know."

With a soft sigh, she sank onto the bench again. "Me too."

"Gage wasn't to blame last night." Why was I bringing this up? "I initiated that kiss."

"Not surprised. And it's not like he minded, regardless."

I'd noticed.

"Your making excuses for him doesn't help any," Evie said.

"I don't expect it to." I had a good idea where I stood with Evie. What her opinion was of me. "But don't take it out on him."

Silence sank in.

Now was a good time for me to leave.

I nodded to the empty spot beside her. "Mind if I join you?"

"I don't even know if I care at this point." Exhaustion bled into her voice. Frustration.

Whatever she was dealing with, it went beyond me.

"Why do you know so much about RC planes?" Evie's question knocked me off-balance. It was the same thing she asked yesterday, but let me brush off then.

Did I want to change the subject again? "My knowledge is more about tanks, though there are a lot of similarities and some shared history."

Apparently I was going to let the question ride.

Evie huffed a laugh. "Not an answer."

"My husband built them. He loved them." The memory didn't hurt as much as I expected, but the sting was still there.

"You're married."

Was that surprise?

"What's the line from the ceremony? Right. *Till death do you part.* So technically no. I'm not married anymore."

"I'm sorry." She sounded sincere.

"Me too." It was weird to talk about things this way. As in, directly…ish. "He would've liked you."

"How do you figure?"

"He didn't put up with my shit either." I glanced at her with a wry smile. "Also, he had a great deal of respect for anyone who could solder cleanly."

This time her laugh wasn't so rough. "Grandpa would've hated you."

I had a feeling that wasn't a random comparison. "Why?"

"You and he have a lot in common."

"Ouch. *You remind me of my grandpa* isn't what
most men want to hear. Regardless of the
situation."

"He never gave up either," Evie said. "You two
would've butted heads until you were both bruised
and battered."

"So you inherited that from him."

"I guess I did."

Silence settled in again, this time more
comfortably.

I didn't realize I was inching my fingers toward
Evie's, where she had them splayed over the bench
between us, until she pulled away.

Evie was on her feet in a blink. "I should go."

"Don't." I stepped in her path as if our entire
history didn't say that was the worst way to get her
to listen to me.

She paused anyway, with so little space between
us I was surprised there was enough air to breathe.

Evie caught my gaze, staring at me with the
same intensity in those stunning green eyes that had
captivated me since the first time I saw her. She
licked her lips. "I'm not going to sell to you."

I probably deserved that response, after the way
I'd been hounding her. "That's not what this is
about. Don't misunderstand—I *don't* give up—but
tonight is about two people enjoying each other's

company. And for what it's worth, I truly am sorry. The moment I realized who you were, when we first met, I should've said something."

No clue where that came from either, but it was nice to say it.

"Uh-huh." Evie's skepticism was appropriate. "Why?"

"Why am I sorry?"

"Yes."

"Because you're a great lay." Wonderful. Sarcastic me was back.

She raised her hand, and I caught her wrist before she could slap me. "I'm kidding." I pushed the assurance out quickly. "I'm sorry because it was a dick move." I didn't want to let go of her wrist, and the sparks flitting between us were more potent than the stars.

"But the sex was still good."

Was she asking or telling me?

"The sex was incredible," I said. "You don't need me to say that, though."

"Almost every woman likes the reassurance sometimes."

Why was she still standing so close? Why hadn't I let her go? Why were the scents of sawdust and ozone that lingered on her skin so intoxicating?

"Then allow me to reassure you. The sex was great, and on top of that, it was fun. Do you know how many people don't know how to have fun during sex?"

Her smile was back, mischievous and tempting. "Too many."

"You do know. Next question, which is better—sex after more than twenty years of longing, or sex with the guy you hate?" There was that part of me I didn't understand, daring her to compare me to Gage.

She searched my face and relaxed some of the weight in her arm against my grip. "I don't hate you, and I'm still not picking a favorite."

Uh-huh. "You've already picked a favorite." And it wasn't me. "But tell me you're not tempted by the thought of Round Two."

"In the interest of your newly found appreciation for honesty..."

Was I holding my breath waiting for her to finish the thought? "Yes?"

"Very tempted."

I let go of her arm to drop my hand under her chin. She was alluring in ways I couldn't define.

Evie stepped back enough to place her out of my arm's reach. "Tempted. Not a sucker."

"It's not like you're *with* Gage."

She raised her brows. "Not the point, and regardless, it is like you're still you."

This had just become a challenge again. Not only was she enticing, from the memories of how she sounded when she came to the defiance she faced me with over and over, but she was fun. Smart. Gorgeous.

"Would you let me kiss you if Gage was here?" I asked.

"Why would that matter?"

"The three of us had fun last time."

Evie sighed. "Yeah, we did."

Fuck the drive to prove I was right. This wasn't about anything but her and me, like I said earlier.

And maybe a little about quieting the voices in my head. I had a feeling she was struggling with something similar, though I didn't know what made me assume that.

Maybe the fact that she hadn't left.

This time when I reached for her, she didn't move. I placed a finger under her chin and closed the distance between us. When I dipped my head near hers, her breath caught.

"You know who I am now," I said.

"I'm not sure I do."

Clever. "You do. Tell me you're not tempted anyway."

Evie bit her bottom lip.

"No response?" I prodded.

"I'm trying not to lie to you." One corner of her mouth tugged up.

I brushed my lips over hers, and forced myself to pull away rather than diving in and deepening the kiss.

Her eyelids fluttered before she opened them again, and her lips stayed slightly parted.

"My room is across the street." My voice was

rougher than I meant it to be. "No commitment. No pressure. But a lot of fun and the world will cease to exist for a few hours."

"That's a big promise."

"No. Just the right kind of escape from reality."

The way Evie slipped her hand into mine was an impossible combination of bold and shy, and the action instantly made me hard. The walk to my room took an eternity and then some. Why did I feel like a teenager about to get laid for the first time?

It didn't matter, because I was done thinking. The instant we were inside, I pinned her to the door, hand pressed to her throat, and claimed her mouth in a hungry kiss that devoured her groan.

She rested her palm on my chest, pushing me back until I hit the bed, and fell onto the mattress.

Evie straddled my legs, and I flipped us both, pinning her to the mattress with her hands above her head.

"See? Fun," I said.

She smirked. "Very."

I could taste the electricity around us, and it was impossible to ignore my own desperation.

Just the right kind of escape from reality.

I kissed her again, harder, and let myself fall into the moment.

I pulled back to look Evie in the eye, and the immediate future splashed in front of me.

If I did this with her tonight, it ruined my chances of buying.

Worse, it ruined my chances with her. She already thought so little of me…

I lost every other connection I'd made here too.

Did I care?

"I can't do this." Evie sighed.

I rolled onto my back. "Me neither."

"Is this where you say this has never happened to you?"

I looked to the side to see her staring at the ceiling. "Something like that." I sat up and offered her a hand, pulling her into a sitting position as well. "Do you want to go?"

"No."

As basic as a reply could get. One word. Two little letters. It was the first time I'd heard her say *no* and liked it.

We moved to put our backs to the headboard. I tossed the pillows that were in my way onto the other bed, and she pulled one into her lap.

"How long were you married?" Evie asked.

Ouch. We were diving this deep right away? "No sex means no fun, huh?"

"Apparently."

"Fifteen incredible years." My mouth provided the answer before my brain could decide if it was a good idea. "And then I watched him waste away, devoured by the same cancer that killed my mom when I was a kid." That went downhill fast.

"I'm sorry."

Me too. "Hey. The hard-on is gone."

Evie's laugh was tight. "I think—I'm pretty sure —one of my employees is ripping me off."

"Oh?" I was surprised she shared that with me.

"Don't use that against me."

Did she really think I was that big an asshole?

Fair. I really had been. "I wouldn't. I promise."

"Is it fucked up that I want to believe you?" She fiddled with the hem of the pillowcase, folding into zigzags with whatever tension the fabric allowed, then letting go, so it all fell apart.

As long as we were being random about our past and present. "Why did you enlist?" I'd rather she not put the focus back on me.

"GI Bill. Help me pay for college. Isn't that why everyone does it?"

"The real reason." I had no idea why the truth mattered, or how I knew that wasn't it.

"My entire family is military. Grandpa, my parents, my brother... Eddie and I were supposed to both be boys. They weren't prepared to raise a girl and I wasn't willing to be a princess. I spent a lot of time proving I was at least as good as my brother at everything. When we turned eighteen, he followed in Mom and Dad's footsteps and went Navy, and I was going to impress Grandpa, so I enlisted in the Marines."

That sounded exactly like the Evie I'd seen since I met her. "But you weren't in for long." According to the basic notes I had about the hardware store, she'd owned it for almost twenty years.

"Turned out chasing someone else's dreams wasn't for me. I did my four years and came home. Why did you lie to me about who you were?"

Back to me. I saw it coming, but I wasn't prepared. "I don't know."

Evie was quiet.

I couldn't sit here, not moving, just talking. My limbs itched, and I hopped to my feet to pace the short distance of the room.

She was waiting for a different answer. Or had decided the conversation wasn't worth pursuing. It was impossible to tell from her blank expression and the way she watched me.

"When Tony passed away, I cried so much." Fuck, what was I doing? "Then I got mad. Furious. The only thought I had for the longest time was *how dare he*? Since then, I've been pushing to get back into my family's good graces."

Evie hadn't asked me for my fucking life story, and I barely vocalized those things to myself. Why was I saying them out loud?

"Win by any means necessary. That's my motto." That answered her question in a flippant, brush-it-off kind of way.

Evie was still silent. What else did she want?

"I guess I thought if I found a new place to fit in, the family business for instance, it wouldn't hurt so much." What the fuck was wrong with me?

"I didn't do a full four years in the Marines, though it was close." Evie's voice was soft, but it startled me regardless. "Grandpa died a few months before my term was up, and I came back for the funeral. They discharged me early. He left me his store, and I did everything I could to lose myself in the people around me, including…" She blew a puff of hair out of her eyes. "I made a stupid mistake with a guy. The lies he told hurt a lot of people, not just me."

"It wasn't stupid."

"It was. And then I did it again years later, with another man."

I would much rather focus on her than me. "They were the ones who made the mistakes."

"Uh-huh." Evie radiated disbelief.

"If they lied and you chose to believe them, that says shitty things about them and good things about you." I refused to examine those words closer, no matter how blatantly obvious they were.

Evie rolled her eyes. "We must have something in common that's not depressing."

I perched on the edge of the bed. "My car. You like my car. I like my car."

"Your car is also depressing."

I turned to face her, letting exaggerated disbelief show through. "My car is *amazing*."

She snorted. "It leaked in the rain and ruined your clothes."

"It's a work in progress. Something doesn't have to be perfect to be great."

"Motivational. No. Really." Was her tone shifting toward lighter? "And I'll agree, it is a wicked cool car."

"See?" At least I'd made my point about something. One point: Sawyer.

We kept talking, sometimes drifting toward the dark or sad, and other times sliding back toward dry humor and sarcasm. At some point, we both laid down again, mostly because a person could only sit on a hotel bed for so long before their back started to protest.

I didn't realize I had drifted off to sleep until I felt the mattress shift next to me. The only light in the room was what spilled in under the curtains, from the parking lot. It was enough for me to see Evie slide into her shoes, and slip from the room, making sure the door latched quietly behind her.

The clock next to my bed said it was four. *Oof.* I should get some real sleep.

My eyes drifted shut, and drowsiness engulfed me. I rolled onto my side, and the faint scents of sawdust, ozone, and Evie's shampoo teased my thoughts.

A sharp ache pinged in my chest at the reminder, and memories tumbled into my half-asleep brain. I wanted to stay in this cloud of barely-consciousness and Evie, and I kept my eyes shut, sinking into the visuals.

Her laughs when she was having fun. Her soft, sweet lips, hard against mine. Her bare skin and warm body underneath me.

The ensemble was enough to make me half-hard. I kicked off my pants and freed my cock. While I recalled her taste and the way she was both power and yielding, I stroked myself to fully erect.

Unlike a few hours ago, in my fantasy we didn't stop making out. She was pinned under me. Then on top of me. Our clothes were gone, and our hands roamed everywhere.

The flash of thoughts had me gripping my shaft harder, as desire built inside me.

And now I was fucking her. Feeling her slick, wet warm wrapped around me. In the vivid but chaotic vision, Gage walked in on us. There was no argument or disbelief. Instead, he joined in. Kissing Evie. Kissing me.

Distinct images blurred to flashes of all three of us touching. Of me tasting both of them. Separately. Together.

Need tightened in my balls, and my dick was hyper-sensitive. My arm was tired, but I was so close. I couldn't stop stroking. Faster. Harder.

I came hard, shudders racking my body as I jerked until I was spent.

As the consuming need faded, I slumped back against the mattress, and lay there. My eyes were closed, and the bliss lingered. I wanted to sink into the pleasant thoughts longer. To lose myself in them.

Consciousness bled in. Sleep wasn't going to happen, and the waking dream had faded.

I had a few calls to make anyway. Hudson would be up already, but I'd need to make the other call in a few hours.

And until then, I had to try my damnedest to not think too hard about what happened last night.

19 /
evie

I was running on fumes and confusion as I got ready in the morning to deal with the day.

I couldn't stop thinking about Gage. About Sawyer.

About the fact that I didn't know how I felt about either one of them.

In Wendover, it all seemed so easy. Almost a game.

Correction—*definitely* a game. One with so much subtext I missed. That I was still missing. Who was the real Sawyer?

The man in Nevada? The one who walked into my store the following Monday? The person I talked to last night? Because that man seemed so real. So hurt. Had so much more in common with me than I wanted to admit.

And Gage was a whole 'nother bundle of questions.

What a ridiculous problem to have. I should feel the same way I did a few days ago. That Gage was the guy I could count on no matter what, and Sawyer was an asshole who wasn't worth the breath it took to say his name.

It was shitty of me to get pissed at Gage because Sawyer kissed him, and then for me to turn around and kiss Sawyer. Then again, as I stared at myself in the mirror, searched green eyes while I finished my makeup, I had no idea what Gage and I were to each other.

Friends. Right? That was what he kept confirming for me.

But did he?

Sawyer seemed so certain that Gage and I had some sort of soul mate connection. As if I just refused to admit that we were always going to be.

Why was I giving headspace to any of this when I had real problems to consider—Terrance may be stealing from me. I was still only a few weeks from losing my store.

And instead of focusing on those things, I was wondering about my heart.

Maybe I was an idiot, but I couldn't do anything about the big problems right at this moment—I had to wait for my plans to play out—so talking to Gage made the most sense.

I found him in his restaurant, in back, working with Knox in the brew house. They both saw me at the same time and Knox's "I'm gonna go some-where else" overlapped with my "Can we talk?"

"Yeah. Good call." Gage seemed to be talking to both of us.

I held my tongue until Knox was gone, as much because I was searching for the right way to start this conversation as anything.

Gage opened his mouth.

If I let him go first, I'd lose what I needed to say. What did I need to say? "I-have-to-tell-you-some-thing," I blurted out the words in a blur.

"Me too, but you first."

"I know I don't have to tell you every guy I sleep with, and you keep saying we're still friends no matter what, but..." I trailed off as I watched Gage's expression shift from neutral to a scowl as I talked.

"Who?"

"Sawyer. But when I say *sleep* I literally mean *sleep*." As I talked, Gage raked his fingers through his hair. "We were talking, not fucking. Though there was some kissing."

Gage was pacing now, tiny back and forth steps that halted when I paused. He puffed out his cheeks and focused on me. "I like this woman, and I don't know how to tell her."

The coffee in my stomach soured. That was the last thing I expected him to say. This was Travis all over again—except Gage wasn't borrowing me into bankruptcy. But how did I read the situation so wrong?

And why did he think this was the right time to say something?

Because now he could. Because of me and Sawyer.

There was no *me and Sawyer*.

My brain didn't like that thought any more than the notion that Gage might be interested in someone else. "We're grown fucking adults. Tell her. Ask her out or something." I couldn't keep the irritation out of my voice.

"Can I buy you dinner tomorrow night?"

What the...? "If you don't want to have a real conversation, just tell me." I shouldn't be angry, but the way he was jumping from one subject to the next...

Was easier to focus on than my fracturing heart.

"You said to ask her out." Gage's voice softened. "*Who?*"

"The girl I like."

My brain was catching up, but I refused to let the thought form. Gage wasn't keeping that kind of secret. I hadn't missed... We didn't keep secrets from each other, because those had nearly destroyed us in past relationships.

Gage cupped my face between his hands, and my heart leaped into my throat. The way he kissed me made a little voice in my head chant *it's you, it's you, it's you*. I wasn't focused on anything but how good his mouth felt against mine, though. His tongue probing my mouth. One hand sliding to the back of my neck to hold me captive. This was like Wendover, like in my kitchen, but with a passion behind it that erased the rest of the world while we were locked together.

"What is this?" I asked when we broke apart. I was pretty sure I knew, but he hadn't said it yet and I was terrified he wouldn't give me the answer I wanted.

"It's you. The woman I like is *you*."

Told you so. "Yeah?" *What about Sawyer?*

My brain could turn off now, please. This gorgeous, amazing man who was so good to me and did so much for me and who I had so much fun with and who filled me with warm fuzzies *liked* me. As in, kiss me until my heart grew wings kind of liked me. "I like you too."

Gage's grin was cocky but sweet. "I really want to drag you into the supply closet and prove how much I *like* you, but I feel like there's another conversation we need to finish. Why Sawyer?"

"You kissed him." It was a bad counter on my part, but I didn't know how to answer his question.

"*He* kissed *me*. You slept with him." Gage teased. There was no meanness in his voice.

Nope. I still didn't know how to answer Gage's question. "*Slept.* Exactly. And it was more like a fitful doze."

Maybe Sawyer wasn't all asshole, but he wasn't

Gage, who was always here for me. "I was so stressed yesterday." I was trying to explain this to myself as much as him. "And I think Terrance is stealing from me—"

"Whoa. What? How do you leave that out? Isn't he working right now? Why didn't you fire him?"

I didn't appreciate my decisions being called into question again and again. "I have to be sure. I installed cameras yesterday."

"And talked to the police."

Shit. I should've done that, or at least clued someone in that I had my suspicions. "Not yet. I was going to do that today. Soon. Next."

Gage flexed his fingers and clenched and unclenched his fist. "So I can't walk down to your hardware store and beat the shit out of Terrance."

How incredibly caveman, but also sweet. "No. But I will head to the police next and tell someone what I'm up to, and about the cameras."

"I want to ask all the questions," Gage said. "How you found it, how long it's been going on, but I feel like we can do that after. Have dinner with me tomorrow night?"

Because I was closing tonight, and he already knew that, because he kept track of my schedule. "Definitely. Yes." I was giddy at the idea of Gage and me. Officially. A couple. Dating. More kisses like those amazing ones I'd already experienced.

And I was upset all over again about Terrance,

and still had no idea how I felt about Sawyer or why it was anything besides a strong dislike.

I didn't get nearly enough sleep for this emotional roller coaster.

20 /
gage

I was so busy watching Evie's ass as she walked out, I nearly missed Sawyer walking in.

But when I noticed him, it was impossible to ignore the way he turned and stared at the same view. "Give me ten minutes, Evie," he said.

Seriously? He came in my restaurant to—

"I can't, Sawyer. I have things to do." She kept walking.

I had absolutely nothing to be jealous of. I'd told Evie how I felt, and it went so well.

Was I envious that she had his attention?

No.

Sawyer turned to me with a smirk. "She left in a hurry. Want me to talk to her on your behalf?"

He didn't think I knew about last night. "Not necessary, Richie Rich." I turned away from him to the dining room. There was opening prep to be done.

"Are we back to the name calling?" Sawyer joined me. "Does that mean she told you she couldn't get enough?"

Uh-huh. "She told me you weren't worth the lube. What do you want?" I pulled a chair from a table and set it on the ground.

"To talk about Evie." Sawyer mimicked my actions, grabbing another chair.

If he was going to work, who was I to argue? "What do you really want?"

For each chair I pulled down, he did the same. "I just told you. I came in here because Evie was here, but I'll settle for talking to you." The smugness vanished from his voice.

I couldn't figure out his game. "Talk to me about what?"

"I may know how to get Evie back on her feet."

No. There was definitely a trick in this. I had yet to see otherwise from Sawyer. There was always a move or a game or a plot. "Does that mean you're going to stop trying to buy her out?" I asked.

"No."

And there it was. "Okay then. Out you go. Or I can throw you out."

"You're such a fucking caveman. You don't think Evie actually likes that, do you?"

I was pretty sure. "She fucks me, rather than *just sleeping*, so yeah."

"Hmm." Sawyer glanced at his watch. "Okay. I'll stop wasting your time."

God damn it. I was torn between giving Sawyer any time, and hearing any solution that could help Evie, regardless of who it came from. "What are you up to, and why?"

Sawyer shook his head. "I'd rather tell you both at the same time."

I was going to deck this man. "You already know she's not here, and you dragged this out anyway? She's working the rest of today." After she talked to the police. "So why are you still here?"

"I don't know." Sawyer frowned. "I guess... I don't have anywhere else to be." He sounded reluctant to admit it. "My plan was basically *tell Evie the news and take up space on her calendar.*"

"You don't strike me as the kind of man who doesn't have a back-up plan."

"I didn't need one."

Arrogant fucker.

"Don't you have some sort of picnic you can torture me with or something?" Sawyer asked.

I was wishing yes.

Did that mean I wanted him hanging around?

Not so much.

"Hey. I put together a flight of the new flavors if you want to—" Knox stopped talking when he stepped into the dining room. "You're not Evie."

Sawyer looked down, patted his chest, and looked up again, a horrified expression in place. "Oh my God, I'm not Evie," he said in a horrible falsetto. He grabbed his crotch. "But I'm well hung, so…"

Color me unimpressed. "Evie had to go." I told Knox.

"Ah. Bummer. I thought you both might want to taste test these." He set the two wooden trays of drinks on a nearby table.

"You're drinking at ten in the morning? And you tell people *I'm* the bad one?"

There was no way I was going to let Sawyer shame me for enjoying this. I pulled up a chair next to one of the flights. "Perk of the job. Do you want the second order, or should Knox take it away?"

"Someone's got to drink it." Sawyer slid the glasses closer to himself, and he sat as well.

Knox clapped me on the shoulder. "Let me know what you think. I'll be in back."

"Thanks." I wasn't surprised to see Knox walk away. He preferred the company of people he knew. I was surprised I was about to have beers with Sawyer. Willingly.

Maybe I'd accidentally traded places with Alys overnight, and stepped through the looking glass.

"What are we drinking?" Sawyer's question drew my attention.

The glasses weren't labeled, but I knew what our fall flavors were, so it was easy to guess. "Apple wheat pale ale, pumpkin—not pumpkin spice—IPA, chocolate porter, and molasses oatmeal stout." As I talked, I pointed to each drink, light to dark.

Sawyer puffed out his cheeks and exhaled. "Those could either be really good or really bad."

"Knox is the best. I guarantee they're good." We did have a bad first attempt with both the apple and the chocolate, but this was round four flavor-wise, and we'd gotten closer each time. Sawyer didn't need to know how many iterations we'd gone through.

I watched as he picked up the apple wheat, and took a decent sized drink.

"Enjoying the show?" He asked over the edge of his glass.

"I'm watching for a reaction. This is a taste test." Not that I expected to get much of one out of Sawyer, unless he had the chance to tell me the beer sucked. Then I was sure he wouldn't hold back.

Sawyer shrugged and took another drink.

I was also watching him. It was impossible to not notice how attractive he was, especially when he wasn't putting on a show. The hints of silver that streaked his hair, his strong jaw that I happened to know delivered incredible kisses... His furrowed brow and mussed hair.

This was a bad time to tumble down the *he's hot* rabbit hole. Especially with Sawyer. I should obliterate thoughts of how attractive he was. Or at least save them for when I was alone. "What do you think?" I asked.

"It's good. Subtle. More of a hint than a smack in the face. You're drinking too, aren't you?"

I was. I took my own taste, and the flavor was exactly what we'd pushed through multiple iterations to achieve. It wasn't a sweet drink. This was still a pale ale, with just the lightest essence of apple and buttery crust. "Nailed it," I muttered.

"You sound surprised."

"Not at all. Of course Knox got it right."

"Uh-huh." Disbelieving Sawyer was back. Or never left. "Gage's friends never make mistakes. That's why they're part of this warm, happy Main Street family." He rolled his eyes, but the sarcasm didn't come through as strongly as I expected.

Was I feeling a buzz already? Was he? We were about to down four pints, with no food. That seemed like a big mistake. Usually Evie and I got just drunk enough to feel it, and then we'd eat. I wasn't going that far with Sawyer.

"We need breakfast. I'll be back in ten." I pushed back from the table.

Sawyer shook his head. "I'll try not to wander off and get lost."

I was getting used to the dry sarcasm, and if I was forced to, I might admit there was something sexy about it.

It was definitely a good time to put food in me.

In the kitchen, I let the fryer and one grill heat up while I gathered supplies. Fries went in the basket and into the oil. While those cooked, I scrambled eggs and diced sausage next to a pile of diced, grilling onions.

When it was all cooked, fries went on the plate first, with everything else next, topped with generous helpings of cheese, salsa, and sour cream.

I brought the large plate back to our table, and Sawyer's eyes grew wide when I approached. "What is that?"

"Secret menu item. Breakfast nacho fries."

"I fucking love it."

We dug in while we finished the first beer.

We'd moved on to the second flavor when Sawyer said, "Tell me how Gage's Grub came to be."

"Not a terribly interesting story." My tale was nothing like Sebastian's or Aubrey's. Hell, even Deacon had a more interesting story, though his came long after he took over. "My great grandpa was Gage too, and the store was passed down. I took over about five years ago."

When we'd started on the fries, Sawyer was being careful. Fork. Knife if needed. Nothing that looked like it might drip on the table or him. So it was fascinating to see him struggle with a lump of several fries, and toppings barely balanced.

"You didn't want to be the Grub Guy growing up?" he asked after he swallowed the food.

"I was going to be a *real* cook." I wanted to laugh at how insistent I was to anyone who asked that it was the only way to cook.

Sawyer didn't do much of a job of hiding his

snort. He took another drink. "Like Emeril or some shit?"

"Something like that. It turns out though that I'm happier working with a short order medium." Sure, a steak dinner that took four plus hours to prepare had its place, but I was more of a breakfast nachos guy.

"You're good at it."

What? I scoffed. "Say that again."

"Fuck you. You heard me the first time." Sawyer's mouth quirked into an unformed smile.

I grinned. "I did hear you, which means it still counts. What about you? What made you become…" an intolerable asshole? "*Diverse*." I used the same word he had when we first met him.

"Are you talking about my work or my sexuality?"

There it was—he'd just avoided my question. Not something I'd noticed before, but this time it stood out. He was good at dancing around a direct answer when he didn't want to discuss it.

I wouldn't push. Despite the food, the pleasant fuzzy headedness of beer was sinking in, and I didn't want to wreck the feeling. "Whatever you want to tell me."

"Nothing. I don't want to tell you anything."

"All right." I shrugged.

"You're more pleasant when you're drunk."

So are you. "I'm mean and I beat people up for

looking at Evie wrong when I'm drunk. This is maybe a quarter of the way there."

"So you're drunk most of the time?" Sawyer teased.

Fucking joked. And didn't sound mean about it. I didn't know how to respond to his tone.

"I was in real estate with my— Not big, high-end deals. Residential. New families. Sitcom shit." Sawyer's tone was smooth and cold, but covering a stronger emotion. "He lef— Died. He died. I was numb for months after, and then it hit me and I just — I can't believe I'm telling you this. Fuck that."

He was self-editing so much that he wasn't telling me much of anything, but I didn't see a benefit to pointing that out.

"I married Grace—my ex-wife—because Evie enlisted." I'd never phrased it out loud that way before. The thoughts were there, but not pieced together so cleanly. *Fuck.*

"Poor baby had to share his woman with the world even though he never grew big enough balls to tell her how she felt before she left."

And now we were back to this. *Hurray.* "Were you born an asshole, or do you have to work at it?"

"Last night I found out that my father's been fucking my brother's wife, so I'm pretty sure it's genetic." Sawyer moved on to the third glass.

Wow. Fuck me. "You win. Your life is *way* more fucked up than mine."

"Should've pegged you for a Deadpool fan."

"What does that make you if you got the reference?"

"At least as weird as you."

I couldn't argue that. Or I didn't want to. "I married so young." Apparently I still wanted to talk about this, despite it being a bad idea. "I thought as time passed, some of the doubts—all of the doubts would go away—but I never got rid of that question... Did I let the right one get away?"

"If you could tell eighteen-year-old you anything, what would it be?" Sawyer asked.

Where did that come from? "Really?"

"No. I asked for my health. Yes, really."

"Back then—both when I got married and when I got divorced—I figured if I just had the answers... if I knew what came next... I wouldn't make so many stupid mistakes. I've thought variations on that so many times over the years."

"That's not an answer." Sawyer stuffed another fry in his mouth.

No, it wasn't. But that was the point—I used to think I needed all the answers, and I really didn't. If I put that into words, would he understand? Did I fully understand?

Why was I drinking with this man, anyway? This was becoming a dangerous slope to understanding each other. Did I want that?

21 /
sawyer

I was enjoying this, and I didn't know how I felt about that. Gage made a decent plate of breakfast nachos, the beer was good, and his company wasn't bad either.

I was a little annoyed he hadn't answered my question, but not nearly as bothered as I was letting him think. "Horny teenage Gage— What would you tell him?"

"I'm getting there." He gave me an infuriatingly wry grin. "I'd tell teenage me that life is better when you get to discover it along the way. Sure, sometimes it hurts to fuck up, and sometimes it feels like your heart is being ripped out and you're never going to survive… But in the end, life is as much about the discovery as anything. Knowing what comes next ruins the fun."

"That's it. You've stopped making sense. I'm

cutting you off." I slid his drink flight away from him.

Gage tugged the tray back to himself. "If you don't understand, I'm not the one who needs to be cut off."

The problem was, I did understand. It all made perfect sense, including that burst of wanting to know. I'd played that game too many times with my memories of Tony. *What if I could've...* But I wasn't drunk enough to admit that. "Next flavor."

Gage raised his brows, but picked up the third glass. "You'll like this one. It starts bitter, but it moves to smooth and rich quickly."

"Cute." According to what Gage said earlier, this was the chocolate porter. This was where I should excuse myself and leave. Two beers, and I was still in control. If I kept going, I was going to slip and say something I regretted.

Then again, walking away now felt a lot like giving up. I took a sip. Once again, they'd nailed the flavor. It wasn't sweet or candy-like. Like the others, it was more of an essence of chocolate than an overwhelming flavor. And it didn't taste fake.

"Well?" Gage prompted.

"It's good." I admitted begrudgingly.

Was it better or worse that he hid his smirk behind his own glass, rather than owning the reaction?

I wanted to knock him off-balance, and I hadn't yet.

Or I wanted to reach across the table and kiss him again. Do more with him. Fuck him until we were spent and he walked bow-legged for a week. While Evie watched, and enjoyed every fucking second of it.

I needed to stop drinking.

"We should get this to go or something." *Not* what I meant to say. Some of the words were right, but the meaning was the opposite end of the field from *I should go.* And who got a beer flight in to-go cups?

"I didn't picture you as a lightweight," Gage said.

Fuck him and his smug-ass, witty retorts. "I thought I could do morning-drunk, but it's not clicking for me. I'd like to at least wait until after noon to be three sheets to the wind."

"We could go back to my place."

"Are you hitting on me?"

"You wish."

I didn't. Or maybe a teensy bit. "Don't you have to work?"

"It's supposed to be my day off. I came in for the beer."

That was one hell of a life. I'd wrapped up a lot of my work early this morning—*thanks, insomnia*—and I was buzzed enough that Gage's suggestion sounded like a good one. "Sure. Let's go back to your place. Drink the rest later."

"Be right back." Gage pushed away from the

table, took our half-finished flights into the back room, and emerged a short while later with a four pack of beer bottles and a to-go box.

He made quick work of transferring the remaining fries to the container, and we were on our way.

We decided his truck could stay at the diner, and we were better off walking. As we headed to his house, the serenity of the town sank in. It was barely ten in the morning, and aside from the occasional car or pedestrian, Main Street wasn't busy. The shops had customers, but they were inside the respective buildings.

It was both comforting and eerie that a place like this still existed in this world. "How do you not go insane from the mundaneness of this town?" I asked Gage.

"You've been here for several days now, you tell me."

That was a shitty counter. Mostly because it meant he'd turned the conversation back on me again. Fortunately, this time I didn't have any emotional attachment to the answer. "I've been working a lot. Hanging out with a few people. I leave town when I get bored."

"And there you have it. My life, Evie's life, most of our lives, in a few sentences." Gage made it sound like the most reasonable answer ever.

"And when it all gets to be too much, you drive to Wendover?" I asked.

He shrugged. "More or less."

"And not to gamble."

"Sometimes to gamble. Depends on the day and the person, but we went just because."

I didn't understand him at all. Or rather, I wanted to say that was the case. I wanted to look down my nose at everything Gage said, the way he lived his life, and his entire appreciation for this small town experience.

And I couldn't do any of that because part of me agreed with how good it sounded.

"Whatever," I said.

We reached his place, he stuck the beer and left-overs in the fridge, and turned to me. "What now?"

"This was your plan."

Gage looked around him. I doubted he was seeing the same things as me. I was taking in the Victorian with the original wood unpainted and polished. The threadbare but clean throw rugs. The real wood table and chairs in the kitchen, and the sofa in the living room that looked like it had seen more good and bad days than most people.

And the massive TV on one wall, with the gaming consoles, sound system, and beanbags in front of it.

The entire house was a twisted combination of classic and modern.

"Death match?" Gage's words startled me.

"Excuse me?"

He nodded at the gaming console setup. "We've

got the day off, we're not doing anything but waiting to get drunk. You're not afraid I'll kick your ass, are you?"

Fuck no. I wasn't losing *anything* to Gage. "Name the game, and prepare to lose."

"You're on, Richie Rich." Gage grabbed two controllers and handed one to me, before he started powering things up.

We both positioned our beanbags where we wanted them near the TV, and a game loaded with soldier characters.

First person shooter? He was going down.

We spent the next several hours alternating who kicked whose ass. I wasn't nearly as frustrated as I wanted to be that we were evenly matched. Morning bled into afternoon, and somewhere along the way we finished off the fries, and a couple of pizzas from Gage's freezer.

As early evening arrived, my eyes were protesting enough that I had to call it quits.

"Can't take the punishment, old man?" Gage teased.

I scrubbed my face, but couldn't wipe away my smirk. This had been too much fun. "I know how to wrap things up when I'm ahead."

"By two matches." Gage huffed and hopped to his feet. "Be right back."

While he was in the kitchen rummaging around, I moved to the couch. Tony would give me so much grief if he could see me now. Eyes dry and strained, back sore from sitting in a bad position for so long, and a stupid ass grin on my face.

I paused, waiting for the thought to carry the same grief with it that memories of Tony usually did, but I only tasted the slightest hints of bittersweet.

Gage returned with the beers. "There's more in the fridge—current flavors not new ones—and it's after five, so I'm hoping your reservations about day drinking have passed."

I took a bottle from him and flipped up the rubber stopper attached to a metal bar. "They have. Let's see if this is the kind of chocolate I'd give someone on Valentine's Day."

"I have such a hard time imagining you celebrating Valentine's Day." Gage took a long swallow of his drink.

He had no idea. Then again, I'd made sure of that. Without being conscious of it, I'd worked hard since I arrived to make sure I was the Sawyer I used to be before Tony.

Why?

"When did you know you were bisexual?" I asked Gage rather than answer my own questions.

He clenched his jaw. "It wasn't— I'm— I didn't—"

"You did know?" I didn't just out him to himself, did I?

He gave a terse shake of his head. "Why would you assume one way or the other?"

"Because of that kiss." Because of the way Gage watched me. Had I read his stares, his mouth on mine, and everything else wrong? I didn't make that mistake often. "Aren't you?"

"I am."

"I'm not going to out you, if you're not out," I said. "I'm an asshole, but not like that."

Gage took a long drink and let out a longer sigh. "It's not a secret. Rather, I haven't told anyone except Evie, but I figured it out a few years ago, and it's not... I've never acted on it. I don't care if people know, there's just nothing to tell."

Oh. That had a few implications. "I was your first? I popped your boy cherry?"

Gage rolled his eyes. "Pretty sure it takes more than a kiss to do... whatever that means."

"You know what it means."

Beer sloshed up the lip of Gage's bottle when he set it on the coffee table. "Seriously. Why are you like this?"

I hated hearing the same question I'd been asking myself off and on for too long. Hearing him voice the thoughts in my head summoned my frustration, and something inside me snapped.

"I'm almost fifty fucking years old. I was married to the love of my life. We had our entire future ahead of us. Do you think I want to be chasing down shitty sales, from people who aren't interested in talking to me, like some greenie who just graduated from State? If I were a more insightful man, I'd say I've been sabotaging the entire thing because I don't fucking want to be here."

I didn't mean to say any of that, but *fuck* it felt good to put words to it. It also hurt like hell.

"Then why are you here?" Gage asked.

God damn him. "Because I don't give up. I'm not Tony. I don't throw away my future because things get hard."

"You're doing something you don't want to do, because you lost someone you love. Sounds to me exactly like giving up."

I really did hate him. "Fuck you. Fuck your perfect little grill in this perfect fucking little town and your perfect fucking childhood sweetheart. You still have the love of your life, you just have to stop being a pussy and go fucking be with her."

"And you *just* have to yank the pity dick out of your mouth, walk away from this job, and go back to being who you want to be."

I should hit him. Punch him square in his smug face.

Instead, I gripped the back of his neck and dipped my head in.

Gage pressed his hand to my chest and pushed me back. "Nope. Not nearly drunk or off-guard enough for that this time."

At least one of us was thinking straight. I picked up my bottle. "Funny you should say that, because

I'm pretty sure I'm too sober for any of this." I drank the rest of my beer and grabbed another.

Hours later—I didn't care how many—I was drunk enough to stop thinking. "This feels good." I meant to keep that to myself. Oops.

"What's that?" Gage moved his mouth like he was tasting the words.

"When my brain shuts off."

"Sounds dangerous." He was definitely slurring his words. "You know what else felt good?"

"Wuzzat?" I asked.

"That kiss at Joystick's."

I smirked. "Yeah, it really was."

Gage raised his eyebrows. "No smart quips or comebacks?"

"Not sober enough for either of those things you just said."

"You're a nice drunk. Go figure." Gage laughed.

"I'm nice in general." I frowned. "I used to be." The thoughts were coming back. Fuck, fuck, fuck. I'd rather they stay away a lot longer.

I leaned in and crushed my mouth to Gage's in a sloppy, desperate kiss.

"Are you fucking kidding me?" Evie's voice drilled into my sleep and mingled with a potent ache behind my eyes.

How much did I drink? Fuck, my head hurt. Why was I half naked and half under Gage?

And why was he staring at Evie with a dorky looking grin?

She stood at the edge of his living room, watching us with disbelief. She raked her fingers through her hair. "Is it me? Am I the problem?"

There were a lot of possible answers to her question, and I didn't think she wanted to hear any I would come up with. On the one hand, I wanted to see Gage try, for the amusement factor. But I didn't want to see them argue. I was tired of that.

"Nothing happened." I pushed him off me enough that I could set up.

"Why are you here?" Gage winced at his question. "I mean, I'm glad you're here, but we didn't have plans, did we?"

"No. But I wanted to talk some more after yesterday." Evie studied us. "Nothing happened?"

It was the next morning. Ouch.

Gage pushed away from me. "Kissing happened."

"Drunk kissing. Not his fault."

"I don't care." Evie turned away.

"You obviously care, because you're looking around the room for a weapon," I said. "Probably not to hit us with, but more because it'll make you feel better."

She scowled at me. "Get out of my head. Stay out of my head. I'm here to talk to Gage."

"I'll tell you what happened," Gage pushed to his feet, putting even more distance between us. "Sawyer has to tell you some of it. He's got a secret…"

Evie looked like she was ready to yield. She grabbed Gage's T-shirt and tossed it at him. "I'll go make coffee." She walked out of the room.

"What are you going to tell her?" I could wait, but now I was curious. It wasn't as if there was much to say beyond *we got drunk*.

Gage grabbed my pants and tossed them at me a lot harder than Evie had thrown his clothing. "The truth, and then you'll share your idea."

I wanted a reason to be smug about all of this, and I couldn't manage. I felt things for both Evie and Gage—warm fuzzy things that made my stomach flutter and left an ache in my chest—and I didn't know how to deal with those feelings. I didn't want Evie mad at me and I was starting to like Gage.

What was wrong with me?

22 /
evie

I couldn't be upset with Gage, could I? I *just kissed* Sawyer two nights ago.

But I hadn't done so after telling Gage *I like you. A lot.*

I had done so after being all wishy-washy about my own feelings for him.

Damn it all.

I headed into the kitchen, barely processing their conversation as I walked away. Seeing them together, both of them half-naked, summoned a rush of heat flamed by jealousy.

I spent most of last night with my head only half on my work, because I was focused on the conversation Gage and I had. Why hadn't he told me sooner how he felt? Would I have reacted as well if he'd said something a month ago? Two weeks ago?

The hints were there, but I convinced myself nothing else was each time I asked *are we still friends* and he said *yes*. I never asked *are we more?* The idea terrified me as much as it enticed me.

I grabbed the coffee pot and filled the reservoir, then added the filter and grounds to the coffee maker. I'd moved around in his house so much that it felt as natural as being in my own.

My big revelation last night sat at the end of a jumbled knot of thoughts. Clear, but only after I unraveled everything around it. The idea of falling for someone again, someone I had as much fun with as I did Gage, was terrifying.

And almost as frightening, but in a different way, was the knowledge that if I told Gage *yes, let's be together*, that I might miss out with Sawyer.

Which, honestly, was the most idiotic thought ever. Hadn't I learned my lesson with Don and again with Travis? Even if I convinced myself the physical relationship with Gage was nothing more, that was actually the case with Sawyer. It was *just* sex. Bold, let's-be-daring-and-dumb-because-you're-hot sex. He was still here to destroy my business.

Sawyer and Gage took a long time to join me for two men who had less than an outfit's worth of clothing to put on between them. Gage looked sheepish and Sawyer was stoic.

Sawyer took a seat at the kitchen table, acting like he belonged here as much as we did.

My feelings about that were more complicated than they should be.

Gage grabbed mugs and sugar out of the

cupboard, then moved to the fridge for milk.

I kept my distance, leaning against the counter with my arms crossed. "I'm listening." I tried to keep my voice cool, to make the words sincere. Did I succeed? Maybe not so much.

Gage looked me in the eye, then dumped milk and sugar in a mug, and added coffee on top, before handing me the entire thing with a spoon. Exactly the way I liked my coffee. Not that he ever got it wrong.

"Here's the truth," he said when I didn't take a sip. "Sawyer has an idea to help you get back on your feet. I don't know what it is because he wouldn't tell me, and since you were busy, and we weren't... we spent the night drinking and gaming instead."

Coming from anyone else, coming from Sawyer, I wouldn't buy it. From Gage, it made sense. He and I had done the same so often. But his story was missing one thing.

"Gaming and drinking and taking off your clothes," I said.

"We were *really* drunk." Sawyer finally spoke.

Gage poured himself coffee and set the pot on the table for Sawyer. "Not that drunk."

"We were." Sawyer mixed his own drink.

"Go with Sawyer's version this time." I felt tugs of both satisfaction and guilt when Gage winced.

He sank into a chair, watching me most of the time. "It was hate kissing," Gage said.

Sawyer scoffed. "You liked it just fine."

"But I still hate you."

That didn't seem to be the case. They were arguing the way I expected, but the edge was gone. I sighed, not sure what to say.

"Hear him out." Gage sipped his drink. "If he can help you, it's worth listening to, and if it's a shit idea, it's worth knowing as much so we can redouble our efforts to ignore him."

Sawyer clenched his jaw.

I sipped my coffee. Yup—it was made perfectly. "I'm listening," I repeated.

Sawyer sat up and put his mug aside. "Those parts that you machined for Kurt? I have a friend back home who owns a model store."

"Like... Victoria's Secret models?" Gage asked. "Can you buy those at a store? I suppose you'd know."

I wanted to laugh and scowl at the same time. "As in, model planes and tanks?"

"Yes, thank you," Sawyer said. "He also works with competition bot builders. He's highly involved in his local scene. They always need custom parts, and have a hard time finding places to get them made. If you can produce what they need, you get their business, and they'll tell their friends."

Fuck me. That sounded like fun, like something I could do, and like something that wouldn't destroy me. Was this actually good news? "What's the catch?"

"You have to prove the parts can hold up in combat. They've had a lot of issues with that as well. Their suggestion is—my suggestion to them was—you build a bot and take it into battle."

I stared at Sawyer in disbelief. The good kind. There was no way he was laying this opportunity out for me.

"Easy peasy." Gage scoffed.

The idea was. The execution? "Not so much. I've never built an actual combat robot before."

"You've designed them." Gage seemed to read the rest of my thoughts. "You've analyzed them. You've studied them for years both for fun and to learn."

"You don't have to win any contests," Sawyer said. "You just have to prove that your parts don't fail, and showing an understanding of the sport will help, too. He's not asking you to do this for free—he will provide a stipend for the parts and time."

No. Really. Did I only dream of getting out of bed this morning? Was I still asleep? Did I start with a nightmare that became an intense fantasy? Would this conversation slide to both of them getting naked and ravaging me again? "That's it? That's the only catch."

"One more thing."

There it was. I should've expected that from Sawyer. "Of course there is. Do you want a blow job? Anal?"

He shrugged. "Almost always, especially if

you're offering. But in this case, for this, no. I want you to let Kurt help when possible."

"Why?" Gage studied him suspiciously.

"I like the kid. He wants to learn, he loves the robots, and this is a good way to expose him to both."

Damn it. Next thing I knew, Sawyer was going to be rescuing puppies and donating his car to charity.

I had so much to worry about with my store—the probable thief, the pending foreclosure—but I had done all I could on both of those things. Taking action on this was better than sitting on my thumbs waiting until I could act on more immediate concerns. And if this was everything Sawyer was describing... "I'm in."

"*Yes.*" Gage actually fist pumped.

His enthusiasm made me feel better about the decision, like I wasn't completely dumb for considering it.

"I'm at your disposal, whatever I can do to help," Sawyer said.

Gage grinned. "Me too. Anything. Let's make this happen."

There was a weird feeling inside me. Familiar but one I hadn't dared listen to for a while. Hope? I shouldn't use up something like that on a situation like this, but I wanted it to work. I needed it to work.

Please let this work.

23 /
gage

What was going on?

And why was I looking forward to it instead of being upset about it?

Not the news about helping Evie. Anything and everything I could do there, I was in. But Sawyer being so involved?

It didn't feel right.

He went back to his hotel to clean up, do what he needed to for the day. Evie was going to leave me alone soon, so I could do the same.

Before I let her go I wanted her time, just the two of us.

We were sitting across the table from each other, sipping coffee. I couldn't be the only one who felt a tension in the air that had never lingered between us before a week or two ago. I'd like to say *before Sawyer*, but fuck him, he didn't get credit for everything.

Evie and I would get to a new normal though. We'd find that spot.

"How'd it go with the police yesterday?" I asked.

Her wry smile peeked over the top of her coffee mug. "Rohde was surprised you hadn't already hauled Terrance in on my behalf. They agreed that if I had security footage, it would build a much stronger case, so as long as I'm being safe and smart about it, they're going to give it a few days."

"I hate that."

"I'm not fond of it either, but I expected it."

I supposed that was that. Not much else I could do right now.

There was something else, though. This plan of Sawyer's was good. I hated to admit it, but it was. And I knew Evie well enough to expect that once she dove in, it was unlikely she'd surface for air unless she had to.

I had to get things done today, but before Sawyer left, he and I promised to give her all of our free time. There was one thing for her to clarify. "About dinner tonight," I said. "I want to spend the time with you no matter what, so I leave it up to you. I can either wine and dine you, or we can dive into robot building right away."

She caught her bottom lip between her teeth as she set her mug down. "I want to know where you and I go."

"Me too."

"And I'm gonna be honest, *let's build robots together*

is one of the sexiest things anyone has ever said to me."

She meant me, not Sawyer. She had to.

"I can keep falling for you as easily in one circumstance as the other," I said. "Though, I may hold off on feeding you chocolate covered strawberries until you're not elbows deep in milled aluminum."

"There were going to be strawberries?"

"There still will be." I reached across the table to grasp her fingers. "There's no time limit or restrictions on what happens between us."

A frown whispered across her face and vanished again. "What about Sawyer?"

Not a topic I wanted brought up in the middle of a conversation about Evie and me. I understood why, though. We both seemed to have a problem with kissing him. Or not nearly enough of a problem with it. "What about him?"

"Maybe..." She sighed and twisted her hand so her palm rested against mine. "Maybe whatever happens with him isn't off the table?"

That was a no good, very bad, horrible idea. So why was it tempting? "Maybe?"

"It'd be easier than getting mad at each other every time it happens."

This conversation was surreal. Yes, we had friends in long-term, happy relationships with more than one other person. The idea itself wasn't new to me. But Sawyer...

He was the enemy. He was a threat—an actual one, not just because he kept pursuing Evie. "Or we could try just not kissing Sawyer anymore."

Evie raised her eyebrows. "Could you?"

"Ouch." That was a fairer comeback than I wanted it to be. *Stop making out with Sawyer* seemed like the obvious answer, yet it continued to happen. It wasn't like either of us had that problem with anyone else. Which had me curious and jealous all at the same time. "Okay. We don't take it off the table."

I stood and tugged her to her feet, using it as a chance to pull her closer at the same time. "Go. Get started. I know you want to." I brushed my lips over hers.

She stiffened for a heartbeat, then relaxed in my arms. I liked this. Being able to reach out and touch her. Not holding back. Feeling her warm body against mine and her lips against mine, and hearing that tiny sigh-laugh she made when she was content.

"I'll see you later today." She kissed me before heading out.

The rest of my day was like normal, broken up by the bursts of excitement each time Evie texted me a new idea or image from her planning.

I put together a dinner for three of appetizers and burgers—but left the beer at Gage's Grub—and headed to Evie's house late that afternoon. Today's plan was to talk about what needed to happen— most of the mechanical talk was gibberish to me, but if she told me to weld pieces together, I could do that. And apparently Sawyer was skilled with remote control hookup.

Sawyer's car was parked in front of Evie's house, with her truck not far away in the driveway. Seeing his work-in-progress *baby* next to hers was a clear visual of why they clicked so well.

I let myself in, and found them in the kitchen, a series of large sketches laid out on the table between them. It was an updated version of the bot in the sketch I gave her for her birthday.

Evie looked up when I walked into the room. "Hey, handsome." Her already soft smile grew. She gestured at the plans. "This is what I sent you pics of. Catching Sawyer up."

So he didn't get the same messages I did. Was I smug about that? Only completely and entirely.

We spent the next few hours talking through a series of details and a schedule. Evie needed to turn this around quickly for the client's timeline—to show she was capable of meeting a deadline—and for her own reasons. The faster the extra money started flowing in, the better for her.

The conversation came easily, with minimal jabs from either Sawyer or me. It was weird, but nice, but also disconcerting to just *talk*. I'd say it was like yesterday, but there was no competition today.

For both of us to go so long without insulting each other's manhood was new.

It was almost ten when we started wrapping up, and we had a solid roadmap for moving forward.

"Inquiring minds want to know." Evie glanced at Sawyer between collecting and neatly folding plans. "Where—why—did you learn to line dance?"

Sawyer huffed a laugh. "I assume the same place as most people—a local bar. I did it for a man."

"So you got the Scorpions tattoo for a woman and—"

"You what?" Evie talked over me.

Sawyer pulled up his sleeve to expose the image, faded with time. "Yes. To catch the attention of a girl who liked the band."

Evie quirked her mouth in a half smile. Was she amused or impressed? "You know you can have those covered up," she said.

"I prefer not to forget my mistakes." Sawyer covered the band logo again.

And how's that working out for you? I swallowed the snide retort. I wasn't in the mood to push his buttons. What was wrong with me? "Who was the guy? The one you learned to line dance for?"

"Tony."

I heard that name yesterday, when he was talking about his husband.

"*Oh.*" Evie's soft exclamation made me think she knew who that was too.

Sawyer shrugged. "It's okay. Some of the memories suck, and some of them are really good."

"I'm glad; they should be," Evie said.

"What I want to know, since we're sharing"—Sawyer's tone shifted toward neutral in a blink—"is how Gage has lived here all his life and *doesn't* know how. Isn't line dancing part of the adulthood ceremony in a town like this?"

"Yeah, but I failed that part." I adopted a twangy drawl. "I disgraced my entire family. My mother-sister and father-uncle disowned me, and now I'll never marry my sister-cousin."

The smirk Sawyer wore as he leaned closer was telling. "Does she realize—your sister-cousin—that she wasn't in the running anyway?" He asked in a stage whisper as he jerked his head in Evie's direction.

She gave a light laugh. "You ever live in a town that doesn't have a bar?"

"There are dry counties in Georgia." Sawyer straightened in his seat.

Evie pushed away from the table, and tucked her carefully folded robot plans inside a binder that sat on the center kitchen island. "We didn't have a bar here until a year or so ago."

"You still don't have one." Sawyer's retort was uncharacteristically light. "Joystick's is *not* a bar."

We'd take what we could. "That's as close as it gets here."

Sawyer looked amused. Like he was genuinely having fun. "Backwater town with no booze? Kind of surprised you two aren't way more boring."

"There's booze, there just wasn't a bar. There's a liquor store at the end of the street," I said.

"It's *old*," Evie added. "It's been here longer than there have been laws that said that all liquor stores have to be state owned, so its license was grandfathered in."

Sawyer leaned back and crossed his arms, brows raised. "Does it do any business?"

He had no idea. Haddarville was half openly *sinners*, and the other half was the pearl-clutching alternative. At least in public. I chuckled. "They've been doing home delivery longer than it's been a thing."

"Every time I think I have this place figured out..." Sawyer clucked. "Do you want to learn, Gage?"

"How to drink? Got that down." I had a feeling that wasn't what he meant, but this was far more fun than tossing cruel barbs at each other.

"Smart ass." He didn't look bothered. "I meant how to line dance."

I most certainly did not. Not from Sawyer or anyone.

Did I? "We're working."

"*I* was working. The two of you were keeping me company." Evie grabbed my hand and yanked me to my feet. "We're done for the night."

Sawyer stood as well. "Yes or no?"

I worked my jaw, not able to push out either answer.

"Hey, Xerxes—play *Boot Scootin' Boogie*," Evie called to her home smart system.

This was ludicrous. There was no way. "There's not enough room in here."

Evie jerked her head toward the living room. "There is in there. Especially for just the two of you."

"Is that a *no*?" Sawyer asked.

If I turned him down, I suspected we'd be done for the night. "No."

He raised his brows.

Fuck it. "Yes. I'd like to learn. Help me Obi Sawyer Kenobi, you're my only hope."

Evie laughed.

"God, you two are such nerds." Sawyer's retort overlapped the music.

Evie planted a hand on both of our backs and pushed us into the other room. "It takes one to know one." She was having fun too—I saw it on her face and heard it in her voice.

It really seemed like I should be jealous. Then again, she wasn't the one about to dance with the sexy man who had tossed our lives into disarray.

The song must be halfway over by now. Should've waited to start it. Still, having the beat helped when Sawyer guided me into the middle of the living room. We pushed a coffee table aside, and took our spot, him next to me.

He gave me a few basic instructions, and asked Xerxes to restart the song.

I didn't do any better than any other time I'd tried this.

Sawyer's growl said he wasn't impressed. Good for him.

He restarted the song again, but told it to pause, and moved to stand behind me. "I told you I don't give up." His voice was as much threat as determination.

The way he pressed into my back, his chest hard against my body, and his hands on my hips, was anything but threatening. It was impossible to ignore the heat that zinged through me at the full-body contact.

Evie's eyes grew wide, but she didn't look upset.

The song started again, and this time Sawyer made sure I followed every step the way he did, moving with me through each kick and slide, and every single beat.

The longer we danced, the more I hated this song. But it was easy to ignore the reaction as the heat built between Sawyer and me. His erection pressed into me, and his fingers dug deeper into my hips each time we moved.

Should I feel guilty for enjoying this? For being so turned on?

The way Evie watched us, captivated and bottom lip caught between her teeth, I didn't think so.

Sawyer's breath was warm on my neck. The occasional grunt was temptation. The sway of his body in time with mine. What would it feel like to have his mouth around my cock? To have his dick buried deep inside me?

I was rock hard. When he left tonight, Evie and I were going to—

The song ended, and this time he didn't restart it.

"You nailed it." Evie clapped, a pleased smile on her face.

I mentally cleared my throat, but the tempting thoughts of Sawyer didn't fade. I summoned a great deal more willpower than I expected, and pulled away from him. "I guess that's that."

"Don't stop on my account." Evie still watched us closely.

Sawyer moved into view. "There's nothing more to it. Your man's a pro now." His voice was thicker than usual. Deeper.

She scoffed. "*Nothing more to it?* You were both half naked this morning, because of *just* kissing, and you nearly lit my living room rug on fire with line dancing that was far hotter than should be legal. There's nothing more to it?"

There was so much more to how intensely I wanted Sawyer at this moment.

His derisive laugh didn't match his expression or the mood in the room. "Do you think we're a pair of insatiable beasts who are going to strip down and fuck in the middle of the living room because we shared a dance lesson?"

Evie twisted her face into an adorable *thinking about it* position. "Let's just say I was hoping."

Fuck this. I fisted Sawyer's shirt in both hands, and crushed my mouth to his.

Sawyer kissed me back with a ferocity that stole my breath. This was always a different experience. A hard, demanding power struggle. The burn of scruff from Sawyer's chin against mine, and his soft grunts that rumbled through me while his skilled fingers roamed over me.

I dragged my palms up his chest. This wasn't a fight. Not like the previous times I'd kissed him. This was an unmet need. I wanted to feel every inch of his muscle under my fingertips, and explore this new body until I'd memorized all of it.

My path reversed, and I moved down again, toward his waist, under his shirt. When my touch met his bare skin, he let out a quiet growl, and the kisses intensified.

He was giving as good as he got. Touching me everywhere. I could focus on that sensation, but I was as interested in exploring as I was in how he reciprocated.

I shoved his shirt up and stripped it off, then dragged a thumb over one of his nipples. The sharp gasp that earned me warranted more. I dipped my head to lick his skin. To taste that hint of salt.

In some ways, this was the same as it had been any other time the making out had gotten intense enough to lead to more, with any other person.

There was still kissing and groping and roaming hands and bare skin. What differences there were, were stark.

The push and pull. The demand from Sawyer—from a man used to being yielded to.

I could do this, the kissing and exploring, all night.

Especially with Evie's tiny sighs as accompanying music. Her being here and enjoying this made the entire experience that much better. I didn't need to put on a show, but I was liking it.

I was so hard it hurt. I felt Sawyer's solid body and heat through my jeans, and my cock begged for release.

He yanked my shirt off, putting us chest to chest, and that cranked the experience up several more notches. He scraped his teeth over my shoulder, and moved to suck my neck, while he dug his fingers into my arms.

And then he was using his full body to guide us both, the way he did when we were dancing, but with less rhythm and more desperation.

The couch stopped me, colliding with the back of my legs, and he trailed his fingers along my waistband. Undid the button on my jeans. Sent my anticipation soaring and made my dick jerk in response and my pulse hammer in my ears.

He dragged down my zipper, and I dropped my hands to do the same for him.

Sawyer pushed me away. "Enjoy the moment.

Your first blowjob from another man." His voice had dropped an octave, and held a commanding undercurrent that was working on me. "Lose yourself in it."

The best response I could come up with was to grunt with need when he freed me. His rough, calloused grip zinged through me like a jolt of lightning. He let my pants slip past my ass, barely held up at thigh level, and he nudged me.

I stumbled into a controlled fall, and my bare butt landed on the cushions.

The sound Evie made was somewhere between a squeal and an *eep*, from her spot next to me.

Sawyer knelt between my legs and squeezed my shaft, making my body roar for more. His movements weren't sweet and demure. There was no hesitation on his part. From the start, he stroked, and gripped hard enough to grab my attention and hold it.

He dragged his tongue over the head of my cock, licking away a glistening drop of precum, and a long, low groan tore from my throat. And when he took me in his mouth, my mind was gone. Lost in this new experience.

With each brush of Sawyer's five-o-clock shadow against my inner thighs, a shudder of pleasure spilled through me. He knew when to lick and suck, when to squeeze harder and stroke faster.

Fucking hell, every second of this was incredible.

Sawyer met my swelling need pace for pace, and I jerked against his touch. I dug my fingers into the cushions, needing something to grab onto. The only things that mattered were Sawyer's touch, and the delicious sounds Evie made as she watched us.

Need swelled inside me. Surging forward. Pushing me closer and closer to orgasm. "I'm gonna fucking come." I was pretty sure the grunted out words were mine.

Sawyer's chuckle teased over my skin. "That's the point." He stroked faster. Squeezed harder. Dropped a hand to my balls to tease the tightening skin.

I came hard, emptying myself into his mouth. Nothing mattered except how good this felt. I was still wrapped in bliss when he stood and moved to kiss Evie.

Her shirt was shoved up, held in place under her arms, and her bra was askew before he reached her.

She'd been watching us. Touching herself.

And now she was kissing Sawyer with unbridled hunger, tasting me on his lips. Licking his chin.

I was spent, but watching them like this was almost enough to make me hard again.

24 /
sawyer

There had been an intensity with Evie from Day One. The kind of pull I didn't try hard to ignore. It had been there with Gage, too, but with him it was easier to block out. Mostly because I had Evie to focus on.

Now, his taste was on my lips, mingling with her touch. Her kiss.

And I needed more of all of it.

The way she returned my kisses with ferocity, her licks and bites along my chin, it was all so good.

She was already half undressed from watching us, and I wanted to take her in here, but I needed more room to maneuver. "Bedroom," I grunted.

There was only agreement as the three of us moved in a tangle of limbs and kisses toward the bedroom, like an insatiable lust beast.

Stripping Evie down a piece of clothing at a time… Making her giggle… Making her sigh and squirm... Nudging her onto her own bed and kneeling between her legs, all while Gage watched, should be the ultimate *I win* kind of power move.

Instead, I felt closer to both of them than I had anyone since--

I didn't like the way my walls were coming down, but I *really* fucking liked being with them. The sex was fun, and so was the not-sex. There was no universe where I could come between them, not that I wanted to. Kissing up Evie's stomach to the harmony of her groans with Gage's, was incredible.

Could I give up my heart again?

Nope. That was my dick talking. Babbling whatever it would take to get me to slide inside her again.

But maybe Gage was right—maybe I didn't need to pursue buying Evie's store. Maybe it wouldn't be a big deal if I walked away.

Walk away. The words were repulsive.

What else was I going to do? Fucking stay in Haddarville and have a happily ever after with Evie and Gage? *Grow the fuck up*. That wasn't something people did.

"Hey." Evie rested a palm on my cheek and forced my gaze to hers. "Are you bored?" Amusement danced in her eyes.

"Never with you two." I nipped at her lip, earning me a light laugh.

I moved my body down hers enough to gently press my shoulder into her bare stomach, and lift her now-naked body enough to toss her onto the bed.

Her squeal was intoxicating.

Gage's eye roll wasn't convincing, given he still wore a contented, relaxed grin. "Now who's a caveman?"

"You weren't complaining five minutes ago," I countered.

"Not complaining now. Simply making an observation," Gage said playfully as he knelt next to Evie.

She pushed up on her elbows to press her lips to his, and kiss him with the heat of the brightest star.

I couldn't get out of my jeans fast enough, and my rock-hard cock protested the rough jarring motions. Not that it would be complaining for long. I grabbed a condom from my back pocket before tossing the rest of my clothes aside.

Evie snatched the protection away from me before I realized she'd broken away from Gage. When I knelt on the bed to grab it back, she held it above her head. I assumed out of reach, but it wasn't really, given my arms were longer than hers.

Still, who was I to pass up the chance to lean in and distract her with a kiss. The play was fun. So was watching Gage pull her face from mine again, to brush his mouth over hers.

Whatever the two of them radiated on a regular basis has wrapped itself around me today, and I was happy to be snared.

Admittedly, I'd be happier once my rock-hard cock was buried inside Evie. I reached for the condom, and she fell away from me before I could snatch it back. She tore the package open as she landed on her back, and raised one leg to plant her foot against my chest, holding me at bay.

Now I had a gorgeous view of her calf, leading to her thigh, and showing off her gorgeous, glistening pussy, which I swore called my name.

She nudged me upright and sat. *Fuck* the way she moved was an art form. The muscle, her core, the entire dance of it all. She held my gaze, and without looking, loosely gripped my shaft to roll on the condom.

The shiver of desire that slid over me was impossible to ignore. I needed her laying down, now. I caught her off-guard and knocked her back, then wedged a knee between her legs before she could react.

"Gage is right, you're pushy." She was still laughing.

And she was stunning like this. Then again, I always liked watching her.

I rested my hands on either side of her head, and dipped my mouth near her ear. "I dream nightly about how good it feels to be buried inside you. Now that I have a chance? Of course I'm pushy."

"Dreaming about me?" Her breath caught.

"Since I met you." I shouldn't admit that, but I couldn't help it.

I moved the rest of me between Evie's legs, and nudged her opening with the head of my cock, while Gage reclined next to her. He kissed along her neck and down to her breasts.

The way she pushed into his touch, thrust her against me as well, and I slipped inside her with a long, slow plunge that drew a matching groan from me.

While Gage sucked on her nipples, he also slipped a hand between her legs to finger her clit.

I didn't know which was better—the look of unfiltered pleasure that painted her face, or the way she twitched around me each time he touched her.

I gripped the back of her thighs and pinned her legs to her chest, to slam into her hard and fast. I barely had enough restraint to keep from coming, while I watched her fall into Gage's touch and mine.

Keeping her twisted like a pretzel, I leaned in again, to murmur, "I want to see you come. I need to see how good you look when you get off."

Evie's response was a strained grunt and the flutter of her eyelids.

Gage slipped over her skin at a faster pace, and I matched my rhythm to the way she worked her hips with mine.

Her breathing grew more shallow. Stuttered. The clenching around my cock became more insistent, and she let out a long, loud scream when she came. Milking me. Teasing me. Yanking my shaft as her orgasm slipped then surged again.

My own climax sped in, and I couldn't hold it back. I dug my fingers into Evie's thighs as my balls emptied.

This was so much more than sex. The release was incredible, of course, but the ping in my chest was potent too.

As we collapsed and lay next to each other, catching our breath while the intensity faded to a faint glow, my mind was free to start up again. All my thoughts roared back in an avalanche. In Evie's house, in Evie's bed, with her and Gage, was the last place I should sleep tonight.

Naked in the middle of town would be smarter.

Evie curled into me without disturbing Gage, who was pressed into her back. "I promise not to tell if you stay," she said softly.

Damn it.

"Unless you have work to do in the middle of the night," Gage added.

Double damn it. I wasn't going anywhere. I couldn't make myself even if I had to.

The next morning was simple. No drama. No sarcasm or snipping or expectation. Just casual conversation, plans for later, and then I left.

I went back to my motel, showered, and told my

half-hard cock to stand down when last night rushed into my head without my permission.

I worked, though the enthusiasm wasn't there. It felt more like I was tying up loose threads than pushing forward with any of these clients. In the early afternoon, I was thinking about calling it a day when Hudson called. A few seconds after my cell started ringing, my room phone did as well.

That was probably Elaina. Hudson could wait. I picked up the room phone. "Hello."

"Hey." Elaina's smile was clear in her voice. "We got a package for you. Kind of big."

Perfect timing, and even better distraction. "I'll be right there." The delivery was from Hudson. I'd asked him to send me one of Tony's RC tanks. An ache bloomed in my heart at the thought, but it didn't linger as long as I expected. It hurt, but it was more of a ghost of pain.

Elaina had the box sitting out of the way near the front desk. "What is it?" she asked when I walked in. "Am I allowed to know?"

"Not only are you allowed to know, you get to decide what happens to it next." I grabbed the box and moved it to a more open part of the space. Not that there was a lot of room in here, but there was a reasonable sized lounge area with a few padded chairs and a coffee table, in an adjoining space.

She followed. "Why me?"

I grabbed my pocketknife and sliced through the tape. The crumpled paper came out first, exposing a bubble-wrapped series of pieces. I extracted what looked like the turret first, and then the remote control, and sliced both out of their protective casing.

Elaina gasped. "You didn't... I can't. Thank you, but no."

"At least let me explain."

"I can't have people buying him things." Elaina's voice went soft.

I should've warned her first. "I didn't buy this. I've had it for years. It was"—*exhale*—"my husband's. Now that he's passed on"—this wasn't easy to say, but it wasn't as difficult as I expected—"this sits in storage and collects dust. I'm not going to do anything with it, and if someone can get some use out of it, I don't know anyone who will appreciate it more than Kurt."

"He's ten. He's going to wreck it."

"I don't even know the number of times Tony has crashed this, or the others." The memories nudged the edges of the box I kept them in. "It's the cost of working with RC."

"I know." She gave a wry smile. "You've seen the plane Kurt takes wherever he's allowed." She dragged in a shaky breath that I felt in my soul.

She was thinking of her husband. I had no doubt. "How long has it been since you lost him?" I asked.

"A little over a year ago, and for the most part

the wounds are scars. Tender, but not raw. The pain still surges sometimes, you know?"

"I do." I knew exactly what she meant. "I lost my husband about the same time. Maybe two years ago." As if I didn't know the exact time and date. There was a mental wince every time I said the words, but the feeling was more like what she just described.

"I'm sorry," Elaina said.

Me too. "Anyway, if you're not comfortable with him having it, I won't be offended."

"He's going to love it. I don't know how to thank you or repay you."

Knowing that someone would give it a new life was all I wanted.

The conversation lulled, and awkwardness settled in. This was my cue to go. See what Hudson wanted. Do anything else.

"You and Evie." Elaina said before I could.

Uh-oh. "What about her?"

"I can see her normal graveyard spot from the front desk. We kind of keep an eye on each other, so I know when she shows up there. Who she leaves with…"

As in me, the other night. "Okay?" I could guess any number of things she was getting at, but it would be easier if Elaina just said it.

She twisted a small piece of bubble wrap, making a series of tiny pops. "It's not of my business—"

Right. Everything here is everyone's business.

"But Gage isn't going to take it well if he finds out the two of you are... hooking up," Elaina said. "Do with that information what you will."

Been there, done that. And now I was thinking about last night again. How good it was. How incredible everything with the three of us when I stopped pushing back. "He knows."

"Ah." Elaina ducked her head.

And now random bits of all my past overlapped. Memories of Tony swirling around those of my time here. With Evie. With Sawyer. All the things that had happened in such a short amount of time, in this town I shouldn't even be in.

"How did you lose him?" Elaina asked, and I knew we'd moved on from Gage and Evie and back to Tony. "I know we're not supposed to bring it up, but..."

But she understood better than most how it felt.

"Cancer. Fast. Invasive." That still hurt to say. So much. Like a knife to the heart.

"So you got to say *goodbye*."

More memories. More muddled thoughts. "I did. You?"

"He was Army. Bomb disposal. One of his attempts went bad. I never..." She dragged in another shaky breath. "Before it happened, when he shipped out, I told him like always that I'd see him when he came home, and he never did." A whimper slipped from her throat. "Sorry. I never talk about this. No one here gets it."

Some of them probably did, and even more would be willing to listen, but I knew what she meant. "Me neither."

"He hated goodbyes," Elaina said. "They were too final. He'd always say *I'll see you later.*"

We were here now. Knee-deep in the past, and I didn't see either of us leaving before we were done with whatever we each needed to face. "Before Tony passed, he made me promise…" I shouldn't be talking about this. I didn't want to dive into it.

"Promise what?"

"To keep living. To not stop because he was gone." The conversation with Gage twisted with Tony's words. Gage's taunting from when we were drunk. *You're doing something you hate…* "Tony made me promise that if I found someone new, that I'd love them." Saying it out loud, reliving it in this way, was an unpleasant combination of ripping off a bandage and putting a cold compress on a fresh sunburn.

Elaina choked on her laugh. "We didn't quite have that. Every time he deployed, I had to promise to wait for him and only him. I always told him I would, and I always did."

Which meant she was still waiting.

"But you both thought he was coming home." I was talking to myself as much as her. "I knew Tony wasn't. I might as well have promised him I'd wait anyway, the way I live."

"But you don't have to."

"Neither do you," I said.

She gave a quick shake of her head. "Maybe."

"*Mom.*" Kurt pushed into the lobby and his call filled the room.

Like flipping a switch, Elaina replaced grief with a smile. Any hint of tears or the past was gone. "Hey, kiddo, how was school?"

I recognized the mask, because I'd done it so many times, but not nearly for as good a reason.

"School was good. What's that?" Kurt focused on the box.

"Mr. Rawlings can tell you better. I need to take a call."

Kurt turned to me. "What's that?"

Elaina stood, and on her way up whispered, "Thank you." She walked out of the room.

I explained the tank to Kurt, minus the trauma, and he wanted to pull the entire thing out and reassemble it now. While he and I were doing that, Elaina returned, eyes a little red and make-up reapplied.

While she went back to work, I spent the next couple of hours showing Kurt the ins and outs of the tank. He pouted when it was time for me to go to Evie's, but Elaina made him let me leave.

I got back to my room, melancholy sinking into

my veins and carrying a heavy dose of introspection. So many thoughts glommed to each other.

I had a message from Hudson that just said, *"call me as soon as you can."*

That was both vague and melodramatic for him. Perfect distraction.

I dialed Hudson's number. "What's up?" I asked when he picked up.

He let out a noisy sigh, as if there hadn't been enough of those today. "I've been digging into Dad's financials behind the scenes. His holdings. All sorts of interesting things."

"And?" The tone shift from earlier was jarring, and I was grateful for the excuse to turn off my emotions.

"He owns more than he's told us, and he's got his fingers in more than that."

"Like what?"

"Like sitting on the board of directors for a lender that does high-risk loans." He gave me the bank's name.

The institution that had a lien on Evie's store.

"That property you're there to buy?" Hudson's question confirmed my dread.

Concern twisted inside me. "What about it?"

"It doesn't matter what steps the owner takes. Not now. It doesn't matter if you get them to agree to sell. The foreclosure paperwork is in progress, and will be done by the end of the month. Once the bank owns that property, they can sell it to whomever they want."

Fuck. The information flipped a switch in my head, and doubt scattered. I wasn't going to let that happen. No one—not me or anyone else—was taking Evie's store away from her. I didn't care what I had to do.

25 /
evie

The last few days with Gage had been incredible.

Sawyer, too.

Both thoughts were strange, for different reasons. I'd never thought Gage and I would be this kind of together. And Sawyer... letting my defenses down seemed stupid, but the longer I talked to him, the more time I spent with him, the further I saw past the mask he wore.

Gage and I were spending every night together, and it sucked to send Sawyer home when we were done working. The bot was coming together, and making my deadline would be tight, but with their help, I was on target.

Without their help I didn't know if I'd make it, and without Sawyer I wouldn't have the chance anyway. We were taking today—Sunday—off for the livestream with Adam and Maddox, and while I was super grateful for this chance, I also regretted the building hours lost.

I was at my hardware store now, making sure I took care of any morning tasks, and getting my back room ready for filming. There was space for several people when there needed to be. Normally the pair recorded at Onyx's, but this should be a better backdrop since I was the cause.

I hated that phrasing. I was out of options, though. This stream would be the modern-day version of a telethon. I'd spend most of the day on air with Adam and Maddox, and our friends would drift in and out, and we'd do it all for donations.

Before then, I was reviewing my security footage from the last week, especially on the new cameras around those times when Terrance had been here.

I'd already discovered two instances of him walking out with equipment, including a high end, portable air compressor, and one of my more expensive jigsaws. He'd stuff them in large bins to get them outside without anyone batting an eye.

Currently, I was reviewing footage and store records of him using store credit he shouldn't have to purchase a gas generator.

Was he using all of these? Selling them? Returning them other places?

It didn't matter. He was going down for it. The betrayal at seeing him so blatantly steal from me sank deep. I forwarded my notes and the videos to the sheriff.

"You all right?" Gage's question startled me.

I didn't hear him come in, which meant I needed to climb out of my own head and face the rest of the day. "I just sent the police proof that Terrance is ripping me off."

"Good." Gage landed the word with a firm finality. "I hope that fucker never steps foot in here again."

His certainty was grounding.

"How did it take me so long to realize what he was up to?" I was asking myself as much as Gage, and the question felt like one I'd had too many times in my life.

He pulled me to my feet and wrapped his arms around me. "Don't blame yourself for not seeing deception around every corner. Never." He kissed me softly on the forehead, the nose, and finally the lips.

Then again, I hadn't seen how good things were with Gage, either. I was missing things all over the place, but I was grateful I had this one now. It felt so good, so natural, to slide into his arms like this.

I *did* hear my shop's back door opening this time, and wasn't surprised when a few seconds later, Aubrey called out, "*Hello.*"

"Back room," I shouted in response.

Aubrey and Alys found us. I didn't realize I was holding Gage's hand until both women glanced down, and Alys raised her brows while Aubry smirked.

"We—"

"It's about time." Aubrey cut me off.

I rolled my eyes, but I was grinning, and Gage tugged me closer, to wrap an arm around my waist.

"The party's here." Maddox joined us, and so did Adam and Onyx, all three of them carrying camera and audio equipment.

Now I was in my element. I directed and helped them set up. With all of us working, we were doing a sound and video test in under half an hour, and ready to go live.

The livestream started, and Maddox and Adam did their standard intro, before introducing me.

"For those of you who missed the gazillion explanations before today," Adam said, "We're helping Evie save her hardware store. Which she's going to tell us about."

I'd sort of prepared for this. Run half a dozen different introductions through my head over and over. And now that the mic and camera were on, they all evaporated in a poof of nothingness.

Words. I needed words.

Adam nudged me with his foot, and across from us Gage gave me a thumb's up.

I was a big girl. I could talk about my own business. "The store has been in my family for generations. We were one of the first general stores in the state, and back then we provided tools for farmers and miners. Work boots. Denims. Today we're still offering what people need. One of those icons of small-town America that reminds us we're people, not just part of a corporate grind. It's also my livelihood, and I love this place. I don't want to lose it." A small lump formed in my throat.

Maddox glanced at me. "And to make sure she pulls through okay, I'm matching every single dollar pledged. No ceiling."

"Whoa." What? I wasn't concerned about whether or not Maddox could afford it—his family founded the town, and his mother had left him a sizable trust fund that he never touched. And that wasn't considering how popular this show was.

And maybe we'd only raise ten dollars over the next twelve hours, but *no ceiling* was dangerous. "You can't."

"I just did." Maddox grinned. "Too late to take it back now."

I wanted to argue. Pride said to tell him *no*. But *pride* was part of the reason I let this go for so long. An internal battle started over whether or not to let Maddox do this, and he and Adam moved on before I could voice any concerns.

Relief trickled into my thoughts on top of it all. Maybe this would be okay. Maybe my store would be okay.

Maddox and Adam were two minds who could create a single stream of consciousness when left to their own devices, and over the next few hours they did exactly that, focusing on elements of my store that I never considered interesting before today.

Seeing my world through their eyes was a unique experience.

They talked about the robots I made, too. They didn't have the details of my agreement with Sawyer, but they knew in general about my tinkering. They could see I was working on a new combat robot.

A few hours into the stream, Sawyer snuck in, but he hung back from everyone else. Still, having him here made me smile.

We talked about gaming. I answered silly personal and trivia questions as rewards for certain pledge goals. When things started to lull, Adam or Maddox would toss out a flash goal, and someone would do something silly or dumb or fun when we met it, like karaoke performances—chat's choice.

When Adam walked away for a break, Gage pulled him aside, but I was talking to Maddox about who would win in a cartoon robot death match between Optimus Prime and Leader One.

"They wouldn't fight each other." My reply was a stalling tactic. Was I more flustered that I'd never thought about it before or that Maddox had?

Maddox leaned in on the table, closer to the camera. "But what if they did. What if... the Zentradi leader tricked them into thinking each was the other's enemy?"

"Wait. There are Zentradi now?" What were the rules of this game? "In that case, Leader One wins because he can be fueled by protoculture."

Maddox's eyes grew wide. "How do you know that?"

Seriously? I made it up like the rest of this. "How do you not?"

"I think Evie wins." Adam was back, and Gage was with him, standing behind me. "I also think it's time for another stretch goal." Adam gestured. "This is Gage, Evie's boyfriend."

It was the first time hearing anyone phrase it that way, and while the words startled me, they were also true. I liked the sound of it.

The way Sawyer twisted his mouth was impossible to miss, but maybe that was because I was staring at him.

"If we meet the next pledge goal on the screen, in the next hour," Adam kept talking, oblivious to where my mind was going, "Gage is going to shave his head."

"What?" I spun in my seat to face Gage. "You can't."

He leaned in to kiss me on the top of the head. "I can. I am."

"But..." I tangled my fingers in his locks, holding him in the crouched over position. "Then I can't do this anymore." I pulled lightly.

He grinned. "It'll grow back." He kissed me hard, stealing my breath to a chorus of *oohs* and *ahhs* and whistles.

We met our next goal with plenty of time to spare. I was sad to see Gage's hair go, but I couldn't believe people were donating this much money. To help me. People I'd never met flooded the chat with words of support and encouragement.

Adam let me take the clippers to Gage's head, and shearing off that first strip made me cringe. But when he was done, when Gage's hair lay on the ground around him, he actually still looked sexy. I couldn't help but run my hand over the short, dark fuzz.

The way he shuddered was delicious.

"What do you think?" Gage asked.

"I like it."

"Maybe I should keep it this way?"

I scrunched up my nose. "I don't like it *that* much. But lucky for you, it should grow back before it gets cold here."

Gage pulled me into his lap. "You'll keep me warm."

"Hey. *Hey.* Keep it PG," Maddox teased.

When I climbed from Gage's lap and pulled him to his feet, I couldn't help but notice Sawyer was gone.

Not that I expected him to stick around all day, especially since he was avoiding everyone. The timing of his disappearance didn't escape me though.

Friends and colleagues from around town continued to drop in, to say *hi*, bring us treats, and—at my insistence—do some self-promo.

We were well into mid-afternoon when the

owner of Granny's Yarn joined us. She only had one grandchild, but we all called her *Granny* because she'd looked after most of us in one way or another all our lives.

She was here to do a tarot reading for me, and then for the first ten people after that who donated ten dollars or more. She had me shuffle the cards three times, cut the deck, and draw a single card off the top of the stack.

I handed her the Seven of Cups. "What's in store for my future?"

A mischievous smile tugged up her mouth. "You've been daydreaming about what comes next. About what you want, and your perfect world," she said. "But you're uncertain of what will really happen. You want to make the right choice, and you want all the pieces and all the knowledge to do so."

Damn. *Way to call me out, cards.* I kept my mouth shut.

"You need to realize that sometimes instinct can guide us better than any logic, and the future is only limited by what we can dream," Granny said.

Adam whistled. "Deep."

I was stunned silent and pondering the words as she read for the people who had just donated. Was that about Sawyer? The store? Gage?

Or was it just the whimsy of chance?

When Granny was done, we moved on to the next challenge, and the next. By the time we hit the twelve-hour mark on the livestream, we were the kind of tired that was the same as being drunk. Adam and Maddox signed off, and the room erupted in a huge cheer when they told us how much we'd raised.

It was more than enough for me to keep my store. I could pay what I owed, I could get myself out of the loan that held a lien on the property, and I could breathe again.

I couldn't believe it.

We all focused on cleaning up, and Maddox pulled me aside. "Transferring these kinds of funds takes a few days, but I'll start the paperwork tomorrow morning," he said.

Tomorrow? "You just finished the livestream. You won't have the money for, what? A few weeks? We have that much time."

"*I* have the money now," Maddox said. "We're not leaving this to chance or shitty bankers who might change their mind."

"You can't." I was already asking so much of them.

He nodded. "I can. I promise I've got this covered. Besides, Alys would never forgive me if I let bad things happen to you."

I could keep arguing, but I wanted this to be all right. I needed it to work out. "Okay. Thank you."

Knox and Rohde showed up a short while later with food and beer for everyone. We ate, we drank, and we lingered in the rush of an amazing day.

Rhode told me they had Terrance in custody.

That was fast, and I was grateful.

When yawns became contagious, we all decided it was time to break it up and head home.

Things were going to be all right. I hadn't felt this kind of relief in months. Longer.

When it was only Gage and me left, he pulled me into him, and rested his chin on my head. "You've been wearing a goofy grin most of the night," he said. "What's up?"

"Nothing." As in, there was nothing outstanding. Nothing to worry about.

Maybe things were going to be all right.

26 /
sawyer

I had fun watching Evie and her friends do their livestream. The energy in the room was tangible.

I didn't think for a moment that I was part of it.

As I stood in front of Evie's Monday morning, my mind kept going back to the same thing it had since I left here yesterday.

Of course I wasn't a part of what Evie and Gage and everyone here seemed to share. But I wanted to be. What would it feel like to be one of the living again? After the conversation with Elaina, after watching everyone here... I wanted to find out.

I didn't hate this stupid town. It was growing on me.

God damn it. This felt like the point where I should be upset or annoyed or plotting something stupid. Though, considering I was waiting for Evie so early, I may still be about to do something stupid.

There was no way I didn't look suspicious, waiting outside her store for half an hour. Gage's SUV pulled up, and he parked as close to me as the curb would allow.

Of course he was dropping her off. And giving her the longest, sweetest-and-simultaneously hottest kiss…

The jealousy. It burned.

Evie hopped out, and Gage shouted, "Catch you later, Richie Rich. Work calls."

That was the first time I'd heard him call me that without animosity.

Gage drove away, and Evie strolled toward me wearing a broad grin.

I didn't stick around yesterday, but I did watch the rest of the livestream in my motel room. I knew she met her fundraising goal, and I had no doubt that was followed by a night of incredible sex.

Why wouldn't she look like she was on top of the world?

"Eager to get to work?" Evie asked as she unlocked the front door.

"Something like that."

She locked the door behind us when we were inside. "You could've stuck around yesterday."

I followed her through the store. Had it really only been a few weeks since we were arguing in the same aisles? Since she held me at bay with a post hole digger? "I really couldn't have."

"Okay, Mister Tall-Dark-and-Stoic." Evie sounded amused.

I stepped into her path, and she stopped abruptly, her eyes wide.

"Just listen to me for a minute." Story of my life these days—trying to get Evie to talk to me. It was almost amusing that the reasons for it were becoming varied.

She licked her lips, gaze locked on me. "I'm listening."

But what was I saying? My brain had been telling me *talk to her* since yesterday, but had yet to provide a script.

"I'm done trying to buy your store." That was a relief to say. Who knew? Like that, it wasn't only the tension that faded, but the expectation, the pressure...

Evie cocked her head to the side and studied me. "Why? Not that the stopping matters now that I have a solution, but... why?"

"It's yours. It's part of the soul of this town, and so are you." Where did that come from?

The puzzled look on Evie's face said she was wondering the same thing. "Thank you." Her voice was soft.

A noise rattled in the background. Keys. A lock. One of her employees must be here, and I should wrap this up. Instead, I searched Evie's face. I so desperately wanted to reach out and touch her. Kiss her. More.

She leaned closer, never taking her eyes off me.

How was she so irresistible?

I laced my fingers in her hair and traced my thumb along her hairline.

She sucked in a sharp breath, and flicked her tongue over her bottom lip again. I wanted to be the one doing the licking.

"Evie." Gage's call made my heart slam into my ribs, and shifted the tension in the air. "You left your — *Huh*." He rounded the corner and stopped, as he stared at us.

He looked good without the hair, but not as good as he had with it.

"Socket wrench set." Evie didn't pull away from me. "I left it in your truck."

There was a thunk as Gage put said wrenches on a nearby shelf. "Are we having this conversation now?"

"Sawyer's going to stop bugging me," Evie said.

"Not what I said." I tightened my grip on her hair, and she gasped.

Evie's smirk was the sexiest thing. "True. That's not what he said."

"Does Sawyer know how to share?" Gage was focused on Evie, but I had a feeling the question was meant for me.

"Sawyer's never been very good at that." Great, they had me referring to myself in third person. "But he might make an exception for this."

Gage's phone rang.

"Oh. My. God." Evie huffed. "Are these interruptions scripted?"

Gage looked at his phone. "It's Knox. I gotta go." He approached us and kissed Evie on the cheek I wasn't covering, then glanced at me. "I trust her." He walked away, answering his phone as he walked.

"What does that mean?" I asked when he was gone.

"It means he trusts me."

"You two drive me insane."

"And you love every minute of it."

This was too much. And not enough. And so bizarre. I nipped her bottom lip. "Not *every* minute." I bit harder, earning me another gasp. "But I do like quite a few of them." I kissed her, and she leaned into the gesture, pressing her body to mine. Digging her fingers into the back of my neck. "So what now?" I asked between kisses.

"Be more specific."

"You. Me. Gage... He doesn't have a problem with it?" I couldn't stop kissing her. Tasting her.

She dragged her nails up my back. "He and I talked."

About me? They said good things?

"We decided he and I could be together and still see where things go with you," Evie said.

"That sounds... vague." I nipped her earlobe.

She tilted her head, giving me a better angle. "Unless you have a more specific answer, vague is what we have until we figure it out."

Her body was hard and soft at the same time, and I wanted to keep holding her. "No answers. Just curiosity," I said.

"Me too. So you gonna stick around long enough to figure it out?"

"I think I might." But in the very immediate future, as in *now*, I was tempted to lift her up and see how sturdy her store shelves were. I also wanted this to be about more than sex. "Should we get to work?"

She pulled away enough to show me her pout.

Evie pouting? Fucking adorable. Not fair, but very cute.

"You're right." Her tone was light, and she stepped away enough to put some space between us. "Pin me to the wall and fuck me later."

I definitely would. And now I had a hard-on.

Meeting her deadline was important, though. She may have raised the funds to get out of immediate danger, but she needed to keep going long-term, and this would provide that for her.

We headed into her work room and got to it. For the next few hours, the conversation flowed easily. Then again, it always did when we both let our defenses down. She teased me a few times about staring at her ass instead of getting things done, and I had no reason to deny it.

She was sitting on a high stool with her back to the door, making some refinements to her blueprints, when Gage walked in. He had a drink holder with three iced coffees, but she was focused on her task and didn't look up.

He pressed into her back, and she let out a light *eep* as she straightened into him. He trailed his nose along her neck as she rested more of her weight against him. He reached around her to hand her a coffee, and kissed her on the cheek.

The exchange left me conflicted. Turned on. Jealous. In awe of how good they were together. Wanting.

I cleared my throat.

Gage straightened and looked at me. "Jealous?"

I raised my eyebrows. *Yes.*

He crossed the distance between us. "I didn't forget about you." He handed me one of the drinks.

As I reached for it, he leaned in and kissed me on the lips instead. I grunted in surprise. That felt good too. I smirked against his kiss and stole my coffee. "I see why she likes you," I said.

Gage leaned his mouth near my ear. "The big dick doesn't hurt either." His voice was a stage whisper.

"It hurts a little. That's part of why I like it." Evie sucked on her straw, a look of deceptive innocence on her face.

This was good. I could get used to it. To spending this kind of time with them.

Gage settled in and started on his checklist as well. All three of us were quiet as we focused.

Evie handed off her changes to me, so I could

work on the remote, and she shifted her attention to some financials.

For a while, the only sounds in the room were metal scraping metal, and Evie's fingers clacking on her keyboard.

I shifted my attention to testing radio connectivity between the wheels and the remote.

"You unbelievable fucking asshole." Evie's angry voice shattered my concentration.

I looked up to see her glaring at me with a venom that rivaled that first day I walked in here, and she realized who I was.

No. This was worse.

"What did I do?" I asked.

27 /
evie

Today was a good day.

That warm *everything is good* feeling lingered from yesterday, mingling with the conversation with Sawyer this morning, and culminating in an incredible afternoon with him and Gage.

Sure, we were just working, but it felt right.

Maddox sent me over a little information about the money transfers, and asked for data in return, so I moved to my laptop to grab his answers.

Before I could reply, there was another note from him.

> Maddox: Xander says it's a good thing you're getting out. This bank has a reputation.

Xander was Maddox's older brother, and the two were night and day. Xander was a partner in a tech investment firm.

I figured the bank that held my loan wasn't the best—they made shitty loans to people who couldn't get them anywhere else—but I'd been desperate at the time, and now that I was paying them back, it was done and over.

> Maddox: And Don is connected with them. He buys a lot of their foreclosures.

Don. The name made my gut curdle. The first boyfriend I had after my deployment ended. He'd been sleeping with Alys and me at the same time, without telling either of us, and had convinced us it was in our reputations' best interests to keep things quiet.

Another example of me trusting the wrong guy.

I had such bad instincts when it came to men, but a glance at Gage, assembling bot pieces, and Sawyer working on the remote control…

Wait.

Don was also a real estate developer who had been trying to buy buildings on Main Street, to tear them down and *revitalize*.

Sawyer was originally here to buy me out. He couldn't be connected…

No.

Now that the thoughts were there, about the bank, about Sawyer and Don, about deeper connections, I had to dig.

Whatever my brain was trying to tell me about

Sawyer, it wasn't true. He'd proven himself. I just needed to see proof and then I could shut up the doubt.

Proof of what? I wasn't sure.

That Sawyer was who he said and nothing more.

I should've dug into the bank when I took out my loan, but I'd chosen to stay ignorant. Now, as I searched their name for a starting point, the bad news unfolded in front of me.

So many negative reviews.

About people being foreclosed on abruptly. Forced out of their properties without the proper warning, thanks to legal loopholes. Properties sold out from under business owners before they knew it was happening.

I should've sold to the guy who tried to undercut me on price just a few weeks before they foreclosed on me.

The text from the review glared at me, and I glanced at Sawyer again.

No.

Whatever my brain was trying to tell me, I wasn't listening.

I had a new branch of the path to follow, though. Reviews talking about that buyer who showed up just a few weeks before they lost their buildings. The one person saying they discovered the buyer was associated with the bank.

And another reviewer saying the same thing.

And a third person, saying that Hudson Rawlings Sr was both an internal board member at the bank, and owned the real estate company who bought the reviewer's property right before foreclosure.

Rawlings Real Estate.

Sawyer Rawlings.

The full picture slotted together in my mind, and I couldn't deny it anymore.

Sawyer, who had lied to me the first time within moments of meeting me. Who worked for a company that had some serious conflict of interest business practices. Who was here to buy me out of a store I would've lost to foreclosure if I hadn't raised the money yesterday...

How did I not see this?

I had to fight to keep a whimper from escaping.

How did I convince myself he actually cared, after the way he walked in here?

How did I let myself fall for the wrong man? Again.

Because I was a fucking idiot.

A furious one.

"You unbelievable asshole." I focused on Sawyer.

He looked up, surprised. "What did I do?"

"What do you think you did?" Faking fucker.

He faltered, but recovered quickly. "I don't know."

But he did know. That hesitation said it all.

"Your father is Hudson Rawlings?" I asked.

"So's my brother. Family name."

Wonderful. Not. "What's the *family name* of the person who you're buying on behalf of?"

"It doesn't matter." Sawyer had recovered, and was all confidence again. "They can't, because you're in the clear."

Gage was paying full attention to the conversation, and the tension coiling through him was visible.

"Who is trying to buy my store?" I repeated.

"Some guy named Don Spader."

I had never been this furious. Not when I found out about Don and Alys. Not when I realized Travis had scammed me out of thousands.

This was a whole new level of rage. I spoke through clenched teeth. "So your father owns the real estate company you represent. He sits on the board of the bank that owns my loan—"

Sawyer went pale, as if I'd just said something he didn't expect me to know.

"And you're here to push me out of my shop, regardless of what I say. Regardless of what you've said," I finished.

"No." Sawyer shook his head. "I *was* here to make you a fair offer—"

"Stop. Fucking. Lying to me." I bit off the words. There was no way I could believe anything he said. He'd known who I was in Wendover the instant he heard my name, and I never saw for a second that he was lying to me. Not then, and apparently not now.

Since then I'd let down my defenses. I'd let him in…

"Leave. Now," Gage said to Sawyer.

"Listen to me." Sawyer didn't move. "I didn't know."

"Which part?"

I was grateful Gage was talking, because the red haze licking at my mind made thinking difficult.

Sawyer worked his jaw. "I didn't know about his connections to the bank."

There it was. My confirmation that the information was true. "Bullshit."

"I know it doesn't sound real, but I swear to you both, it's the truth."

Nope. I wasn't doing this. "You're not going to tell me any more lies. I'm so done with men fucking me and then fucking me over. I can't believe…" I swallowed hard. I wouldn't break in front of Sawyer. He didn't get to see that. "Get out." I growled the words.

Gage stepped toward Sawyer. "Go."

"Listen to me. I didn't—"

"Get. Out." I pushed more threat into my command.

"*God damn it,* Evie. Just let me explain," Sawyer shouted.

My mind was a mess of the past and present. A

jumble of every time Don told me I was being unrea-sonable. Every time Travis reminded me *we're just good friends* before taking advantage of me. Every single fucking time I believed one of them or let them belittle me into compliance because I thought they cared. "*Get out.*" My yell came out more shrilly than I expected.

Sawyer stepped toward the door. "Okay. But this isn't over."

Oh, this was *so* over.

I hated Sawyer and I hated myself more for buying into his bullshit. For the way my heart was shattering. For ever thinking that someone like that could be anyone more than who he showed me on our first meeting.

But I'd still fallen…

What was wrong with me?

28 /
gage

I wasn't there for Evie after Don or Travis, but I sure as fuck wasn't letting her deal with this alone.

I was furious on her behalf and for myself. Sawyer seemed sincere. He was good with us. The three of us had something.

And to find out we didn't?

The revelation didn't feel real.

But Sawyer didn't deny any of it. Except the bit where he was part of a deception. Then again, how could he confirm what Evie found was real if he didn't know about it?

"We need to walk away from this for the night," I told Evie.

The anger and hurt etched on her face sliced through me. "We have so much work to do. If this project is even real." Her voice went soft.

I understood the doubt. If Sawyer lied about

some things, then was this project even attached to a real offer?

Why would he make it up, though? For kicks? For the company? Money had already changed hands. He spent last week helping us with this project, and as far as I could tell, he was doing real work, not sabotage.

None of this made sense, except the part where the lies hurt, and where Evie was hurt. I hated seeing her like this. "We'll double down tomorrow. I'll make arrangements with Knox, so you can have as much of my time and help as you need. We're taking the rest of tonight off."

Evie stood. "You're telling me the truth, aren't you?" There was a vulnerability in her voice that I wasn't used to.

I could ask her what I should be telling the truth about, but it didn't matter because it was all real. "I promise. About everything. I'm here for you, and I love you and the only thing I want from you is you."

Oh. I did not mean to say that. Especially now.

"You love me?" Evie repeated.

"Most of my life."

She frowned.

"I'm not saying that to manipulate you." I couldn't tell what she was thinking. "I can't take it back, because it's true, but—"

"Neither of them ever said that. Not Travis or Don. They said a lot of other things—Sawyer said a lot of other things—but they never said... *that.*"

I tucked her hair behind her ear. "Good. Because you deserve to hear it when it's real. You deserve the world."

Evie let out a tiny exhale. "You're right. We should take the rest of the night off."

Neither of us said much as we cleaned up, and I drove us to my house. I didn't know about her, but I wasn't sure there was a reason to rehash what happened. It would come up enough over the next few days and weeks and months anyway, as we tried to make sense of it.

Because for some reason, somehow, Sawyer had already become that kind of part of our lives.

As we pulled onto my street, Evie muttered, "are you fucking kidding me?" at the same time I saw my ex-wife sitting on my front porch.

Seriously? *Now?* I parked in the driveway. "I'll see what Grace wants and she'll be gone. You can come with me or wait here, it's up to you."

"I'm coming with you." Evie hopped from the truck as she talked.

That was good for me. Grace could've called or texted or emailed. Even if this conversation needed to be in person, there had to be a reason she didn't let me know she was on her way.

What did we have to say to each other face to face anyway?

When Evie and I approached, the look Grace gave her was half disdain, half disinterest. Grace stepped past her, to try to hug me.

I stopped her, gripping her arm and keeping her at that distance. "Why are you here?"

"I just." Grace's chin quivered and she bit her bottom lip.

No. I wasn't up for this any day, but especially not now. "You what?"

Her eyes filled with tears. "I'm sorry." She sniffled and glanced at Evie before looking at me again. "Can we talk alone?"

"We cannot." I wouldn't be cruel, but I wasn't getting sucked into whatever this was.

Grace made a noise that sounded like *hmpf*. "I miss you, Gage. I never should've done what I did. Please talk to me."

I might've felt bad if she was mourning the loss of a family member. Or something actually bad happened to her. But to hear she was here to try to apologize? After all these years?

What. The. Fuck?

"We *are* talking. Is that why you're here?" I asked.

She nodded.

"And not because something happened to your housing situation in Idaho Falls?" The realization struck me."

Her expression wavered, and was back in an instant. "No."

Uh-huh. "So you need a place to stay, and you thought *Gage has been my sucker before?*"

"I still have feelings for you." Grace's chin

quiver was back. "You can't just turn those off."

Evie's arm tightened where it was pressed against mine. I'd hate to see her get in trouble for hitting Grace.

"You're right, I can't," I said. "But I can tell you I don't feel the same and ask you to leave." I was surprised at my own reaction. Sure, I'd spent the last few years dealing with what she did to me, and getting over her, but there was nothing inside except a little pity that she thought she could do this.

"Is it because of her?" Grace nodded.

I looked at Evie. "*Her?* You mean *Evie?*"

"You've always loved her more than me."

Had I?

That wasn't right.

"No, Grace. I've always loved her differently than you. And I *did* love you. Past tense. Once upon a time."

"Bullshit." Grace's pouty tears vanished. "I never would've ch—"

"Cheated?" I finished for her. "You're going to tell me your mistakes are my fault? Evie's? *That's* bullshit. You fucked another man without telling me, and now you want to pretend that wasn't all on you?"

"I want us to have another chance," Grace said. "If you and I could just go somewhere and talk."

Evie stepped in front of me, between us. "So help me, I desperately need to hit something."

"Are you going to beat me up?" Grace scoffed.

"I don't know why I ever thought I could compete with your memory. And then you were here again. Why did you come back?"

"Because she belongs here." I draped my arms over Evie's shoulders, pulled her back into me, and kissed the top of her head. "Grace isn't worth bruising your knuckles on."

Grace's face contorted into anger.

I was so done with this. "Last time. Leave. I'm not going to talk to you." I wrapped an arm around Evie's waist and pulled her into the house with me, not checking to see if Grace walked away or not.

"That was almost stone cold," Evie said when the door closed behind us.

"Maybe."

"Would you have done the same to me? Treated me like that, if things kept going with..." She swallowed hard.

With Sawyer.

"You didn't cheat on me." I hadn't drawn the parallels before. There was jealousy with Evie and Sawyer, but I never compared her to Grace. Why not? "She snuck around behind my back. After we were married. After we made promises to each other. You've always been honest with me, even before we were *together*."

"Well, yeah. It's not right otherwise." Evie shrugged.

"Exactly."

She scrubbed her face. "I can't believe he had

me—us—fooled. I really thought…"

That things with Sawyer were what they looked like. That he was a good guy under the asshole facade. That he cared. "Me too."

It was strange to have this conversation with Evie. To have just pushed Grace away again because she slept with another man, and moments later to be talking to Evie, because she'd had her heart broken by another man. To still adore her.

When I put it that way, it sounded fucked up, but the whole train of logic made sense to me. I understood why the scenarios were different.

Evie rested her cheek against my chest, and I wrapped my arms around her.

"I'm so glad I have you." Her breath seeped through my shirt, teasing my skin.

"We have each other."

"We do."

Evie and I spent the rest of the night watching movies, but not saying much. It felt good to have her here. Right.

I hated that it felt like someone was missing. It was probably wrong of me to keep thinking about Sawyer. How close he and Evie had gotten. But him and me too. How did she and I both read him wrong?

Did we really?

We must have. All signs pointed to *yes*.

So why couldn't I stop questioning whether or not he was really guilty of trying to fuck her over?

29 /
sawyer

I was going out of my mind.

After Evie and Gage threw me out, I wanted to camp on her doorstep, maybe hammer on the door, until one of them talked to me.

I told myself I was nixing the idea because it was ludicrous and I needed to move on. The real reason was because I didn't want to have to hit Gage, and I fully expected his police friend would show up and haul me off. I couldn't fix anything from a holding cell.

What I really needed was to sleep off this feeling. Sure, Evie refused to hear me out, and of course Gage took her side, but it didn't make any difference to me.

It did. I very much did. Sleep didn't make that clawing feeling in my mind and chest go away.

Was this about not giving up?

Yes. Because these two people had abruptly become part of my life, and I couldn't give them up.

Neither of them answered my texts or calls on Tuesday. Gage wasn't at his grill, and when I went by the hardware store it was locked up tight. There was a sign in the window, in Evie's familiar and precise handwriting.

Closed for the week. Apologies for the inconvenience.

What?

I headed around back, and hammered on the roll-up door leading to Evie's workspace, until my fist was sore. Then I hammered some more, because apparently I was losing my mind.

"I need you to stop." Rohde's voice came from behind me.

I turned to see him standing in the alley, in full uniform, a blank look on his face. "I need them to open the door."

He sighed. "You can leave, or I can bring you in, and find an excuse to send you to a bigger jail in a different city."

I wouldn't mind hitting him. The outlet for my frustration would be nice.

Kurt would be upset if I beat up his Uncle Rohde though.

It took the last of my willpower to jam my bruised hands into my pockets. "I'm going."

That night, sleep didn't come any more easily than answers, and the next morning, the driving need to make this right hammered in my skull.

I was surprised when my room phone rang. "Yeah," I answered.

"If anyone asks, you didn't hear this from me." It was Elaina. "Gage is at his restaurant, and he's alone."

I started to ask how she knew—that he was there or that I cared—but I was on a short schedule. "Thank you."

A few minutes later, I pushed through a thankfully unlocked door at Gage's Grub, to find him behind the counter, prepping for the day.

The look he gave me was impassive, which I'd take over angry.

"Hear me out," I said.

He nodded. "Okay."

"Just like that?"

Gage grabbed a glass from under the counter and twisted a rag inside it. "Why did you lie in Wendover?"

Not an answer, but a reasonable question. There was the reason I'd given myself since I did it—I was here to conduct business and that had the potential to give me an advantage.

That wasn't the real reason, and now that I'd pushed aside so many of the lies I'd told myself, the answer was clear. "The two of you spark. Fireworks on the Fourth, even when you're just having breakfast." I vividly remembered them together.

"I was jealous," I said. "What the two of you have, it reminded me so much of what I had with

Tony, and you were blissfully unaware. I saw it when I saw you, and something inside me clicked. I didn't think it so much as feel it—that sensation of *fuck you both for ignoring something most people would give anything to experience just once*."

Gage was going to rub a hole in that glass, or crack it, with as white as his knuckles were. "Did you know about the bank?"

"Not until a few days ago. It didn't occur to me to share, because it didn't matter anymore. I should've said something, but I didn't keep it from Evie to trick her. I promise you. I've been honest with her and with you. Why would I—" Go through so much trouble if they didn't matter?

"I keep asking myself the same thing." Gage answered the question despite me not answering it.

"I'm sorry. I want to tell Evie the same thing, but I won't ask you to be my go-between."

Gage finally set the cleanest glass in history on the counter. "Evie's mad because she's scared and because she cares. Anything else, she should tell you herself."

I agreed, and I understood where she was coming from. I'd pushed away a lot of people after Tony, though none of them as wonderful as Evie.

"We're heading to a private garage in a few hours, to run some tests on the bot," Gage said. "I'll tell her what you said. I don't know what will happen after that."

I should be going with them, but I understood

why I wasn't invited. This wasn't the final test drive anyway, based on the schedule we'd laid out. "I'm not doing much of anything, so…" I stepped on the rail running around my side of the counter, leaned across, and brushed my lips over Gage's. "Call me."

"I will. Evie will." He said it with so much certainty I couldn't argue.

As I left, the clawing inside shifted. I still felt high-strung, but the *I can't lose them* feeling was more hopeful. I wouldn't lose them. I didn't know how it had happened, but somewhere along the way during the last few weeks. I'd fallen for Evie. And Gage.

There was no reason to fight that pull. Not a good reason, anyway. I could take my time and let myself feel it.

That was both terrifying and a relief. It'd been so long since I let myself care, and this went beyond the basic idea of giving a shit. I wanted them in my life. Needed them.

And the instant they got back this afternoon, I was going to tell each of them.

The next few hours of waiting were torture, but not as much as the last couple of days.

Regardless of what came next, I wasn't continuing to work for my father. I saw now why Hudson was pulling away from the family business. I dove into wrapping up more of my accounts, so I could walk away.

Forty-eight and starting over. Again.

When I lost Tony, the idea made me ill. Now it was a relief. Almost exciting.

It had been a couple of hours, and I was fully immersed in my work, when I received an email alert. I had one for every property I was working with.

This was for Evie's, and it had just gone up for sale.

What the fuck?

It was a quick auction that ended at the end of the day. Eastern time. That meant in about three hours, someone besides Evie would own her property.

I doubted she knew, given how quickly and quietly this had happened. Whether or not it was a legal move didn't matter. It would be far harder to fight if a sale went through, and there was already a bidder.

I called Evie.

No answer.

I got the same result from Gage.

I couldn't let this happen to her. I called them both back and left them the same messages. "You need to call me back the instant you get this. You're about to lose your property. They're selling it out from underneath you, and you need to put a stop to it."

I sent them text messages too.

Time was ticking away, though. I needed to do something *now*.

30 /
evie

For the last two days, since I kicked Sawyer out of my shop, two thoughts had been in my head above all others.

Gage loves me.

And "I don't want things with Sawyer to have been a lie." I didn't mean to say that out loud. So far I'd kept the thought to myself.

I was an idiot for feeling that, wasn't I? Every instinct, every bad experience, every mistake I'd made around me, said *yes*.

Saying the words aloud felt good, though. They were a relief.

Gage glanced at me from the driver's seat. He was currently taking us to the garage out west, where we could test the bot. We were driving an identical route to the one we took the day we met Sawyer. Today our exit came earlier, but the familiar road had me remembering.

"I don't think they were a lie," Gage said.

My heart skipped. I wanted to believe him. It was so dangerous to let my guard down, though. "But how do you know? How would I know?"

You could've heard him out. That voice sounded smart, but also completely irrational. Hearing people out meant giving them room for more lies. Travis. Don.

But I listened to my friends all the time. Misunderstandings happened.

"He called us both dozens of times yesterday," Gage said.

"Because he's already told us, he doesn't give up."

Gage took the appropriate exit, which looked like it led to salted sand dunes and nothing else. "But he already had. He walked away from trying to buy from you."

Yeah. He had. And yesterday, I doublechecked with his friend in Atlanta, to make sure I was still on to use this bot to try to win a contract for parts making. That was a lot of effort for Sawyer to go through to meet his goals.

"I talked to him this morning." Gage navigated the roads as if we'd driven them dozens of times, despite us never being out here.

The news should surprise me. I should be upset that he'd talked to Sawyer. I didn't know. "What did he say?"

"He said he didn't know about the bank thing

until a few days ago. He didn't keep it a secret to try to trick you, but because he didn't think it mattered at this point. He said he's jealous of how good we are together."

But he's good with us.

Fucking brain. I hated that thought. I loved it at the same time. "What if I listen to him… and I can't tell if it's the truth." Admitting that was what scared me was hard.

"Have you noticed how aggressive he tends to be with the truth?" Gage asked. "To the point where he's said some shitty things?"

I had. "That's not my question." I fixed my gaze on the salty dust that kicked up around us. By the time we stopped, Gage's black SUV was going to be a mottled gray. "What if I put my trust in the wrong person again?"

"You trust me."

"Yes."

"And Alys and Aubrey. Elaina."

I clenched my jaw, mostly to bite back the war raging inside between what experience had taught me and what was in front of me now, with Sawyer. "Your point is?"

"Sometimes you have to go with your gut. And sometimes your instinct will be wrong. We all have those days, but don't walk away from something that could be good because bad things might happen. What if you don't get this contract?"

The thought sliced through me from a new angle, and I couldn't hide the fresh hurt.

"I'm not saying you won't," Gage added quickly. "You've worked hard, and no one deserves it more than you. They'd be idiots to turn you away. But… the option is always there. You're trying anyway, right?"

"Of course. If I don't, I automatically lose." Fuck. I was pretty sure I saw the parallel he was drawing, and I wasn't sure I cared for it.

Or maybe I loved him even more for pointing it out. "Are you really telling me to go after another man?" I asked.

Gage parked in front of what looked like an airport hangar or a warehouse in the middle of nowhere—sheet metal walls, a huge footprint, and a high roof.

This was our place.

He turned in his seat, and searched my face. "Yes. I'm telling you to make things right with Sawyer, and I'm telling you I intend to do the same. Weird, right?"

Three people in love, when none of us had managed to make it work with just one other person before?

Not completely true. Sawyer had something incredible before, and he'd put his heart on the line again. For both of us. For two fucked up people who couldn't tell when someone cared about them.

"Alys makes it work." That was easier to say than trying to put the other thoughts into words.

Gage grasped my hand and traced his thumb along the back of my knuckles. "Alys *is* pretty smart. Though not as smart or as pretty as you. But she's got a good head on her shoulders."

I did want things to work out with Sawyer. I wanted to try. It already hurt that I'd pushed him away, and if for some reason we crashed and burned...

But we wouldn't.

And I wouldn't with Gage either. I wanted him in my life even more than he was now. I was more with him than without him. I should probably tell him, "I love you. I really do, so much. And I don't know why it's taken me so long to figure it out, and I'm sorry—"

Gage kissed me. It was a fast dip of his head, then his lips were pressed to mine, silencing my words and my thoughts and searing passion into the space between us. He kissed me until the world fell away and there were no worries, there was just now.

I let out a tiny sigh, contentment mixed with the tiniest disappointment that the moment was over, when he pulled away. There would be hundreds more like this, though.

He kissed me on the forehead and lingered. "Never apologize for that."

I'd argue that wasn't what I was doing, but this felt too good to ruin with details.

We sat like that for a moment, but we had an appointment to make. I wanted to call Sawyer, tell him we needed to see him tonight. Maybe he could meet us here. But we were so far from any cell towers that my phone was in *Emergency Only* mode. I was fairly sure that was like having negative bars.

Gage and I talked to the building operators, and got instructions, then backed his SUV up to the loading docks.

It was a shame Sawyer wasn't here with us. For the company, but also because he should've seen this maiden flight. This happened because of him.

I'd take video, and he'd be here next time. He had to be.

We tested the robot's weapons against stationary structures—wood piles, pumpkins, and milk jugs filled with water.

It was raw, entertaining-as-fuck destruction. An hour later, when we wrapped up, my cheeks and throat hurt from laughing and shouting so much. This was the best kind of exhaustion.

We loaded the bot back into Gage's SUV, and headed home.

We were an hour or so into the trip when my phone lit up with a dozen notifications. Most of them from Sawyer.

Gage's phone went nuts too, and when he handed it to me to check, I saw it was for the same reason—Sawyer's messages.

I started with my own texts. They all just said *Call me now.*

I was about to check the voicemails and see if they had more info, when my phone rang with a number I didn't recognize.

Uneasiness clawed at me as I answered. "Hello?"

"Evie? Hey, this is Xander Haddar. I got your number from Alys."

None of that made me feel better. "What's up?"

"Did you decide to sell your hardware store?" He asked.

So much for small talk. Though given the question, I was glad he cut right to it. The acid in my gut was churning up a storm. "No."

He muttered something I couldn't make out over the road noise. "I have a series of alerts for several of the buildings on Main Street," he said. "I like to keep an eye on the properties, so I know if they hit the market, things like that."

That made sense.

"Your store went up for auction earlier."

I couldn't have heard Xander right. That wasn't... I still had time. I had until the end of the month. Maddox was taking care of things.

The things I'd discovered online a few days ago rushed back. People with loans like mine, situations like mine, having their property sold out from underneath them. "What do I do? How do I stop it? Buy it? Something."

Gage shot me a concerned look.

"You don't." Apology hung heavy in Xander's voice. "Bidding closed at three. The winning bidder was one Sawyer Rawlings."

What?

No.

"If you can find out how it happened, I might be able to help," Xander said.

"I don't know what happened." But I did. Sawyer...

No.

This wasn't right.

"I'll let you know." I managed to keep my voice cool. "Thank you for calling." I hung up on Xander before I could hear his response. I wanted to be numb, but the disbelief was starting to ache.

"What's wrong?" Gage's voice barely penetrated the fog filling my head.

Everything. The world was ending.

No. I wouldn't let it. I told him what Xander told me.

Gage pulled over to the side of the road, and turned the hazard lights on. "It can't be right. Xander's wrong." He sat there, staring straight ahead.

"What else is there to think? There aren't a lot of other explanations." I didn't want it to be true. I wanted so badly for Sawyer to be who he said. Who I saw when we were having fun.

"I don't know." Gage shook his head. "But he does. Did you listen to all his messages?"

No. I pulled up the first voicemail and let it play.

"You need to call me back the instant you get this. You're about to lose your property. They're selling it out from underneath you, and you need to put a stop to it." Sawyer's voice filled the cab.

That didn't explain anything. He'd tricked me.

No. That wasn't what the message said. I needed to call him back. I needed him to tell me this was bullshit.

"He was panicked in that message." There was a hesitation in Gage's voice, as if he was searching for something he didn't know was real. "Have you ever heard Sawyer panic?"

Two days ago when I kicked him out of my store. That was the only other time. He had to explain. I called, but there was no answer.

This was probably a conversation better had in person anyway, but I wanted answers now.

"Get us home," I said to Gage.

He nodded and we were on the road in an instant, going as fast as we could, speed limits be damned.

It felt like an eternity when we pulled into town, but it was maybe forty-five minutes later. We found Sawyer near my sliding rear entrance when Gage parked in the alley. Sawyer was pacing, and looked up with a wide-eyed expression when we stopped.

I didn't want to get my hopes up, but they were.

They were so high up there that he could explain this, and I was about to crash hard, wasn't I?

"Thank fuck you're here." He approached the instant I was out of the SUV.

I needed him to make this better. *Please, please be able to explain.* "Did you buy my store?" I couldn't be demure or coy about this. I needed answers *now*.

He nodded. "Yes."

"Why?" It was safer to scream at him now. Tell him to fuck off. Giving him the time to come up with a pretty story would hurt, but I couldn't do this with him long term. I couldn't cut him off whenever bad things happened.

I wanted to be able to talk to him the way I did with Gage. The way I did with Sawyer when things were good.

"So no one else could," Sawyer said. "I bought it because I needed to make sure Don didn't get it, and neither did anyone else."

That was... good? "Then I'll buy it from you. How much."

"Nothing. I won't sell to you."

What?

"You have to." Gage had joined us.

Sawyer reached in his back pocket and handed me an envelope. "I told you—this building belongs to you. It's part of this town and so are you. I'm not going to take that away from you, and I had to make sure no one else did either."

I still didn't understand. I opened the envelope.

It looked like a receipt, and it was notarized. It was transferring this address back to me.

"I don't have the paperwork yet," Sawyer said. "But this is a promise that the property is still yours."

"You can't." I was starting to wrap my head around this, but I didn't believe it. He bought my building to give it back to me? "That's so much money."

"What am I doing with it? Chasing a shitty legacy built by the kind of man who's made this a business practice? I can afford it and you're worth it."

But was I? "After the way I reacted on Monday..."

"To be fair, I have a history." Sawyer twisted his mouth in consideration. "Also, I should've told you when I found out about the bank."

This was easy—the talking to him. Like it had been in the graveyard. Like almost every moment after. I wanted to believe him, and I didn't see a reason not to.

"So I'm gonna go." Sawyer stepped away.

Gage moved into his path. "Like that? You're not going to stick around? Ask about the bot trials? Have a beer with us?"

Talk about if all three of us have a future. I swore I could hear Gage thinking the words. I certainly was.

"The building is a gift, not me forcing my way

back into your life. It's no strings attached. It's yours, Evie. Goodnight."

I grabbed his arm, and the shock of my skin on his sped through me. "Don't go," I said.

The last few weeks flashed in my mind. The way Sawyer did things. The walls that had come down. How well we all clicked. The heat. The passion. The fun.

Without fun, the rest falls flat.

What we had was real. I could see it. I *knew* it. "Don't go. I love you." Twice in one day. Wow.

Sawyer looked surprised. "What about Gage?"

"I love him too." And I liked saying it. Over and over. To both of them. About both of them. "I have multiple best friends, why can't I have multiple boyfriends?" It felt good to have Sawyer here. To have Gage here. To have picked them because I wanted them in my life and not because I was lost or lonely.

This—they—were incredible, and I was so excited to see what came next.

31 /
gage

I was so glad this was how things turned out with Evie's building. I'd hate to have to track Sawyer down and hurt him.

But that had never really been the issue, had it?

There was so much possibility that spread out before us, and I wanted to explore it all. While I wanted one thing specifically—Evie and Sayer in bed and naked—it probably shouldn't happen quite yet.

"I hate to be the responsible one in the group..." I said.

Sawyer studied me. "But do you really? Hate it, I mean? I kind of feel you like holding it over us."

I liked the teasing. "I do. Gage is lord and master now."

Sawyer snorted, and Evie looked like she was biting back a smile.

"Make a guy feel small, why don't you?" I fake-scowled at both of them.

Evie pressed her body to mine and teased her hand below my waist, to trace the outline of my cock. "Not small in any way."

My voice caught and I turned half-hard under her touch.

"You were saying…? Something about being responsible?" Sawyer prompted.

I forced myself to back away from Evie enough that my brain gears started grinding again. "There's a large metal beast in the back of my truck. We should put it away before we do anything else. And let Sawyer take a look at our success." I opened the tailgate.

Sawyer's expression shifted in an instant, as he focused on the robot. "Wow. You finished her."

"Not quite." Evie hovered her hand over the steel without making contact. "We found a few issues today that need to be ironed out, but we're ninety percent there."

"She looks good. How does she drive?" Sawyer asked. He helped me shift the small vehicle, and lift it from the back of the SUV to set it on the ground.

Evie reached into the box that had been next to it, and grabbed the remote control. "Amazing. Smooth reaction time. Smooth drive. You're going to love it."

"Can I…?"

Evie handed Sawyer the remote. "Of course. She needs to get inside somehow." She stepped away to unlock the door, and she and I raised it.

It was amazing to see Sayer take the controller with so much reverence. This man was like day to night compared to the man we met in Wendover. He maneuvered the robot with immense skill, rolling it inside, accelerating and decelerating as if he'd been driving RC all his life. He smiled the entire time. He didn't hesitate to take control.

Okay, that last one was Sawyer no matter how he was acting.

"We took video," I said, as he navigated toward its resting spot.

"Does anyone get naked?" Sawyer asked.

I pretended to consider the question, though he wasn't looking at me. "Evie was masturbating during the speed run, but the camera wasn't on her."

She slapped my arm playfully. "You weren't supposed to see that."

"I want to see that." Sawyer glanced at us.

She shrugged. "I'm sure we'll get around to it."

Sawyer made *tsk* sounds, and parked the bot. He put the remote on the nearby table, and spun on Evie, causing her eyes to go wide. "I'm going to need a more concrete answer than that." His voice was abruptly deep and gravelly, and he stepped toward her until she collided with the table.

Hot. To watch. To imagine being on either end of. The two of them were going to be so much fun.

Evie managed to look simultaneously demure and defiant. "I can fit you in two months from Thursday."

"I don't need you to *fit me in.*" The sound Sawyer made was somewhere between a growl and a bark. "That's the point of masturbation."

"Now? You want it now?" she asked.

"No." His answer came instantly. "Tonight, we're fucking you."

"Both of you are?" Evie looked between us.

I was on board with that plan. "Yes." I'd always loved the back and forth with Evie, but with Sawyer it was just as good. A different flavor. Peanut butter on top of chocolate. But they blended so well together and with me.

With Grace, there was never this kind of connection. Sure, the sex was all right, but not as good as with Evie or Sawyer, and that spark... I never had that with her.

Sawyer, Evie, and me, we lit things up when we were together.

"So what you're saying, if I understand correctly, is Evie is dinner and dessert tonight." I took my time raking my gaze over her.

Sawyer shook his head. "That's not at all what I said, but I do like the way you think."

"So... wait. There are two of you." Evie held up

her hand and stuck out two fingers. "And two cour-ses." She put up two more digits. "Does that make me four servings?"

"You're overthinking it." I certainly didn't want to put that much thought into it.

"Says the man who earns a living selling his large meat," Sawyer said.

Evie frowned. "Now I'm confused. Are we having burgers, or me?"

"I don't even know where the two of you are going with this." Sawyer laughed. "Do you?"

"Of course." I thought it was obvious. "Sex."

Sawyer wrapped an arm around each of our waists and steered us toward the door. "Why didn't you just say so? All this beating around the bush."

"No. That's masturbation, and we're not doing that tonight," Evie said.

He pulled her closer to him, and made loud chomping noises while he nipped at her neck.

She squealed in response.

"The shop is locked." I didn't know why he was trying to move us somewhere else. "No one's going to walk in on us here."

Evie playfully pushed Sawyer away. "Nope." She popped on the *p*. "We're going back to Gage's place."

"Any particular reason?"

"The very specific reason is that my toothbrush is there," she said. "Also, once I get naked tonight, I don't want to have to get dressed again."

I had no arguments. "That's smart."

"I guess." Sawyer let out an exaggerated sigh.

Sore sport. "You're just pouting because it wasn't your plan," I said.

He gave me a deep scowl. "Let's get two things straight right now—first of all, I do *not* pout, and second, I'm never upset when sex is on the table."

I opened my mouth to make a joke about sex on tables.

He pressed his finger to my lips, silencing me. "I swear to God if you take us on another tangent, instead of driving us to your place..."

I could let the threat hang, but I wanted him to finish the thought. "You'll what?"

"I won't kiss you the rest of the night."

And? Best not to push my luck. "Effective threat. You win."

Evie locked her store up behind us, and the three of us climbed into my SUV. Me in the driver's seat, and Sawyer pulling Evie onto his lap in the front passenger seat.

I pointed us toward home, eager to make the trip fast, and grateful it was a short drive. As I navigated roads I'd traveled most of my life, Sawyer reached across the center section, and glided his hand up my thigh. Inside my leg. High enough to tease me and send heat rushing over me.

By the time we reached my place, I was more than primed and ready to go.

This was all so amazing. It made me so happy.

To be with Evie, and that I hadn't lost my chance with her after all. And then to get double lucky in finding Sawyer...

Whatever came next for all three of us, I couldn't wait.

32 /
evie

A lot of bad things had happened in my life because I trusted the wrong people.

But so had a lot of good things.

And it took all of the above to lead to this. To Gage kissing me on his front porch like I was his lifeline. Or maybe that was the best description for how I clung to him. He fumbled with the keys, hitting the lock then slipping. Fumbling and almost dropping the entire ring.

Sawyer was with us too. "You're taking too long." His grumbling was good-natured.

Gage shoved the keys at him without moving his arm from around my waist. "You do it then."

Sawyer slipped between us, rather than taking the keys, and glided his mouth up the side of my neck in a chain of tiny kisses.

This was so much more playful than when they

met, and it was a lot of fun. I wanted to do this away from prying eyes, though.

I slipped from both of their grasps and grabbed the keys from Gage. "If you're both going to be like this, you can stay out here and kiss each other."

The men exchanged glances and shrugs, then pressed their lips to each other. And their bodies. And... I was sure if they pressed any closer, they'd merge. I loved watching it, because I could feel the draw between them. The realness of their attraction to each other was tangible.

We were going inside. I unlocked the door, let us in, and tugged them after me. "I was promised I was on the menu."

"You very much are." Sawyer turned to me, and dragged his tongue up my neck then back down, laying tiny nips with his teeth along the way, and finishing by biting my shoulder enough to make me yelp and sigh.

Gage scooped me into his arms, and I squealed in surprise as I threw my arms around his neck.

"How do I get you to do that for me?" Sawyer asked.

"Learn to squeal the way Evie does."

Sawyer twisted his mouth, as if in thought.

"Well?" I asked.

He gave a brief shake of his head. "Trying to decide if it's worth it or not."

I snuggled closer to Gage, burying my face in his chest. "It's worth it."

"It's also not something you can fake." Gage turned away, and headed toward the master bedroom with me in his arms.

Sawyer followed. "Last thing I'm going to do right before sex is brag about *faking it*."

In the bedroom, Gage set me on my feet, and I turned to Sawyer. I brushed my lips over his. "Bragging about that is probably a bad move any time."

"I swear to you"—Sawyer grabbed my face between his hands and crushed his mouth to mine with an intensity that stole my breath and my thoughts. —"this is all so real it nearly drove me insane." His voice was breathy and desperate.

I could sink into this forever. It was so good. So solid. Enough to stop the talking while all of our mouths were occupied with other things.

Gage pulled off my shirt. Sawyer was behind me, to tease his fingers up my spine and undo my bra, while Gage leaned past me to kiss him.

I liked being the filling in this sandwich.

Gage cupped my breasts and teased his thumbs over my nipples, only pausing long enough to let me yank off his shirt.

Sawyer pressed into my back, bare skin on bare skin, to tease his hands down my sides. Lower, over my jeans, between my legs. Pressing into my slit through denim. Teasing. Keeping up the attention until I was squirming and squeezing my thighs together.

I reached in front of and behind myself,

fumbling with Gage's and Sawyer's zippers at the same time. Was I coordinated enough to undo one of their zippers one handed? Let alone two?

Sawyer made a sound that was half groan, half chuckle, and nipped at the shell of my ear. "Greedy girl."

I did my best to lean into his touch without pulling away from Gage's, and my fingers slipped off the button of Sawyer's jeans. "What does that make you, stealing kisses from both of us?" I countered.

"Just as greedy."

Gage grabbed my wrist and dug his fingers into the skin, drawing a gasp from me. He pushed my arm behind my back, and Sawyer grabbed both of my hands, to hold me captive.

Gage never let up on the attention he was giving my nipples. Sucking and biting and stealing my breath. He dropped his hands to my waist to undo my jeans, and shoved those and my panties halfway down my thighs, exposing and binding me.

In Wendover, I thought being trapped between the two of them in a competition was hot. This, with them both working together to play with me and each other? A billion times more scorching.

While he held me captive, Sawyer slipped his free hand along the curve of my ass, and over my thighs. His touch was light enough to tantalize and tempt, growing the throb of need from my core. He glided along my skin that was already slick with my juices.

He slipped inside me as much as he could with my legs trapped, and that lingering feeling of being penetrated zinged through my senses.

Gage brushed a touch over my clit, and I bucked into the sensation. My entire body was a live wire sitting at the edge of a puddle, sparking and dancing with every nudge.

Gage and Sawyer worked me harder, slipping one way and then the other, rocking me between them, pushing the build of friction higher and higher until my head was light and floaty. I was trapped here, in a tiny circle of pleasure, and the fact that they both held so much power over what happened next was both terrifying and freeing.

The sensations built inside, surging and evening, then pulsing again, until I hovered at the edge of climax. Lingering right there was a unique kind of torture, and oh so delicious.

When orgasm raced through me, I was helpless in its waves. Gage and Sawyer coaxed my body until I couldn't take any more, and sighed away as much as I could, with a wobbly giggle.

We lingered for a moment, them holding me up and letting me catch my breath. The unspoken agreement to pause was tantalizing too, in a new and wonderful way.

Feeling their bodies, being enveloped in their

scents, left me wanting more. They finished stripping me out of my clothes, and made sure I was seated on the bed, then moved their attentions to each other.

They undressed in a hungry wave of kisses and gropes. Gage's jeans came off. Sawyer's pants.

And then they were both naked too, muscled, their cocks standing at attention.

Sawyer gripped the back of Gage's neck hard enough I felt it from where I sat, and pressed his forehead to Gage's. "I *will* fuck you." The promise in Sawyer's growl was delicious. "But we'll work our way up to it... Unless you've been playing on your own."

I knew from my own private play, and the few times I'd been with Sawyer, that a dick like that wasn't going in an ass that wasn't ready for it.

For a heartbeat, Gage looked uncharacteristically shy. "Not like that, I haven't."

"I have." I was happy to volunteer the information. Partly to take the attention off Gage, but also because I wanted both men inside me at the same time.

"Really?" There was a rumbling amusement to Sawyer's reply. "Sweet little Evie has sex toys?"

He crawled toward me on the bed, and I scooted away with a smirk, stopping abruptly when I ran into Gage.

Sawyer knelt between my legs and dragged a finger down the middle of my chest. The combination of threat and promise in his touch sent my mind ablaze with anticipation.

"Sweet?" I repeated playfully. "Me? Or have you been playing with another Evie?"

"I promise you're the only Evie I want." As Sawyer leaned closer, I was trapped again.

I loved every second of it.

Gage licked my shoulder. "He's right about one thing—you are sweet."

I didn't know how to respond to that, but from the heat flooding my face, the answer was probably *blush furiously.* "I'm a forty-year-old, single—previously single—woman. I have enough sex toys to leave you both speechless."

"All these years." The noise Gage made in his chest rumbled through me.

Sawyer clucked. "You could've been watching. Not that you weren't already fantasizing."

"I was," Gage said.

"About me masturbating?" I suppose I could've guessed it, since apparently Gage had the hots for me for a lot longer than I'd realized, but the confirmation added a whole 'nother layer of desire to what simmered inside.

Gage kissed along my shoulder and trailed his fingers up my sides. "I've fantasized so many things about you. About every single fucking way you would come. Watching. Helping. Tying you down and drawing out one climax after another..."

"Told you he's been hooked for a while." Sawyer

grabbed my hips and rolled onto his back, prompting me to follow.

I straddled his legs, hovering over him enough to tease him with my heat, but not enough that he could penetrate me.

Sawyer's laugh was tighter than before. More strained. He gripped my thighs, digging his thumbs into the sensitive flesh. "Protection."

"Birth control." There was a different kind of connection without a condom. A new level of intimacy. I'd only ever dared trust Gage, but I wanted that closeness with Sawyer too.

He traced along my jawline, up to tangle his fingers in my hair, and searched my face. "You sure? Nothing else?"

"Yes." I lowered myself enough to brush against his erection, which was trapped between us.

He shifted my weight abruptly, and thrust up, driving himself deep into me. The penetration, the way he stretched me out, drew a long groan from me that mingled with the delicious sound he made.

We slipped against each other, with him withdrawing most of the way before plunging inside again, while Gage slid lubed fingers along my back side, leaving a generous trail behind.

Sawyer pulled me into him and held me there, not moving aside from the occasion twitch of his cock inside me. If it weren't for the anticipation building inside me, I could lay like this for hours.

Gage nudged my rear entrance, and Sawyer's

warning of, "Slowly," rumbled through me. Gage entered me a little bit at a time, pausing between each slip to let me relax. To make sure I was all right.

And when he was buried in me, it felt so much better than playing with toys. His erection and Sawyer's so close to each other, both stretching me out and building friction without moving.

There was a tug of pain, too. A light kind of whisper that felt as incredible as the rest of the sensations. They started moving again, more of a slow rocking than a frantic pounding, but with both of them here, plunged deep, this felt just as intense.

Friction and pleasure built again, climbing. Pushing me closer and closer toward climax. The way Gage was grunting and the grip from Sawyer digging his fingers into my thighs told me they were as immersed in this as I was.

Sawyer glided his hand along my leg, over the crease where it met my hip, and down to my clit. When he brushed the swollen, tender nub, I jerked at his touch.

He pushed in harder, circling and teasing while they continued to fill both my openings.

The combination of touches, the overwhelm of all of it, tore orgasm from me. I spiraled into climax, letting it wash over me and no longer thinking about each individual touch. It all felt so good. So right.

I could float in this cloud forever, riding this high.

I was vaguely aware of Sawyer moving his hand back to my leg, and the stutter of his grunts. Part of me registered Gage's movements becoming more frantic. More jerky.

And I swore I felt them fill me in a new way as one of them came and then the other.

As the frantic need ebbed, we all sort of fell against each other. Slowly the world bled back in, but it was tempered with Gage's weight against me and Sawyer's breath on the top of my head.

We lay there for who-knew-how-long, catching our breath, before they finally slipped out of me, then we pulled apart long enough to clean up, and collapse in a proper cuddle pile in bed.

"None of this *I have to go* shit tonight, Sawyer," Gage said. "You're staying."

"I'm staying," Sawyer confirmed with a light huff of laughter.

I still didn't have words. I was content to be pressed between them. To focus on how good it was to have them both here.

Whatever came next—and I was so looking forward to every minute of it—we'd all tackle it together, and it would be incredible.

33 /
sawyer

The first day I drove into Haddarville, I couldn't wait to leave.

Now, a month later, it felt like the closest thing to home that I'd had since I lost Tony.

I'd checked out of the motel a couple of days after making things right with Evie and Gage. It didn't make sense to keep that room since we all found ourselves at his house or hers every night, depending on what we'd been working on that day.

But for the last couple of days we'd been on the road, driving Evie's robot in the back of Gage's SUV to Atlanta, for my friend Malcom to check out.

My car wouldn't stand up to another trip like this. Not yet. But Evie had introduced me to Cash, the guy who owned the auto shop in town, and he'd been far more helpful in getting parts and knowing what to do with them than I'd found before.

We arrived in Cumming last night, and even though it wasn't a much longer push to get to our destination, we'd been driving hard to get to Georgia and that seemed like far enough. Now, we were on our way to the testing arena Malcom had set up for this.

The energy in the car was tangible. I'd say I was as excited as Evie, but I couldn't steal her thunder on something like this.

She glanced in back every time we hit a bump.

"It's going to be fine. You're going to do great." Gage was starting to sound like a broken record.

"I know." Evie straightened in the back seat again, facing forward. "I'm just so excited."

Malcom was waiting for us outside when we arrived, with a dolly for us to wheel the bot inside on. Because we were going to be operating on a hard rubber floor, we didn't want the tires to pick up any debris that might tear things up.

Typically the weapons and bent frames did that plenty fine on their own.

I made introductions all around, though all of us had talked several times over video, so it was as if Evie and Gage already knew Malcom.

When we walked into the building, a wave of the past hit me so hard I expected to stumble. This space was used for other things as well, including RC competitions, and the number of times I'd been here with Tony…

For so long, even thinking about it hurt. There was still a knot inside at being here, and I suspected like any scar, I'd notice it for a long time, but it wasn't the same. I could look at then and now and see both with a fondness that warmed me from the inside out.

"How do you want this to work?" I asked when we had the bot in the cage.

"I have a series of more or less obstacle courses for you to go through. Basics first," Malcom said. "Driving forward and backward. Speed."

None of the opening steps would leave an impression, unless the bot failed. If it didn't even drive, there was no reason to damage anything to find out more.

Evie handed me the controller for Destructy 2.0. She insisted I was the better driver. I knew she was as good as I was, but I liked steering so I didn't argue.

I took Destructy through Malcom's instructions, making sure to spin up the weapons despite not using them yet, to show off the mechanics and the balance.

"We couldn't decide which of Evie's manufacturing skills to highlight, so we picked several." I talked while I drove. "Horizontal spinner on one side and a lifter on the other."

Malcom stayed impassive. "Not a great combat design."

"A brilliant exhibition design." I would brag about Evie's brains all day and night.

"Stronger hydraulics than you'll see most anywhere." Gage joined me. "Flipped our test subjects twenty feet in the air, at least."

Malcom looked between Gage and me. "I get it. Pretty girl, big mind." He turned to Evie. "I assume you can speak for yourself."

A glance at her showed that she was smirking. "What they say makes me sound way better than anything I'd tell you."

"That does sound like Sawyer. Nothing but praise for the people he loves." Malcom turned his attention back to the arena.

That hadn't been me for a while, and it was nice to know my friends saw me returning to someone more like my old self.

"I have some pumpkins if you'd like to smash those to show off your weapons." Malcom's gestured to a cart off to the side, stacked with giant orange squash.

Evie's grin was priceless. "Does anyone ever say *no* to that?"

"No." Malcom chuckled.

I handed the controller back to Evie—she should be the one to bash things with Destructy— and helped Malcom and Gage set up pumpkins inside the cage.

Evie sent pumpkin guts flying again and again, until the ring looked like a gourd massacre. To me, her glee was as good as the carnage. Gage and I cheered every time she exploded something with the giant steel blade spinning on her robot.

From there, she switched to the flipper, and tossed a few heavier objects into the air. Last up was running her robot into a few stationary, bot-like creations.

"I'm sorry in advance," Malcom said. "I hate to destroy such a great creation, but I need to see…"

"If the parts will hold up. It's okay." Evie didn't look concerned. "I knew this was coming, and we can rebuild him when we're done."

All of the work we'd done paid off—Destructy 2.0 held up beautifully.

As we wrapped everything up, the buzz was different than it had been on the ride here, but it was still just as incredible.

Malcom placed an order then and there. "Get me these parts, the ones we've discussed, in the next two months, and you can expect referrals going forward.

"Thank you." Evie shook his hand, then turned and threw her arms around my neck. "And you, too." She pressed her lips to my cheek.

Simple. Sweet. And just as good at getting my blood racing. "You did all the work," I said. "I just made the connection."

Evie stepped back and grabbed Gage's hand. "No. You two did as much work as I did. Your help made this possible."

We finished loading the SUV up again, and Malcom pulled me aside.

"I don't believe it, and I'm glad I was wrong," he said.

What? "About what?"

"That you could smile like this again. And that you could make it work with two people."

"I still miss Tony. I haven't forgotten him."

Malcom shook his head. "I know. We all do. I see no better way for you to honor his memory than to keep living."

And I was. When I lost Tony, I never imagined having enough left in me to love again. He had consumed me. But I still felt the same about him, and had room for Evie and Gage too. I wanted the world for the people I was with now.

"Thank you." I couldn't put better words around it, but I hoped he understood the gratitude was for today, as well as for his support. "We'll drop by with the other stuff in a few hours."

"Sounds good."

I was bringing him some of Tony's old model stuff that Malcom had uses for. I'd held onto it for so long, and it should be used and loved and seen rather than hidden away in boxes.

We headed to my old house next. Hudson had been staying there since he left his wife, and there was a certain amount of apprehension about seeing my brother again. A man I'd never really gotten along with, but I was starting to.

We parked in the driveway, and Gage whistled. "Look at you, Richie Rich. Wealthy city boy living in the suburbs."

It wasn't that grand, but compared to the hundred-year-old houses in Haddarville, the modern glass and concrete were definitely different.

Though this was still my house, I didn't live here anymore. I knocked, and waited for Hudson to answer. As we'd talked a few times recently, I kept expecting him to turn up his nose at the relationship with Evie and Gage.

So far, Hudson had been polite about it. *If it makes you happy, who am I to knock it? God knows what I was doing didn't offer any sort of joy.*

That made me a bit sad for him.

When Hudson answered, he wore an odd look. Somewhere between concern and confusion.

"What's up?" I asked.

"You didn't hear?"

"We've been locked in the throes of destruction for the last few hours." I heard Gage and Evie join me.

"What's wrong?" Gage asked.

I wasn't the only one who noticed. "Don't know. Hudson, this is Evie"—I pointed to her—"and Gage. Everyone meet everyone."

"Pleasure." Hudson didn't sound like he meant it. In fact, there was little emotion at all in his voice as he focused on me again. "They arrested Dad this

morning. Wire fraud. Conspiracy. Money launder-
ing. The list goes on."

Oh. *Fuck.*

"That's good, isn't it?" Gage asked.

Hudson scowled at him.

"I'm sorry, I am." He was sympathetic. "But the
man tried to fuck Evie over, and he fucked over who
knows how many others. And both of you."

Part of me saw this coming, but the news still hit
hard. And he was my father. I... "Gage is right."

"Is that weird?" Hudson sounded snide. "Telling
someone else they're right?"

I didn't want to argue today. Especially not over
this. "Not as long as I'm right too."

I stared Hudson down for several seconds as he
clenched and unclenched his fist, and his nostrils
flared.

He finally let out a long sigh. "You're right. This
is what needs to happen, and he brought it on
himself."

"Are you safe?" I expected he and I would both
be subjected to more questioning over the next few
months, but he was a lot more involved in the business, for longer. I could prove I was ignorant.

Hudson on the other hand... He'd been elbows
deep in the business for years, and while I believed
him when he said he didn't know what was going
on, that didn't mean the people enforcing the laws
would.

Hudson shrugged. "So far, yes. My only real

choice is to keep telling the truth. The business though? I don't see that surviving."

I was pushing so hard to take over, so he couldn't have it. The entire situation made me laugh, in a dark, twisted sort of way. "I guess no one inherits it, then."

"I guess not." Hudson gave a rough chuckle. "Maybe my ex can have it in the divorce."

"So you're both good? Okay?" Evie asked.

I was still processing, and I doubted I'd be done anytime soon, but overall, "Yeah. We're good."

We spent the next hour or so loading what we could into Gage's SUV, for me to bring back to Utah, and more into Hudson's truck for him to drop off with Malcom.

I'd come back for everything else later, or have movers bring it to me. I had some more clothes now. And I was leaving Georgia with what mattered the most—Evie and Gage—and a whole life spanning out in front of us.

"We're going souvenir shopping." Evie announced when we were done. "Call us when you're done?"

I brushed my lips over hers, and Gage's. "I will."

They were on their way.

"So you're staying out west," Hudson said when they were gone.

I nodded.

"You deserve this. To have this."

His words surprised me. That wasn't the kind of sentiment we tended to share. "Thanks."

And I couldn't argue with him. I wouldn't trade Evie and Gage, what I had with them, this next chapter in my life, for anything. Not money or power or prestige or pride.

I wouldn't give them up for the universe.

epilogue 1 / aubrey

"There's no way I'm going to be on a team with one of *them*." Elaina shook her head and took a step back from us.

Evie frowned. "What's wrong with us?" She sniffed her armpits. "I promise I showered this morning."

"Evie's a good team member to have." Sawyer had to raise his voice to be heard above the growing din in Joystick's, as people around us broke into trivia teams without the drama, and took their seats.

But not us. *No.* We couldn't do this nicely and neatly. Instead, Elaina was arguing about why she wouldn't take Alys's place this week, to play boys versus girls.

"She has a point." I agreed with Elaina. Sawyer versus Evie was ultra-competitive. These days the matches ended with the two of them kissing, regardless of who won, but they got intense before that point.

Ravyn sank in her seat. "So what are we doing instead?"

Elaina pushed Sawyer toward our table. "You go over there." She pointed behind her. "And I'll go play with the boys."

"Whoa. No one wants to hear that." Sawyer's protest carried above all other noise.

Somehow over the past few weeks, he'd more or less adopted Elaina as a little sister. Rohde wasn't impressed, but he also wasn't here tonight.

I was glad to see it, though. In school, and even after, we didn't hang out with Elaina much, because she was one of those girls who kept her head down, always followed the rules, and never had time for those of us who fucked around—literally or figuratively.

Not that I had a problem with that, but it did make her difficult to get to know.

Evie was urging her out more and more these days, and I liked when she hung with us.

Sebastian grabbed Elaina's wrist loosely, and tugged her into a seat with his team of Adam and Eli.

It didn't matter how competitive Evie and Sawyer were, we were so going to get our asses kicked.

For the next hour or so, it looked like we might have a chance. We kept things neck and neck, and just like a month ago, when Sawyer first walked into this place, our teams found ourselves tied and in the top spots with one question left.

All we had to do was name every single movie in the pictures, and we'd tie with them. No one was delusional enough to think Adam's team would get one wrong.

We kept our voices low as we listed out the easy titles first, and then worked our way through the more obscure ones. There was one image left, and all four of us squinted and examined from every which way, trying to figure it out.

"Is that... Joystick?" Ravyn asked softly.

Holy shit, it was. He'd been a child star, and done nearly a dozen different, direct to DVD movies after his TV show ended.

The problem was... which one was this?

"I've seen that one," Sawyer said.

We stared at him in disbelief.

"When?" Evie asked.

"I don't know. Sometime? Nephew's birthday party?"

"Your brother doesn't have kids," Evie said.

I shook my head. "Doesn't matter. If you know what it is, I don't care how." Evie opened her mouth, and I silenced her with a look. "Do you, if it means winning?" I asked her.

She snapped her jaw shut again. "Nope."

"It's *All Roads Lead to Rome*." Sawyer spoke with the kind of finality that was difficult to argue with.

I was going to anyway, to be certain. "Are you sure? Because I guarantee you, Eli is sure."

"Positive."

We wrote in our final answer, just as time was called.

The judge read out the answers, and we cheered each time we got one right. Of course, Sebastian's team got them all right, too.

When we got the last one, the Joystick movie, I realized I was holding my breath.

"*It's all Greek to Me*," the judge said.

Our entire table groaned in unison, and I smacked Sawyer's arm. "You said you were certain."

"I was. None of you had the answer."

That was a fair point.

"*Aubrey*." A new but familiar voice drew my attention to the front of the bar.

It was my younger sister, standing in the entrance, grinning and waving at me. She strode across the floor to join us, with the kind of purpose that said nothing would get in her way.

Not that anyone would in here, but she'd always been like this. Determined. Living with purpose.

"Sylvie." I grinned and hurried toward her, wrapping her in a hug. "What are you doing here?"

She squeezed me tight and stepped back. "I know I should've called, but I had a last minute meeting out this way, and really this is something better done in person."

"What is?" I asked.

"I want you to be my maid of honor. I'm getting married." She squealed.

I couldn't believe it. "I'm so happy for you." I wrapped her in another hug.

The pit in my gut could just fuck off now. I would not ruin my sister's wonderful news because I hated that I was still single.

epilogue 2

one year later

sawyer

I'd been in a tattoo chair enough times over the years that the sounds and sensations didn't faze me. I was a bit concerned about sitting for someone I didn't know.

Hudson assured me if I was in Vegas, this was the best place to go, and unlike a year ago when he sent me to Wendover, we were on friendly terms now. I trusted him.

I was saying that more and more these days, and it was odd, but it was nice.

Gage sat next to me while the guy with the gun laid fresh ink over my Scorpions tattoo. For the last few hours, Evie had been in a meeting with people from the combat robot TV show, and we were killing time until she was done.

She had enough clients in the business now that they'd all recommended she be on site during the shooting of the next season. When we picked her up in a little while, she'd have the contract, and we'd be here again in a couple of months, this time working from a tent on The Strip.

Evie tried to remind us this morning that she didn't have the contract yet, but Gage and I both knew she was going to get it.

"You're all done." The guy put down his gun, wiped away the last of the excess ink, and handed me a hand mirror to get a better view of the work.

It was a heart with a Celtic trinity knot inside it. I had probably butchered the meaning, but the concept of eternity—the intertwining of the past, present, and future—and also recognizing what I had with Evie and Gage, was the perfect new image as far as I was concerned.

Plus, it looked way cooler than the Scorpions logo ever had.

The artist wrapped my upper bicep in plastic while I thanked him, and Gage and I were on our way.

We were a couple of miles off The Strip, where things looked like any other Southwestern town, aside from the slot machines in every other business. We drove a wide circle around the touristy parts of the city, to return to where Evie was in her meeting.

Gage and I still gave each other grief as often as not, but it was fun and lighthearted now. The jabs were never cruel, and it made for some intense sex. I wouldn't trade what I had with him for anything.

Evie was waiting outside when we pulled up at the front curb. The building behind her was deceptively simple—stucco, a few windows, a basic etching on the door. One wouldn't know unless they were looking that this place housed the secondary headquarters for such a massive sport.

She looked both adorable and sexy-fucking-in-charge, in a button down white shirt, with a tie, suspenders, and pin-striped trousers. Aubrey had picked the outfit for her. Said it conveyed power and presence, and that Evie would rule the room in it.

Logic I couldn't argue with.

Evie didn't look up from her seated, head-bowed position as we approached.

"She looks unhappy." Gage's words echoed what I saw with my own two eyes.

I didn't want to consider the possibility she hadn't gotten this. I couldn't and wouldn't believe it. Evie was the best.

Her furrowed brow and what little I could see of her expression looked like a scowl.

She didn't move as we approached. Didn't look up until Gage said, "Evie?"

As she finally gave us her attention, I saw the twitch of her lips. If I'd blinked, I would've missed it. She was fighting a smile.

Okay, I'd play along. "How'd it go?" I kept my voice kind and cautious.

Her sigh landed heavily. "I don't know."

"Are you all right?" Gage was concerned.

He hadn't noticed yet that she was fucking with us. I'd bet on it.

Evie let out an exaggerated huff. "I don't know."

"Do you want to talk about it?" Gage asked.

"Not here." Evie looked like it took immense effort to push to her feet.

This was too silly, and God help me if I was wrong, but I wasn't. "She doesn't need to talk. She needs a thick dick in her mouth and to fuck this off."

Evie met my gaze, eyebrows raised. "You're an asshole."

"And you're making Gage feel bad. He believes you."

"I— Oh." Gage twisted his mouth in understanding.

Evie's grin finally cracked through. "I'm sorry, Gage. You were both supposed to fall for it."

I pulled her closer to us. "Truth now."

"I got the contract." Her grin was brighter than the Vegas summer sun.

Joy bloomed inside me, on her behalf, and I crushed my mouth to hers, swallowing her playful laugh. "I knew you would," I murmured against her lips.

Gage wrapped an arm around Evie's waist and pulled her to him. "Why does he get kisses first?"

"I figured it out first." Duh.

"Because he's a grabby bozo." Evie rose on her tiptoes, draped her arms around Gage's neck, and kissed him as she rubbed her whole body against his.

I liked watching them almost as much as being with one or both of them.

This was perfect. It didn't replace what I'd had with Tony, it was the next album in my life. A new volume filled with incredible new songs, and the perfect people to live the entire experience with.

---

gage

Okay, so I was the gullible guy who fell for Evie's trick, but I didn't care. I was just happy she had this. She deserved it. She'd earned every single bit of this opportunity and more.

Besides, I had a secret of my own. "We should celebrate."

"Where?" Evie asked.

"It's a surprise." A good one. One I'd struggled to keep for the last few weeks. I still had no idea how they hadn't found out yet.

Sawyer studied me with suspicion. "You do surprises?"

"I kept your Christmas present a surprise." I'd had Brooke sculpt him a new hood ornament, as the finishing touch for his finally-restored car.

Sawyer nodded. "Fair point."

"Give us a hint." Evie took both our hands and tugged us toward my SUV.

I yanked her back. We weren't ready to leave yet. "I met a guy last time I was here for that restaurant supplies trade show."

Sawyer had helped me remodel the banquet room in my grill. He had an idea for what was both functional and modern stylish, and he knew a lot of people who could get construction supplies for cheap.

And he was still watching me suspiciously. "So you bought... another oven? That's not a surprise for us."

"You got me scrap metal, didn't you?" Evie sounded more excited. "How'd you know?"

I scowled at both of them. "You're supposed to think it means I'm taking you to dinner someplace nice."

"But it doesn't mean that," Sawyer said.

Evie pouted. "It's not scrap metal?"

I loved how impossible the two of them were sometimes, and once they heard what I was up to, they'd love it. I gave all my attention to Evie. "More than thirty years ago, we made each other a promise. I'm a year late, but we're both single—"

Sawyer cleared his throat.

"Neither one of us is single, dork," Evie teased.

I rolled my eyes, but I was still enjoying the moment. "And apparently neither one of you has a single romantic bone in your body."

"I have one." Sawyer grabbed his crotch.

"This guy I met is also an Elvis impersonator and a minister." I pointedly ignored Sawyer's reply. "I had a whole big speech planned about how much I love you both, and he's happy to perform a ceremony for us, and what I was going to say was really romantic, and now neither of you gets to hear it."

Sawyer gripped the back of my neck and held me captive as he kissed me.

This never got old.

When he broke away he pressed his forehead to mine. "I would marry you again and again." His voice was rough with emotion. "Even without an elegant speech, I'd marry both of you."

"I still want the pretty, prepared speech," Evie said brightly.

I managed to glance at her without pulling away from Sawyer. "Yeah?"

"My answer is *yes* regardless. Duh. My answer will always be *yes* if we're talking about all of us together, but you worked hard and I love it when you tell me I'm awesome." Evie was grinning.

I loved them both so much sometimes it scared me, but in the best way possible. I loved the way we all worked together, the playful clashes and the intense coming together. I was so grateful I'd told Evie before I lost her, and now to have Sawyer too...

I'd tell them both over and over, until the end of time, how incredible they were.

---

evie

I was already riding the high of landing this contract, but that was nothing compared to the way my heart swelled to near-bursting when Gage went down on one knee in front of me. This man I'd loved for as long as I could remember, who I almost lost because I couldn't admit to myself how I felt.

"Eowyn Young, you've been my partner in so many things for longer than not. When things were great, when things were bad, whether you were here or halfway around the world, it didn't matter because I knew I could count on you. And I want that for us for the rest of our lives. I want to fall asleep to you and wake up to you and I want to give you all the love you deserve and more."

Gage twisted to look at Sawyer, grasping his hand without letting go of mine. "I never expected to love someone else, and when I first met you..." Gage trailed off with a half smile. "But Sawyer Rawlings, you're this force I can't resist. I don't want to. I need you as much as I do Evie, but in a very different way. We're all better people when we're together."

"Is this where I get to say *yes*?" I'd already said it, but I wanted to accept again, after an incredible proposal like that.

Gage gave me the same sheepish grin that I'd fallen in love with a million times over.

Sawyer pulled Gage to his feet. "I'm not going down on one knee," Sawyer said. "Mostly because my knee won't let me. But Gage is right. We're better together, and I can't imagine a more wonderful way to move forward in life than with the two of you."

It was tempting to stay out here kissing both of them, watching them kiss each other, for hours. But we had an appointment to make.

We drove to the chapel. Gage's *Elvis* friend couldn't perform a legal ceremony, so we didn't need things like a license or witnesses. This was a symbolic promise between the three of us, and I was so happy to do that.

Gage had gotten a jacket from Aubrey to go with my outfit, as well as matching suits for him and Sawyer.

Which meant Gage planned this outside of himself and managed to keep it a secret. Super, super sweet.

We changed, and found the chapel we were supposed to be in.

The elderly lady at the organ in the back of the

room reminded me a bit of Granny. She asked if we had any special music requests, or if we just wanted the wedding march.

"Can you play *Love Me Like a Reptile* by Motör-head?" Sawyer asked.

She tapped out a few notes, and then a whole chorus. "Like that?"

"Perfect." Sawyer grinned.

"My fee is included in the ceremony, but tipping is traditional," she said.

Sawyer and Gage both dropped large bills in her tipping jar.

She grasped my fingertips loosely and winked at me. "Pair of keepers."

"Trust me, I know it." I couldn't wipe the smile from my face, and I didn't want to.

She started to play.

"Hang on. One more thing." Gage pulled his phone from his pocket. "I have to make a call."

What?

I peered over his shoulder as he dialed *Aubrey*. The phone only rang once before she answered on video. She was surrounded by all of our friends. Even Eddie was with them.

Gage and Sawyer moved to the altar, to stand by Elvis, and Gage set his phone on a stand next to them, looking out on the room, so our *guests* could see.

As I walked down the aisle to Motörhead, My smile, the joy in my heart, grew with every step. By the time I reached the front of the room, I was ready to burst with love and joy.

The ceremony was a blur, I caught Elvis telling us something about loving and cherishing each other, and getting three *I dos* from us.

And the kisses…

I always loved the kisses, but today they meant more. The love I felt flowing between all three of us, the cheers from our friends on the phone, it was so incredible. I never imagined I could have something like this.

Having Gage and Sawyer by my side, through sickness and health and strife and good times and everything else Elvis had said…. I couldn't think of a more wonderful way to spend the second half of my life.

Thank you for shouting, crying, and laughing with Evie, Gage, and Sawyer.

For more Haddarville hi-jinx, and to read Aubrey's story, check out PIN-UP GIRL.

Aubrey's best friends have each found not, but two perfect men. Her little sister wants her to be the maid of honor and pick the perfect dress for the wedding. Even the boy Aubrey loved her entire life has found his happily ever after with someone else.

When her online gaming partner, Brodie, suggests she find a Plus One for the wedding festivities, to keep her from looking like the thirty-seven-and-still-single that she is, she turns to her childhood friend, Clint. When Brodie shows up on her doorstep ready to be her fake boyfriend for a month, she realizes he meant himself.

Now Aubrey's caught between her sister-turned-bridezilla and two faux beaus who are better at making love feel real than she imagined was possible.

Until she catches her not-her-guys making out with each other…